GRAVITY

Dark Anomaly, book 1

Marina Simcoe

To my Captain

MARINA SIMCOE

Gravity

This book is a work of fiction. Names, characters, places and incidents are a product of the author's imagination. Locales and public names are used for atmospheric purposes. Any resemblance to actual people, living or dead, or to businesses, companies, events, institutions or locales is completely coincidental.

Cover Design by Naomi Lucas and Marina Simcoe

First Edition

Spelling: English (American)

Editing and Proofreading by Cissell Ink

Gravity is a Science-Fiction romance. It contains graphic descriptions of intimacy, violence, and discussion on topics that may be triggering for some. Intended for mature readers.

Chapter 1

WAS I DEAD?

I felt bruised whenever I moved.

Do dead people feel pain?

I was still inside my spacesuit, which meant unless I'd taken it with me into the afterlife, I must still be alive.

What had happened, though?

The damage from the impact with an asteroid wasn't that big, I had fixed it in minutes. Then, I made it back inside my one-person spacecraft. But before I had a chance to get out of the bulky suit, all hell had broken loose.

The instruments went haywire. The last memory I had was that of the screens of instruments on the control panel blurring into a wide colorful ribbon of light around me. My spacecraft plunged off course, spinning out of control, as I was suspended inside.

Now, all motion had stopped. But I didn't remember when and how.

I must have passed out at some point.

Carefully, I took a deep breath and lifted my head inside the helmet, then moved my arms and legs to assess my body for injuries. My muscles hurt, but my limbs appeared to be functioning. The suit must have saved me from the worst.

Had there been a crash?

I had no idea where I was.

Lying on my side, I didn't get up while wearing the suit. Bulky and strong, it had been built to withstand the enormous pressure of the planet Omphi's bottomless ocean. However, it was not exceptionally comfortable to move in when it wasn't powered on.

Instead, I rolled onto my back and lifted my arm, bringing the screen built into the sleeve up to the glass of the helmet.

The light of the communication device was on, but I couldn't send a message out. Despite the light, the device was not functioning.

The readings of the environment outside of the suit were off, but not by much. The pressure and the oxygen level remained stable. There appeared to be no breach in the ship's hull.

Carefully, I opened the hatch on the chest of the suit, then crawled out of it.

My head swam with dizziness when I attempted to stand. My stomach roiled, and I dropped to my knees, vomiting onto the floor.

Not the *floor*, I realized, staring at the warped and cracked wall panel under my knees. The ship lay on its side. Save for the few emergency lights on the control panel above me, the power was off. However, gravity was keeping me, my suit, and thankfully the mess I had just made down.

The gravity was real. If it were the artificial kind created by the ship, I would have been on the floor, not on the wall.

I had most definitely crashed.

But *where*?

The Anomaly was the nearest space object to my ship when the asteroid hit it. However, I was well aware of the Anomaly's enormous gravitational field, and I had stayed far away from its reach.

I had studied the mysterious space abnormality for years. At first, it was thought to be just another black hole. However, it had exhibited behaviours vastly different from that.

Shortly after my graduation from the Academy, I applied for the mission to explore the Anomaly.

It'd been well into my first year of working on the station orbiting Omphi, the closest planet to the Anomaly, before we had enough data collected by unmanned probes to send a person even closer. I'd volunteered.

It was supposed to be a day trip. I had stayed the calculated safe distance away from the Anomaly. The blow from the asteroid might have nudged me a little closer, but still nowhere near close enough that I would have to worry about the Anomaly's pull.

Something had happened, and I needed to figure out what.

First things first. Where was I?

Had the computer on my ship somehow activated the return route after the incident with the asteroid, sending me back to Omphi?

Then I might now be in that planet's ocean.

Why the spaceship had crashed, instead of safely docking with the station, remained unknown, but its system would have sent a distress signal upon impact. The search and rescue team should have already been deployed, as per the protocol.

I needed to see if the ship's communication system was still functioning, even if the suit's wasn't.

A faint screeching noise caught my attention.

Hands on the wall, I listened carefully. It seemed to come from the outside.

Omphi was a water world with no land. If I'd crashed into its ocean, shouldn't I feel the rocking of the waves? The vibration of them splashing against the hull, maybe?

Yet the spaceship remained stationary, albeit on its side.

The screeching noise grew louder, then bright sparks shot out in a spray from the opposite wall.

Someone was trying to get on board my ship by cutting a hole in its hull.

Why would the rescue team damage the ship like this? Unless the crash had been bad enough to disable all entrance points at once?

I moved over to the control panel. The stream of sparks had completed a full circle. The cut-out fell with a loud thud. A stream of smoke or steam blew in, filling the interior. Its chemical scent was unfamiliar, and I held my breath, trying not to inhale too much of it.

The smoke cleared quickly, revealing an inky silhouette in the glaring light streaming through the hole in the wall.

From the first glance at the person, it was clear—they were not from my station.

Tall and broad, the being had a humanoid form with male proportions. Dressed only in a pair of worn dark pants and heavy boots, he was holding the tool he'd used to cut the hull.

Tossing the tool aside, he stepped inside my spacecraft, remaining but a large shadow in the faint light.

"It stinks in here." He rubbed his nose with his forearm, then added a long curse that got simply translated as "fuck" through my device.

I touched my fingers to the universal translator implanted in the back of my head.

My entire team had gotten the implants before leaving Earth. It had been only a few decades since the extra-terrestrial Federation had made the first contact with Earth. Humans had finally discovered another intelligent life form in our galaxy. However, it came not as a single race, but dozens of them. The Federation included representatives of seven populated planets from five different solar systems. All of them were much closer to the Anomaly my team had been studying than to Earth.

The male who had just barged into my spaceship must have been one of the species that belonged to the Federation. He obviously spoke a language recognized by my translator, though I couldn't immediately place him.

If I understood what he had said, chances were he'd understand me. The translation implants had been mandatory for thousands of years among the members of the Federation. Many nations had them implanted within the first year of a person's life. His would now be automatically updated with a number of languages from Earth, even if this was his first contact with a human.

Hope sparked inside me. As a member of the Federation, he would be obligated by law to assist me.

While I was gathering my thoughts to come up with an appropriate greeting, he clicked on the light strapped to his upper arm, illuminating my empty spacesuit on the ground.

At its sight, the newcomer leaped back. Raising both fists in defense should my suit attack him, he seemed fully prepared to fight back.

"Wyck," he said over his shoulder.

Another one of his kind climbed in through the hole. Just as intimidating in size, with wide shoulders and massive arms, this one wore dark pants similar to the first one. In addition, he also had on a short leather vest.

A chain was wound around Wyck's thick wrist. He yanked at it, and I nearly yelped in shock as a large, terrifying animal leaped into the ship. Black, with red markings, the monster had three heads, each maw open, displaying several sets of sharp, translucent teeth.

"See if this one is alive." The first newcomer ordered Wyck, tipping his chin at my spacesuit.

Wyck led his animal to it. The three-headed hound from hell took a sniff at the suit, then pivoted my way instead. All three of its heads lowered to the ground, the middle one gave out a loud hiss. My insides leaped from fear, but I straightened my spine.

"Greetings..." I cleared my throat, addressing the one with the flashlight on his arm, since he seemed to be the one giving orders here. "Under the interplanetary law of the Federation, I request your assistance. My ship—"

The one with the flashlight twisted my way, illuminating me. I blinked at the beam of light directed at my face and quickly covered my eyes with my arm.

"Well, *this* one looks very much alive," the male sneered. Something thick and heavy in his voice sent icy shivers of dread down my spine.

This didn't seem right.

These individuals and their behaviour were unnerving and intimidating. Their rugged appearance raised concern. The clothes they wore were not recognizable uniforms. Several rips and slashes in them seemed to have been made by teeth, claws or blades.

My throat went too dry to speak.

The monstrous animal moved my way. "Back, Lesh." Wyck yanked on the chain.

"I've got to get out of this stench." With an enormous hand, the first one grabbed me roughly by my arm, dragging me to the hole in the wall.

"Wait..." I tried to protest, but it was like attempting to stop a tugboat. I could either hurry and catch up or fall and be dragged behind.

"Vrateus will want to see this, Crux," Wyck pointed out.

"We didn't break any of his precious rules...yet," Crux scoffed, shoving me through the opening into the bright light outside. "He'll see it soon enough. But *we* got here first."

The "outside" turned out to be a long corridor, lit by strings of light suspended from the ceiling. The panels on the walls and the ceiling here were cracked and bent out of shape, just like the interior of my ship.

Did our spacecraft collide in space, somehow? Was that the reason for their unjustified rude behaviour toward me? Were they angry with me for crashing into them?

"Let me see what was sent to us this time." Painfully squeezing my arm, Crux yanked me closer.

His skin was the color of clay with a reddish tint to it. It darkened to charcoal gray on the three bumpy ridges that ran along his bald skull. Similar ridges stretched the entire length of his massive shoulders and down his thick arms.

A wide rugged scar crossed one side of his face, narrowly missing his eye. It must have been a nasty wound when it was fresh.

"Excuse me, but..." I started, hoping to reach some understanding here. Could it be that this male lacked the implant for some odd reason? He didn't appear to understand me at all.

He touched his nose to my temple, making a loud sniffing noise.

"A female," he growled low. "What a boon."

A shiver of revulsion ran through me. I fought to free my arm from him, but he wouldn't budge.

"I'm Svetlana Kostyk," I said as loud and clear as I could manage, hoping that if he didn't understand my words, he would at least catch from my tone of voice that I disapproved of his behaviour. "I'm on a peaceful research mission from Earth. Our station is orbiting the planet Omphi. I need your help in contacting my team, please."

It remained unclear if Crux understood any of that. He stared at me with his yellow eyes, focusing on my mouth for a moment then sliding his gaze further down my body. His wide nostrils continued to flare as he sniffed the air around me.

Surely, this brute couldn't be the leader of any spacecraft.

"I need to speak to whoever is in charge here." I desperately looked around, hoping to find someone with a better grasp of the situation.

The wide corridor was quickly filling with all kinds of creatures. Some had humanoid body shapes. Most were bipedal. However, I didn't recognize any of the species here. They all gaped at me, their mouths open, drool dripping off their fangs, and their tongues rolled out. It was impossible to tell if any of them were at all intelligent.

"If you just could…" I made another attempt to free my arm from Crux's grip, wishing to put some distance between us, but he only held tighter. Fear pulsed inside me. Crime had been all but eliminated back on Earth and on most of the civilized planets of the Federation. I'd never been threatened in my life, never felt as vulnerable as this man was making me feel. "By intergalactic laws, I am guaranteed personal freedom and respect," I desperately reminded him.

A memory from a history class rushed to mind. Centuries ago, space pirates had travelled these parts of the Galaxy. Could some of that remained here?

Was this a pirate ship?

I regarded this motley crew of individuals of all shapes, textures, and colors. None of them were dressed in anything that resembled a uniform of any known government.

Fear vibrated through me, but I inhaled deeply, forcing myself to act as calmly as possible. Pirates could still be negotiated with. Hopefully, even the one who kept holding me…

My hope for any intelligent communication with him had quickly evaporated the moment he licked my ear then bit on my neck.

"Hey! That hurt!" I yelled, trying to twist out of his grip once again.

He finally let go of my arm, but only to grab me around my waist next.

Stricken by panic, I forgot all about diplomacy.

"Let me go!" I jammed an elbow into his gut.

"Yesss," he hissed into my ear, his hot humid breath slinking down my neck. "Fight me. I like it."

Was he insane?

"Crux. Drop her," suddenly came from the crowd. It was said not exceptionally loud but in a firm voice that carried authority.

I exhaled with relief. Finally, someone in charge here.

A tall man stepped out of the thickening crowd. Subdued whispers from others reached me.

"Vrateus…"

"Captain is here."

Nearly as tall as Crux or Wyck, the newcomer appeared to be leaner. His silver-white hair looked more like long fur, streaked with black. It had been shaved off above his pointy ears, the skin there decorated with intricate tattoos. The same fur covered his forearms and the back of his hands. He flexed his fingers, and a set of black, curved claws slid out.

This one definitely could be a pirate. He even dressed the part, complete with a wide-sleeved white shirt and tall boots. Two long swords were strapped to his back by embossed leather belts. Huge gems glistened on his fingers, and a row of golden hoops decorated each of his ears.

His outfit appeared to come straight from some theater play. To my knowledge, no one in the Galaxy dressed like that anymore. No one.

The noise of shuffling feet and rumbling voices lowered to a hum with his appearance.

"Sir," I said with renewed hope. "I am Svetlana Kostyk, on a research mission from Earth. My spaceship suffered an accident…"

The newcomer paid absolutely no attention to me. His focus was fully on Crux.

"I said, drop her," he growled, baring a pair of long, white fangs.

He slowly raised his arm. With a hard click, a metal gun appeared in his hand, seemingly coming out of nowhere.

I stared at it in shock. Was it an actual weapon? I had never seen one before.

He pointed the gun at Crux.

Chapter 2

VRATEUS

His eyes on Crux, he mentally dared his second in command to disobey. That would finally give him a legitimate reason to shoot the *errock*.

Vrateus had given him an order, twice. There was no third time.

Crux knew it. With a hard swallow, he finally released his grip, letting his prize drop to the ground.

Vrateus suppressed a sigh of relief. With Crux, open disobedience was just a matter of time.

"I saw her first." The *errock* took a wide stance, not moving away from the girl.

Vrateus didn't spare her a glance. She didn't matter. If Crux got his way, she'd be dead before morning anyway.

And if the *errock* didn't get his way, Vrateus risked a mutiny.

There was no place for a woman on the Dark Anomaly. The last few females brought to the Anomaly by its gravitational field had died within hours, brutally raped to death, their bodies eaten by the *ognats* and *kreers*.

That was ten years ago.

Vrateus had been the captain for seven years, now. He'd fought hard to gain control over the feral shipwreck population. And he had been working even harder to maintain the fragile order ever since.

Now, the sudden appearance of this female threatened to undo the results of his labor in seconds.

"She is mine," Crux gritted through his teeth.

The *errock's* jaw muscles twitched, his massive hands fisted at his sides. He was obviously waiting for a better moment to start a fight, to claim what he had already believed was his—the girl.

Vrateus's hackles rose in response. His tail lashed against his boots.

"Yours?" he forced himself to lower his arm but didn't send the gun to its holster. "For how long?"

"For as long as I want her." Crux glowered at him.

"Which would be an hour. Maybe?" Most likely less than that. At least a decade older than Vrateus, Crux had taken an active part in that last brutality. The lives of at least a few females killed that night were on Crux's hands. Rough and vicious, he would give the woman zero chances of survival. "Then what?"

Crux rubbed the back of his neck. "Who cares?"

"I'm sure the rest of them would." Vrateus tipped his head over his shoulder, gesturing at his crew.

"Let all of us have her then!" one of the *ognats* yelled, Naizu, the most bloodthirsty of them all. His eight pairs of skinny limbs were undulating impatiently.

Vrateus's law forbidding cannibalism was especially detested by *ognats*. However, they were not the only race on the Dark Anomaly that would eat sentient beings if given a chance. Most of Vrateus's crew would want to fuck the girl first, but some might also eat her afterwards.

"And how is that going to work?" he asked, sarcastically.

"We'll take turns!" someone excitedly shouted from the crowd.

Several growls supported the idea.

That would create a fuck frenzy that Vrateus wished to avoid—for the female's sake, he realized with annoyance. Part of him wished the girl would have died in the crash. Saving her life seemed to be a nearly impossible task now.

Maintaining power over his people meant carefully balancing the often-opposing interests of different groups and species. As long as Vrateus kept them divided, he held control over all of them. The presence of the female now gave them a reason to unite against him.

The simplest thing to do would be to give her to them. Let them do whatever they wanted with her—fuck her or eat her.

There were over seven hundred of them, though. Most wouldn't get anywhere near her before every trace of her ravaged body would be annihilated. Then there would be fights, murders, and more cannibalism.

Restoring order would take everything he had with no guarantee of success.

He rubbed his face. Running this place was exhausting.

A huge issue was that he had already stopped Crux. Letting the *errock* have his way now would make it look like Vrateus was giving in. He did *not* give in to anyone. For seven years, Vrateus had ruled with undisputed authority. He could not afford to have his decisions questioned publicly—even the decisions he hadn't made yet.

He had no idea what to do with the girl.

"Yeah, so, who's going first?" Naizu hissed, inching closer on his skinny legs. Saliva dripped from both corners of his lipless mouth. His long, body—black, glossy back and beige, mottled belly—slithered her way.

"Me!" Crux stood over the girl, his fists raised to defend his prey. "I saw her first."

"But you didn't fight for her," Krakhil, a huge *dimo*, roared, placing all four of his hands on his hips.

"We need to pull numbers! Lottery!" The shouts came out of the crowd.

"That's fair," others agreed.

The air in the corridor was charged with lust and aggression—an explosive mix waiting for the slightest spark to detonate into violence.

"Fuck the lottery. I want her now." Naizu dove for the girl, grabbing her ankles. His long black tongue slicked out, running over his sharp teeth.

She jerked back with a grimace of utter horror, letting out a panicked scream.

That scream...

It pierced Vrateus's brain with memory, painful and toxic.

"Back, I said!"

He shot. The bullet hit Naizu in the back of his head.

Thick, greenish blood splashed over the pristine white of the girl's bodysuit. The scream caught in her throat, turning into a gurgle of shock as the *ognut* dropped to the ground, dead, his head landing between her legs.

"Anyone else want to try?" Vrateus released the second gun from its holster inside his sleeve and wrapped his fingers around the smooth metal handle.

He had a laser gun strapped to his thigh, a knife hidden inside each of his boots, two swords attached criss-cross to his back, and a dagger concealed in its sheath at his chest. That was his light, everyday armament. Had he known there'd be a female on the new shipwreck, he'd have at least doubled it.

His crew stilled, those in the front shuffling back. No one but him was allowed to wear weapons of any kind on the Dark Anomaly. Vrateus was the only one armed. He had made sure of it.

"All right." He took a pause, sweeping the crowd with a heavy stare to make sure all attention was on him. "There are seven hundred and forty-four—" he glanced at the dead body of the *ognut*. The girl had shrunk away from it, hugging her legs. "...forty-*three* of you. And only one female."

"We'll take turns," Brel, a *kreer*, suggested again, only in a slightly less sure voice now.

"*Seven hundred and forty-three*, Brel. She'd be dead within the first hour if you all get on her at once. Most of you would get nothing at all."

"We'll space it out." Krakhil elbowed a *yourlu*, shoving his hard-plated elbow into the *yourlu's* soft shoulder. "Qen here wouldn't mind waiting for his turn. Would you, Qen?"

Qen rubbed his shoulder with one of the three tentacles he had instead of a left arm.

"How long would I have to wait?" he squeaked.

"Good question." Vrateus shifted his weight to his other foot. "If each of you got her for a day, how long do you think those at the back would have to wait?" He paused for effect, not expecting an answer—math skills were not one of the strengths of his crew. "Almost two years."

Groans of frustration filled the corridor.

"She can be fucked more than once a day," someone grumped, disheartened. "Twice? At least?"

"That would still be nearly a year wait for those at the back," Vrateus retorted. "And that is if the guy before you has been gentle enough for you to get her alive." He leveled a pointed stare at Crux. "You know there's an excellent chance she will not survive that long. Not all species have the endurance for that lifestyle. And she is..." He finally took a good look at the girl, trying to identify what species she was.

She glared at him with her big, dark eyes, the color of aged bronze. The long filaments on her head looked more like hair than fur—a deep shade of brown. Her skin was of a similar color to his, maybe a shade or two lighter. He saw no wings, horns or claws on her. The only tail she had was on the back of her head, but it didn't seem to be functional, hanging limply down her back. She might have injured it during the crash.

What was she?

"Who are you?" he asked.

She straightened her back. Her composure was admirable, though it wouldn't help her situation.

"I told you, my name is Svetlana Kostyk. I am the mission specialist with the research team from Earth. My planet is the newest member of the Federation—"

"Species?" he cut her off.

Her dark eyebrows moved closer together as she levelled him a disapproving glare.

"Human," she gave him a clipped reply.

He searched his memory for the species with that name and found nothing. He was certain he'd never seen anyone like her before.

Staring at her, he'd lost his train of thought and had to gather his focus before addressing his crew again.

"As I said, the wait for those at the back would be nearly a year." He still had no definite plan, working on it as he went. "Do you want to spend that much time, not getting a thing from our bounty here?" He glanced down at the girl again, and she gave him another glare, filled with shock and resentment.

"What other choices do we have?" came a question from the crowd.

Over the years, he had trained them to expect solutions to problems from him.

"I'd say, fuck the waiting. Let's have fun now!" Krakhil roared, his deep, rumbling voice rising over the noise.

"It would be a very short-lived fun, I'm afraid." Vrateus kept his own voice calm and even. Showing any emotions would only fuel the excitement of the males already charged with lust in the female's presence.

"You want to keep her to yourself!" Crux growled accusingly.

Vrateus considered that option briefly and quickly dismissed it. Taking the girl for himself would ignite a riot. Crux would be the one to start it. The *errock* had laid his hands on her—in his mind, the girl was already his property. If denied any access to her now, Crux would snap, all *errocks* would follow, quickly joined by the others.

All seven hundred united against Vrateus.

The exact situation he had been masterfully avoiding for years.

"Give her to us," several voices demanded. "Even if for just one night of fun."

The strangled gasp of the girl reached him. Without looking at her, he sensed her tension. Her fear.

"It might be fun. But only for some." He let his words sink into their minds. An idea formed in his head, but he knew he needed to lead them to it carefully. "What do you do for fun now?"

"Fight!" many yelled.

That was true. Most of them participated in the nightly fights he organized to let them work out some testosterone and aggression.

"What else?"

"Eat!" someone shouted.

After the years of hard work Vrateus had put his crew through, the Dark Anomaly finally was producing enough food to sustain them all. There was enough to eat for fun, not just for survival.

"Gardening," came a quiet voice.

Malahki.

The *damirian* spent a lot of time in the in-door gardens, taking care of plants. Vrateus didn't expect to see Malahki here. The *damirian* had no gender. It was neither male nor female. Lust didn't affect its species at this stage of their development.

Curiosity was not a gendered quality, though. Anything out of the ordinary passed for entertainment on the Dark Anomaly.

"What else?" he prompted. "What else do many of you do for fun before falling asleep?"

"Fuck!" Trox, one of the *errocks*, smirked.

"You can't call it *fucking* if you're on your own." Nocc, another *errock*, guffawed, shoving an elbow in Trox's side. "You jerk off."

"Right." Vrateus tilted his head, carefully keeping the mood of his crew in focus. "How about if you had a female sitting next to you while you did that?"

"While I'm jerking off, you mean?" Nocc huffed another laugh. "She wouldn't be sitting *next* to me! She'd be right on top of me!"

"Or under!" Someone yelled, cheerfully.

"With both of my cocks deep inside her!" Nocc guffawed.

The crowd grew loud with approval, threatening to get out of control at any moment.

"We've already established *that* can't happen!" Vrateus raised his voice, speaking over the increasing noise. "You can't *all* have sex with her and make the fun last. But you *can* have her next to you—"

A series of confused exclamations interrupted him.

"What for?"

"Naked?"

"Is she gonna touch me, Captain?"

He lifted his arm in a wordless call to silence.

"No touching. But you can *see* her." He gazed over their faces, gauging their reaction. "And yes, she'll be naked."

"Watching her while I'm jerking off?" Crux stared at him with less hatred and more confusion.

"You can see her naked flesh as you stroke yourselves," Vrateus explained, evenly. "You can hear her moans as she touches herself—for all of you to watch."

Crux's green-spotted yellow eyes flashed with lust. Vrateus forced down the uncomfortable feeling. Sexually exciting his second in command was not his intention tonight, or any night for that matter.

The words worked, though. He put an image in the heads of the males. Now he needed to firmly nail that idea to their brains.

"You will be able to watch her every week, for as long as she shall live. And *this* way, she shall live much longer than just for a night. We'll start tomorrow."

It was time to leave.

He needed to remove the girl while the males mulled over his idea. Having her sitting here as an invitation for immediate action was dangerous.

Vrateus also needed to keep Crux from touching her again. He had to put the scent of another male on her, to eliminate any trace of Crux's claim.

"Wyck, get her up," he ordered to the youngest *errock*.

As soon as Wyck complied, Vrateus motioned for him to take the woman down the corridor, keeping the rest of the crew in his view.

The crowd's excitement ran too high to settle right away.

"Why tomorrow? Why not right now?" they shouted at his back as he headed after Wyck and the female.

"She's hurt and filthy," he threw over his shoulder, not slowing down the pace. "Once she has eaten and rested, she'll moan louder."

Chapter 3

WHAT ON EARTH HAD JUST happened?

Could any of this be real? Or was I hallucinating, still lying unconscious after the crash?

With Wyck's meaty hand around my arm and Vrateus walking on my other side, I was hurried down the corridor to keep up with their pace. It was especially challenging over the uneven floors, bulging up in some places and dipping in others. It required concentration not to trip.

More creatures stared at us from side corridors and doors as we passed. Some moved my way, but Vrateus and Wyck shoved them aside.

My stomach was tied in knots, my head swam with dizziness, and my legs barely obeyed my brain.

There must be something wrong with my translator. Otherwise, I would have to believe that the leader of this bizarre group had just promised his people some sexual favors on my behalf.

It was absurd. Illegal. And unethical. Immoral, too. Yet he seemed to find it absolutely acceptable.

I hesitated to clarify anything with him while we remained in the presence of others. Though I wasn't looking forward to being one on one with him, either.

"Here." Vrateus stopped in front of a round, pewter double door. "She'll stay in this room." He hit the side panel with his palm, making the doors slide open, then walked in.

Wyck let go of my arm but didn't follow his boss. Instead, he silently nudged me toward the open doors.

"Are you coming?" Vrateus snapped at me, with an annoyed glance over his shoulder.

The clear resentment in his eyes baffled me. What have I done to deserve any of this?

Anger flared inside me. I dug my heels in defiantly, folding my arms across my chest.

"I believe you owe me an explanation," I said in a much less diplomatic tone of voice than before.

Crux and some of the others came into view at that moment. They rushed our way down the corridor. Wyck's chained monster hissed.

Even annoyed at me, Vrateus still seemed like the lesser of two evils, and I promptly entered the room. He immediately hit the door's side panel, shutting the doors with a soft swishing sound.

"You'll stay here." He stepped aside.

My breath suddenly caught in my throat with a gasp.

The room was made entirely out of glass. Like a soap bubble with a flattened bottom for the floor, it protruded from the wall of the ship into the vast space beyond.

Outside looked like nothing I had ever seen, even after nearly a year of working in space. Shimmering waves of multi-colored lights ebbed and curved through the absolute darkness surrounding me. Beyond the lights, the distant stars twinkled.

Standing on the clear glass, surrounded by undulating lights from all sides, made me feel like I was falling.

"Ahh!" I exhaled in shock, spreading my arms in an attempt to hold on to something.

Then the sensation of floating in space came.

"You're not afraid of open spaces, are you?" Vrateus asked calmly.

"No. Not afraid. It's just..." I swayed, struggling to find a reference point for at least a modicum of balance as everything around me appeared to move along with the lights. "Unsettling. Like a free fall. Or flying. Weird, but not scary."

"Good." He moved back to the entrance, leaving me in the middle of the floor, my arms spread wide like wings. "*Errocks* are terrified of open spaces. They'll never come in here."

His comment hardly registered.

"What's generating the light?" I asked, mesmerized. "I've never seen anything like it."

His chest expanded with a deep breath as he folded his arms across it.

"That is the Dark Anomaly. You must have known you were near it when you crashed."

"Do you mean space anomaly GR-A8502?"

"We call it 'the Dark Anomaly.' But sure, why not assign it a number?" He shrugged on his way to the door. "I have to go. There is always a lot of work with each new ship's arrival. Don't stare at the lights for too long. They can drive you mad."

The space abnormality my team had been studying had looked *dark* on the images. Upon its discovery, it had been initially mistaken for a black hole. Professor Zhang Wei Liu was the first one to calculate a number of dissimilarities in its behaviour. A significant one being that unlike black holes, the Anomaly did not grow. Neither did it suck in any celestial bodies nearby. It didn't absorb planets or stars.

We'd been unable to peer inside it, but the gravitational force of it was strong enough to rival that of a large star or a giant planet. Unlike them, however, its gravity behaved differently, too.

"How did you get this close to it?" I couldn't tear my gaze away from the hypnotic lights. "How come the gravity doesn't pull us in right now?"

"Because we're already inside it, human," he said before exiting the room. "You're looking *out* of the Dark Anomaly, into the open space beyond."

I KEPT STARING AT THE lights long after he had left. After a while, the awareness of this room and the glass around me had completely disappeared. All that remained was the feeling of floating in space, surrounded by the undulating colors and light.

"Don't stare at the lights for too long. They can drive you mad."

I understood what he meant. The sense of reality was no longer there, but I didn't miss it. The brutal aliens, their captain, this insane grotesque world—all seemed to be just remnants of a bad dream. A nightmare I hoped to wake up from soon.

The sound of the doors opening yanked me back into reality again.

"Dinner," the captain's voice sounded behind me, and I slowly turned around.

Carrying a tray in one hand, he rolled a small table in with the other. A group of his thugs lingered outside the door, peeking in over his shoulders. Their smirking faces proved even more sobering.

This was real. I still didn't understand why or how, but this world truly existed.

The wall between the room and the corridor was of the same solid pewter-colored metal as the doors. Both provided a stable point of reference that helped me finally ground myself. Facing the wall, I felt the floor under my feet once again.

The captain deposited the tray on the table. When he turned around to get more things from his crew, his tail came into view.

He had a tail! How could I have not spotted it before? Covered in long, silver-white fur, it swayed delicately, the black tip reaching the tops of his tall boots.

I'd never seen an alien this close before. Despite the dreadful situation, my undying curiosity won over fear for the time being. I openly ogled him as he brought in a roll of blankets and a metal box.

His skin color was that of deep tan, as if he indeed was the captain of an ancient pirate ship, with his skin bronzed by the sun and weathered by the ocean winds. The hard features of his face seemed to be chiselled out of a mountain cliff. He wasn't beautiful, but he could still be considered handsome, in some harsh, rugged way.

His black eyebrows furrowed the moment he caught me staring.

"Sleeping pallet." He tossed the bed roll at my feet. "May I suggest you place it in the part of the room farthest from the door. We'll search for a real bed for you later."

"Listen..." I scrambled to collect my thoughts.

He pressed an open metal box into my hands, obviously uninterested in anything I had to say. "Here are some toiletries. Everyone is allowed a five-minute shower a day. And no, the minutes do not roll over into the next day. Use them or lose them."

I mechanically clutched the box to my chest.

"What is this place?" I asked one of the gazillion questions that crowded my brain.

"Dark Anomaly." He lifted an eyebrow. "I thought we've already covered that."

"Can you...fly your ship in and out of it?"

The Anomaly did not absorb celestial bodies. However, it had sucked in any probe or unmanned research vessel we had ever sent near it. Past a certain point, which was slightly different for each object, all transmissions stopped. And we had been unable to retrieve any of the probes or vessels.

"Dark Anomaly sucks things *in*. No one gets *out*." He said it slowly, as if depositing every word into my brain then waiting for me to absorb it.

"Have you tried to steer the ship—"

He tilted his head, not letting me finish. "Which one of the millions of wrecked ships would you suggest I *steer*?"

Despite the thick sarcasm in his tone, I replied as calmly as I could manage, "Whichever is in the best shape. My spacesuit actually could—"

"No, it couldn't," he cut me off. "The solid part in the center of the Dark Anomaly, where we are, is made entirely of crushed spaceships. For ages, this thing has been sucking them in, smashing them into each other, then squishing them together, into a disk. We are on the very edge of it here, where the newly arrived vessels still have room between the walls. Using the energy we get from the lights of the Anomaly, we have made this sector of the disk habitable. This is home. Yours too, now. The only one you'll ever have. The sooner you accept it, the higher your chances of survival will be."

"This place is not my 'home!'" It could never be.

He barely dignified me with a look in response.

My dire situation was turning into a nightmare, and I feverishly searched for a way to end it.

"How about contacting the ships passing by, outside of its gravitational field? My station is—"

"The Dark Anomaly absorbs any kind of communication waves," he explained with a tired expression. "Reaching the outside world is impossible."

I blinked at him, lost for words for a moment.

Vrateus might fully believe what he was saying, but I couldn't blindly accept any of this as facts without testing them first. There had to be a way out of here. He just hadn't found it yet. Or he simply wasn't interested in helping me.

He obviously mistook my silence for acceptance.

"Well, let's see..." He slid an assessing gaze down my body. It wasn't immediately clear what exactly he was *assessing*. "I'll organize a search for clothes for you tomorrow. There are not enough hours left for that today."

Only now had I noticed the slight slump in his wide shoulders and signs of exhaustion on his face.

"I don't need clothes," I protested. My bodysuit was self-cleaning and required minimal maintenance. Besides, I wasn't planning to stay here for long. "My team will be searching for me."

"The only way anyone can find you is if they crash here, too. We'll deal with that when or if it happens," he dismissed.

Our protocol required for a search party to be sent to look for a missing person. However, I doubted my team leader would send anyone inside the Anomaly. Even if they discovered exactly how I had disappeared, the risk of losing another person without knowing what to expect inside this abnormality would be too great.

With or without the rescue party, however, I was determined to find my way out of here.

"Vrateus, I'll be leaving here, one way or another—"

"No, you won't." He wouldn't listen.

He brushed his hand over his face in a gesture that betrayed how tired he was.

Maybe right now wasn't the best time to argue or even try to reason? Would he be more agreeable if he rested?

He raked his fingers, tipped with black claws, through the fur on his head. It seemed thick and soft, bringing the fur of an arctic fox to mind. It ran in a wide stripe up his nape and along the middle of his head, ending in a thick wave hanging over his forehead. The visual softness of it clashed with his chiseled jaw and sharp cheekbones. And with his hard attitude, too...

"Eat." He pointed at the bowl on the tray, piled high with things not all of which I would consider food. "Then rest. You'll need your strength for tomorrow night."

Alarm shot through me at that reminder.

"You weren't serious about that, were you? You don't really want me to...um, do what you told them I'd do?"

No one would expect a person to do anything of that sort. Would they?

He glanced at me, confused.

"I promised my crew some entertainment. That's the reason you're still alive," he said it as if he had done me a huge favor by bargaining with my body without my permission.

"You must know it's illegal to force me." I shook my head in disbelief. "You didn't discuss anything with me. All I wanted was some assistance—"

"What *you* want is irrelevant." He jerked his head to the side, impatiently. "There are over seven hundred males in here. They all want a piece of you, some literally. The trick was to convince them to want *less* of you. And I have accomplished that."

Lifting an eyebrow, he leveled me a stare. Was he expecting me to be grateful for what he'd done "for me?"

"You've promised them what wasn't yours to give!" I snapped. "How are you planning to deliver it? Surely, you don't think I will act out your perverted fantasies?"

His jaw flexed. He folded his arms across his chest, his tail lashing against his boots.

"What choice do you have?"

"The choice *not* to do it." I widened my stance.

"And who would protect you from the wrath of their disappointment? Do you know what hundreds of sex-starved males can do to one female?" He flinched.

I grimaced, too, trying not to imagine what he had implied.

Was he trying to scare me? Why?

Several interplanetary laws guaranteed my freedom and wellbeing anywhere in the Federation's territory. I could recite them all by heart. All intelligent races of the Galaxy abided by the law of the Federation—the crime had been practically non-existent for decades.

"Why are you threatening me?" I asked.

"It's not a threat. Just the simple truth."

My mind flashed back to the scene in the corridor. Vrateus had shot one of his people in front of everyone, with no repercussions.

True, the male who'd attacked me had crossed the line, but I didn't think he deserved to be killed without getting a chance to defend himself. He had been a talking, thinking individual—a life that shouldn't have been disposed of so easily.

Obviously, the captain didn't respect any interplanetary laws.

My mentality struggled to adjust to this new reality. I felt disoriented, outside of my normal frame of reference.

Did Vrateus want me to beg for his personal protection?

"I suspect next you'll say you'll save me from the big, bad guys out there, but there's a price? Is that it?"

He frowned.

"I've already done all I can to save you. The rest is up to you."

With another irritated flip of his tail, he left.

Chapter 4

VRATEUS

There was still so much to do before he could call it a night.

Each newly arrived ship had to be stripped for every piece of equipment that could be reasonably used as a weapon. It had to be done tonight, no matter how tired he was.

As he worked on cataloguing the items and sorting them into boxes, his thoughts kept coming back to the woman who had arrived on this ship.

What an infuriating, ungrateful female she'd turned out to be.

He had left her alone, in the relative safety of the observation capsule of the ship that had crashed on the Dark Anomaly about a decade ago. The decade as calculated here, according to the arbitrary clock he had established and maintained.

He had long suspected that time on the Anomaly did not flow quite the same as it did outside of it. It appeared to run much slower here.

Whenever a new ship crashed, Vrateus would analyze the data, weapons, and equipment it had. He would estimate the amount of time that had passed in the world outside against the age of the data and technology that he'd recovered from the previously crashed ship.

For every year on the Dark Anomaly, about three hundred years passed on a regular, inhabitable planet like Nofoi, the home of his family. Which meant he had been missing from that world for over six thousand years, now.

Not that it mattered, anyway. No one was there to actually *miss* him. Everyone who'd ever known his family must be long dead by now. And no one outside of the Dark Anomaly would ever see him again. As far as the rest of the world was concerned, none of the people inside the Anomaly existed.

This was a world on its own.

Suppressing a yawn, he pinched the inside of his wrist, forcing himself to stay awake and alert as he inspected the rest of the human's ship.

Crux and Nocc stood nearby.

"To keep watch," Vrateus had told Crux.

In truth, he wanted to have the *errock* close by to keep an eye on *him*. By having Crux close, Vrateus ensured he wasn't out there stirring trouble among the rest of the crew.

Crux was ambitious, unpredictable, cruel, and dangerous. He was also the leader of the *errocks* on the Dark Anomaly, the largest and physically strongest species.

Vrateus had relied on their brawn to keep his crew members in order, especially during the first years of his rise to power. Strong, huge, and ruthless, *errocks* proved useful at enforcing his rules and establishing his authority over the rest.

Leading this community of shipwrecks wasn't easy. Being the only one of his species left on the Anomaly, Vrateus needed the assistance of others. Not that he ever could trust anyone here completely.

He blinked, trying to chase away the sleep that had been clouding his brain with increasing persistence.

With a glance at the watch on his belt, he realized he had been awake for over twenty hours now. Dealing with the aftermath of the crash of the human's little spaceship had taken all his evening and most of his night.

"We're done here for today," he called over to Crux, entering the last piece of equipment into the catalogue on his tablet.

The human wasn't lying when she said her mission was peaceful. Judging by its equipment, the ship had a scientific purpose, not a military one. Although unfamiliar with most of it, he realized that the things he had catalogued must be tools, not weapons. However, if they could effectively kill, he qualified them as weapons.

The rest could wait until tomorrow, he decided, sweeping his gaze over the warped walls of the damaged spaceship. In a few centuries, Anomaly time, all of this would move closer to its center. As the disk rotated, the ships crushed and compressed until there was no more space left between the walls. The pressure grew even stronger in the very middle of the disk, fusing all materials in a homogenous matter that bulged up into a sphere at the center.

In a few centuries time, he would be gone one way or another, and none of this would matter.

Until then...

"Come," he ordered Crux and Nocc.

Each of them lifted a box with the catalogued equipment, taking it down the hall to his room. It was identical to the one he had assigned to the female, located just a short distance down the corridor from hers.

Passing by her door, he realized he wasn't done for the night.

At the entrance to his room, he let Crux and Nocc go, then hauled the boxes with tools inside on his own.

He had chosen to live in this room for the same reason he had put the female in hers. The *errocks* had an extreme fear of large open spaces. They would never enter a room made entirely out of clear material, and it was therefore the only place in the Dark Anomaly where he could get some sleep.

The sleep would have to wait tonight, though. After quickly shoving the boxes into the secret storage room he had opened from his bathroom into the wreck of the spaceship one layer below, Vrateus left for the library.

He had promised his crew that the human woman would moan in pleasure. Judging by her words and the glares she had given him, she was not inclined to cooperate in delivering on that promise. Her resistance would end up costing her her life. And the death would not be one he'd wish on his worst enemy.

To keep her alive, he needed her to prove her value to his crew. She had to convince them all that they would get more entertainment from her being alive than from killing her.

He was not against helping her with that, but he needed to educate himself first.

The library was a large room he had expanded into the mass of compressed wreckage, off the main corridor. Here, shelves with opal tablet inserts lined the walls, organized by subject then by the *themul* alphabet of his species.

Heaving a sigh, he contemplated what exactly he needed. Although, he had never heard of humans before, there might be some information on them in the data he had added to his collection in recent years.

The female spoke of the Federation. If humans now were a part of it, there could be mentions of them in the information he'd retrieved from the recently crashed, unmanned ships.

Pulling out the few inserts off the shelves, he grabbed some on mating rituals of *themul* and other humanoid species that might be biologically similar to the woman in his care.

Back in his room, he kicked off his boots, got out of his clothes then unclipped, unholstered, and unstrapped the weapons from his body. Running his hands through the thick fur on his head he arched his back, stretching the muscles and letting the tension of the day finally drain a little.

His gaze drifted to the small figure of the human in the capsule beside his. He had dimmed the glass of his room from the outside. However, he had kept *her* glass completely transparent to keep an eye on her.

As a result, he remained invisible to her, but he could see her clearly.

With her arms wrapped around her, she was sitting on her knees on the floor at the farthest end of her capsule. Her forehead pressed to the glass, she stared straight into the raging storm of light.

He had spent many nights doing the same, wishing he could reach out beyond the lights and into the world.

No one escaped the Dark Anomaly, though. The human was trapped here for life—just like the rest of them were. All she could do was try to survive.

He turned away. Grabbing his tablet frame, he slid the first opal insert in. The surface of the insert came to life, turning into a glowing screen in his hands. Stretching in his narrow, metal bed, he started reading.

As he had feared, there wasn't much information on humans. When the ship before hers had crashed, they had just been discovered, but hadn't been contacted by the interplanetary Federation yet.

The notes on her species were scarce and dry—the expected lifespan, the natural habitat, the general characteristics. Only a few facts on reproduction.

Apparently, some humans mated for life, but some didn't. Breeding was spontaneous, largely unregulated by their governments. Thankfully, like most species he knew, humans appeared to enjoy having sex as recreation, not solely for reproduction.

He found a diagram of male and female bodies and examined it, then compared it to the similar diagrams of other species.

His main goal was to figure out what to do to make the female moan tomorrow night and every night thereafter, but he got sidetracked, watching the mating videos of *themul* and other species.

Vrateus viewed his own arousal as just another function of his body that needed to be addressed from time to time.

When he was hungry, he ate. When his bladder got full, he used the bathroom. When his cock got hard and achy, he stroked it until the climax brought him release.

Never before had he used an outside stimulation to cause an erection. Being in a state of arousal was distracting.

For the same reason, he stayed away from the *irsen* flowers that Malahki grew in a hidden corner of the gardens. The sweet juice from the flowers would make him temporarily forget about the struggle for survival on the Dark Anomaly, about the brutal murders he had witnessed most of his life, about the screams of men being ripped apart alive, and women being brutally raped when his family ship crashed here over two decades ago... One of the women was his mother.

As much as he would welcome the oblivion, losing control over his mind around here could mean losing his life. For Vrateus, survival came with staying alert and aware at all times. All he allowed himself was a glass of berry wine on some exceptionally hard nights.

Like the juice of the *irsen* flowers, the arousal blunted his awareness, which made it just another weakness to him. He never searched for extra stimulation, dealing with physical desire as it came—once or twice a week.

Watching the videos of the different species having sex was an unfamiliar experience for him, causing a wide range of emotions.

He knew that *ognats,* for example, chewed the heads of their females off during copulation. The larvae resulting from the insemination consumed the female's body while growing inside her. The video of that was just as revolting as it sounded, and he promptly skipped it.

Several other species he had chosen, although they looked like the human at first glance, had very different insemination processes and reproductive organs.

Akuks didn't copulate at all, for example. The females of the species detested being touched by males. They laid eggs in a room of their house and left for the day while the males inseminated the eggs in their absence.

Finally, he turned on the videos of *themul*, his own species, which he had tried to avoid, unsure of the emotions they might bring out in him.

Vrateus was the only one left of his kind in this place. As an eight-year-old boy, he'd escaped the bloody carnage and a brutal death by hiding on the day of the crash. He then spent years surviving out of sight of the crude and violent inhabitants of the Anomaly.

He had stolen and begged for food, eating garbage when he had to.

When a ship crashed that had *vasai* centipedes on board, they escaped, populating the deep bowels of the Dark Anomaly. He learned to hunt the giant centipedes, eating some of the meat and trading the rest for things he needed.

During all that time, he had been gathering information on the variety of species occupying the Anomaly. Reading and learning, watching and listening, he had been biding his time until he had become strong and smart enough to take over and name himself their captain.

He had never seen a *themul* female he wasn't related to. Or if he had seen one, he didn't remember.

He had certainly never seen one bare or touched one.

The bodies of the *themul* females in the video were of a similar shape and proportion to the human female. Like her, they were narrower in the middle, with wider hips. Unlike hers, their chests were much flatter. *Themuls* had between two to six young per pregnancy, and had three rows of small, dark-nippled breasts on their chest and upper belly.

In the diagram on his tablet, the human female had two, larger breasts. And he distinctly remembered two lumps pushing against the material of the woman's bodysuit.

The males of one of the tribes on Nofoi apparently had their females collared during the wedding ceremony, the way Wyck had chained Lesh, his pet. The end of the leash was attached to the male's belt.

Something about that tradition appealed to Vrateus. He liked the idea of having his female nearby and of what the collar represented: possession and connection.

Although, he had to admit that it would not work on the Dark Anomaly. It reduced the female's chance of survival if he were killed. She would be trapped, chained to him, with a limited range of movement to fight for her life, and with no way to run and hide.

When the couple in the video were left alone, they came closer to each other, bringing their mouths together. The male then licked down the row of nipples on the front of his female, making her moan and squirm. Flipping her on her stomach, the male fisted his hand in the thick white-with-black fur of her scruff, ramming his cock into her from behind.

She threw her head back, baring her canines and growling in obvious pleasure as he pounded into her, their tails intertwined between their legs.

The primal passion of the couple, combined with the display of their mutual pleasure, shot straight to his groin. He shifted in his bed, making room for his growing erection. This was unexpected—definitely outside of his usual schedule of about once or twice a week.

Setting the tablet aside, he rose on his elbow and fisted his straining cock. It throbbed and ached, growing harder as he slid his hand up and down its length. The images from the video, now stored in his mind, spurred his arousal, sending him to his back with a groan. He arched his spine, pumping faster, the impending orgasm building up.

Rolling his head on the pillow, he faced the human's room. She was no longer in sight, Instead, he saw the outline of her form under the covers of her sleeping pallet by the wall.

The climax hit him, stronger than ever before, shuddering his entire body. He growled, baring his teeth and lashing his tail as the release pumped out of him in thick, ivory spurts.

After that he lay spent, wondering how much more of his measured, carefully organized life of survival was about to unravel because of one little female who couldn't steer her spacecraft away from the clutches of the Dark Anomaly.

Chapter 5

SURPRISINGLY, I HAD gotten some sleep, though it was hard to tell how long I slept. When I woke up, the lights of the Anomaly continued their dance—ever-changing, yet perpetually the same.

I had eaten some of the food that Vrateus had brought last night—a mouldy smelling stew garnished with some leaves and a few pieces of sour fruit that looked like spotted tennis balls.

Thankfully, my stomach felt much better this morning. The food, as unpleasant as it was, must have agreed with it.

Next, I picked up the box with the toiletries Vrateus had given me and headed to the wall with the door in search of the bathroom.

Our conversation last night didn't go well. Maybe, he was too tired to think logically? Now, that he'd hopefully had some rest, the chances to find some understanding between us might be better.

How long had he been here, in this place, away from the real world? That could explain why his perception of things was so different from mine.

The Anomaly turned out to be nothing like what humans had expected. Not once during our mission had the theory of life existing inside it been brought up.

I'd read reports of ships disappearing in this area during the early days of space travel. The last disappearances of live beings had happened centuries before humans made contact with the other species populating our Galaxy.

How long had this crew and their captain been surviving here? What generation of survivors could they be?

The word *errock* finally triggered my memory. It was the name of one species I had learned about in the academy. *Errocks* were a civilized nation, living on Hexol, one of the planets of the Federation.

No wonder I didn't recognize them when Wyck and Crux barged into my ship. The pictures I had seen of the *errocks* were those of well-groomed politicians and scientists, dressed in sleek, tailored suits or lab coats. None of them looked rugged and wild like Crux, Wyck, and the rest of this feral bunch. I was certain their out-of-control behavior would not be tolerated on their home planet, either.

Whatever this place was, my priority remained finding a way out of here.

My mission commander must have sent a search party when I had failed to return to the station yesterday. However, I couldn't realistically expect anyone to rescue me. At the very least, I needed to find a way off the Anomaly on my own to meet the search party outside of its gravitational field.

I found the bathroom behind the door next to the entrance of my room. The door slid open the moment I touched it. The water in the shower turned out to be barely lukewarm, not inviting me to linger. I barely managed to wash and rinse my hair before it stopped running. My five minutes had run out.

Finding a towel, I dried myself then slipped back into my bodysuit.

I was combing my hair with the ornate comb I'd found in the box with the toiletries when the door to my room opened and Vrateus entered, carrying another tray with food.

"Good morning." He stopped by the door, closing it quickly, then gaped at me with a curious expression on his face.

"What time is it?" I asked, since there was no time-keeping device in this room.

He kept staring at me, following the movement of my comb with his eyes.

"It looked just like a real tail," he muttered under his breath, setting the tray on the table.

"Tail?" I touched my hair, confused.

"Never mind." He shook his head on his way out.

"Wait." I rushed after him, stopping him by the door. "Can we talk for a minute, please?"

"About what?" He gave me a suspicious glance.

"I'm afraid we didn't start off well." I clutched my hands together in front of me, determined to give diplomacy another chance. "I'd like to apologize for our misunderstanding last night."

I took a pause, waiting for an apology from him in return, but it never came.

Well, he had obviously been brought up away from civilization. A lack of manners could be expected.

"Anyway," I continued as he just stood there in his usual position, his hands folded across his wide chest. "I offer to organize a rescue mission for everyone on the Anomaly, in exchange for your help in my departure from here."

"Departure?" he scoffed. "There is no leaving this place."

Was he intentionally keeping me prisoner here? The thought was disturbing.

"I believe," I started carefully, "I may have the means to leave—"

"You *believe*?" he smirked, taking a step closer and leaning my way. "You still don't understand. Do you? The Dark Anomaly sucks things *in*. It releases nothing or anyone. Ever."

The job of a scientist was to question generally accepted opinions that were not backed by facts. Fighting the urge to shrink away from him, I stood my ground.

"Well, has anyone ever *really* tried to leave?"

"Plenty of times." He huffed a sad laugh. "All have crashed right back here—smeared on the wreckage along the edge of the disk."

That gruesome description gave me pause.

"How long has it been since the last attempt?"

"A few years now," he said, then specified, "Anomaly years."

"Are those different from the universal year definition of the Federation?"

He nodded. "According to my calculation a year here equals about three hundred universal years."

"What?" Shock suddenly made it difficult for me to draw a breath.

"I should probably get you a watch," he muttered, running his hand through the thick fur on his head.

My insides chilled as I made a quick calculation in my head. "If one year here is about three hundred universal years. Then during the day I've spent here, almost a year would have passed there?"

"About ten months." He rolled back a shoulder. "Give or take a few days."

A universal year was an equivalent of an annual rotation of an average habitable planet of the Federation. It equalled a year and eight days on Earth.

If ten months had passed since my disappearance, any rescue efforts would have been over by now.

I most likely had been declared dead...

"Are you sure?" I struggled to stay upright as my knees shook.

I prayed for this just to be another misunderstanding. It wouldn't be hard to assume that Vrateus had made a mistake in his calculations.

Deep in my gut, though, I feared he was right.

The clothes Vrateus and his crew wore, his weapons and other objects around me weren't costumes or theater props. They were old. Really, really old.

From what I knew about the cultures and history of the nations of the Federation, the comb I used to brush my hair must be from at least a millennium ago. Vrateus's handguns were probably at least a few centuries old.

Even the interior of the ships I'd seen so far, all seemed severely dated in décor and finishes. Though most were in much better shape than they should be, considering their age.

"Are you sure, Vrateus?" I repeated meekly, grasping at straws.

"Nothing can be for sure as far as the Dark Anomaly is concerned," he said firmly. "One thing is certain. You cannot leave it."

I HARDLY ATE ANYTHING that morning.

Over and over, I sifted in my mind through everything that humanity had discovered about the Anomaly, including the knowledge shared with us by alien races.

Somehow things didn't add up. I knew its gravitational field was extremely strong. Yet here I was, not crushed. In fact, the gravity here felt no different from the artificial gravity we had at my research station or that of Earth.

Did the pull of the Anomaly mostly apply to metal objects? Was that why the asteroids moved by freely when our probes ended up being sucked in from much further distances?

We had explored that possibility before. The nature of the gravity had proven not to be magnetic. The probes made entirely of the newest strongest plastics ended up sucked in just as well.

"Nothing can be for sure as far as the Dark Anomaly is concerned."

Was that why humans still had so few results, even after decades of researching this mysterious abnormality in space? There had been so many inconsistencies observed, nothing was definite.

Around lunch time, Vrateus came in again. In addition to bringing food, he also rolled in a rack of clothes. The bright colors of the fabrics rivaled those of the lights outside the glass of my room.

"Choose something else to wear tonight," he said. "I'll come for you after dinner."

He sounded dreadfully serious.

"Hold on." I shook my head. "I said I'm not doing this. I'm not changing, either."

He stopped, sliding his gaze down my body once again.

"Would you rather wear this? Do you want them to associate their sexual pleasure with your regular clothes? You know they will only salivate more over you every time they see you dressed like this. Is that what you want?"

His words sent a shudder of disgust down my back.

"I don't want their *sexual pleasure* to be associated with me, in any way." I frowned.

"That is, unfortunately, not an option I can give you."

His morose composure scared me. I felt more alone than ever before—even more than while spinning through the vastness of space all on my own, my ship out of control.

"Why not? What would happen if I just stayed in here tonight?"

"If you don't show up, they will come for you. *Errocks* wouldn't dare enter this room, but everyone else won't hesitate to break in." He heaved a sigh. "Once they get out of control, they won't stop with raping you. Every trace of your body will be gone before morning."

I fought the horror descending on me.

It couldn't be true. He'd said it to intimidate me.

He was using my fear to get me under his control.

People of the Federation didn't rape and eat each other. The very notion was beyond my comprehension. Sentient beings didn't act like wild animals.

Did they?

The image of Vrateus shooting one of his men came to mind again. I remembered the grip of the alien's chitin covered hands on my ankles, the sinister glint in his black beady eyes. What would he have done had Vrateus not stopped him?

This place could never be my home. I didn't care for whatever mind games Vrateus was playing. Even if the search for me had been called off, I needed to get out of here. And I might have an idea how I could do that.

My ship had been damaged possibly beyond repair, but my spacesuit should still be functioning. The way it was constructed, the suit was basically a little spaceship of its own. I could use the spare fuel cell from the ship to power the suit and leave the Dark Anomaly. A carefully calculated trajectory would send me back toward Omphi and several trade routes that passed by the water world. Once beyond the energy field of the Anomaly, I would send out a distress signal. Someone would intercept it and come to pick me up.

It could work. In any case, it was worth to try.

Then, I would organize a rescue mission to save these poor wretches here. Brutal and uncivilized, many of them might still be sentient beings, therefore falling under the law of the Federation. Their lives were precious, even if they didn't realize it.

Surely, their captain would welcome the opportunity to rescue his people.

"You see," I started, carefully. "This situation here could be resolved easily if you just let me go."

"Go where?" He stared at me with confusion.

"Back to where I came from. Just let me get to my ship—"

"Oh, for fuck's sake!" He threw his hands into the air. "Not this again? As much as I'd love to get rid of you, you're stuck here now. Forever. And I'm stuck with you. Do not make me regret my decision. Do what you're told. Get dressed and be ready to get naked out there."

I fought the rising anger that was fueled by indignity.

"As a figure of authority," I squeezed through my teeth, struggling to keep any kind of composure. "It is your responsibility to ensure my safety from the people under your command." My self-control finally snapped under frustration and desperation, and I yelled at him, "You're giving me to them with no effort to protect me!"

He stared back at me, in shock.

"How can you *not* see it?" His voice rose, too. "I *am* protecting you. This is the only way to keep you alive."

"By...exposing my body? Don't you try to pose as my saviour!" I shouted, my hands shaking. "You're not better than the rest of them. You're breaking the interplanetary law. Which makes you a filthy criminal."

Rage flashed fire-bright in his eyes.

"I invite the Federation Forces to come and hold me responsible, then." He swiveled to leave. "Around here, there is no law but mine!"

EVERYTHING INSIDE ME bubbled with resentment. No, it was no longer just that. Fear and indignation grew into panic and bred hot, searing anger.

Vrateus wouldn't listen to me. He had no intention of letting me go, refusing even to let me try. Obviously, he wasn't interested in being rescued, either. Why would he want to leave this place?

"Around here, there is no law but mine."

He could do anything he wanted on the Anomaly. There was no fear of retribution for him. He could write his own laws and alter them at will.

I didn't change out of my suit. I couldn't even look at the clothes on the rack. They had been collected from the shipwrecks. The women who'd worn them long gone, and I couldn't even bring myself to speculate on how they might have perished.

When Vrateus came for me later, he gave me an exasperated look, seeing me still in my bodysuit.

"I said I'm not doing it," I muttered gruffly.

"Then, I must take you in as you are." He moved my way, and I quickly retreated.

Instead of chasing me around the room, he stopped in the middle. "You know that except for *errocks*, none of the other species would hesitate before entering this room. They will come here if I don't present you to them in a few minutes as promised."

I just glared at him, my head low.

"If they get in here once," he continued, "they will no longer view this room as off-limits. Even if you survive tonight by some miracle, you'll lose your one safe place in the Anomaly. They will come back."

Misery flooded through me, smothering all my senses. I felt helpless as the situation seemed inescapable.

"Can't you see? This is the only solution for them to leave you alone." He took a small step toward me, his voice soothing as if he were talking to a skittish animal. He obviously thought of me as nothing more than an animal if he believed he could put me on display in front of a crowd like that. "You will let them look at you tonight, let me touch you in front of them. Just me, no one else. Only then can I guarantee your life and safety."

"I—I can't..." I hated the way my lip shook, and my voice trembled. I hated the feeling of being all alone, already exposed and vulnerable, even if still fully clothed.

Heaving a sigh, he said in a somber voice, "You have to."

I shook my head, wrapping my arms tightly around myself.

"Svetlana." The sound of my name from him shook me. I snapped my gaze to his face as he stared at me imploringly. "I want you to live."

I hated him so much at that moment. He even somehow schooled his features into a kind expression, using a soft voice with emotion, even saying my name to get his way.

One thing he had been right about: it really didn't matter what I wanted.

He had the means to make me do what *he* wished. Whatever sick game he was playing here, I could only play along. At least for tonight.

Then, I would start working on my escape plan from this hell. On my own. I was now glad that Vrateus hadn't let me share the details of my idea with him. I'd have to do it without his assistance, and against his "rules."

Stepping closer, he suddenly placed his hand on my throat, causing a spike of panic. His expression remained calm, if severe. This gesture, however, could mean anything, from anger, to aggression, to threat. His grip remained gentle enough, though. He wasn't compressing my throat, just touching it.

His face came close enough for me to see the true color of his eyes for the first time. They were of an intense shade somewhere between brown and yellow—burnt orange—with black pupils shaped as vertical slits, like those of a cat.

I stilled under his intense stare, the fur on the back of his hand tickling my chin, the warmth of his hand seeping through my skin.

"Will it be just *you* tonight? Touching me?" I croaked, not believing myself. Was I actually about to go along with this depravity?

"Yes," he said softly.

"No one else?"

I'd glimpsed enough slimy tentacles, hard scales, and sharp talons on some of the males to make my stomach drop with terror at the mere thought of those coming anywhere near my naked body.

"No," he promised.

"And you won't hurt me? I mean there'll be no physical pain?"

The focus in his eyes sharpened with a sudden flash of heat. "Unless you want it to be—"

"No!" I shook my head vehemently. In no way did I trust anyone here, Vrateus included, to deliver any kind of erotic pain. "Please, don't hurt me."

"I won't, then." He held my stare, keeping his hand on my neck.

"I have to change," I half-whispered, unable to stand the contact any longer.

He had made an excellent point when he said I shouldn't wear my own clothes for this.

"Right." He let go of my neck, and I drew in a breath.

Even though his grip on my throat hadn't been tight, his mere proximity seemed to have deprived me of oxygen.

"Can you leave?" I asked. "So I can change?"

"No."

Fine. Over seven hundred men were about to see me naked. It might as well start now.

Something inside me went numb the moment I had agreed to this. Little mattered, now.

I tugged down the front closure of my suit. Vrateus, at least, had the decency to turn around when the suit opened.

Walking over to the rack, I yanked the first garment off the hanger, something in canary yellow. I got out of my suit and threw the dress on over my bra and underwear. It had a long puffy skirt and a wide belt that I tied around my waist.

The entire process took me only a few seconds.

"I'm ready."

He turned around, giving me an assessing look.

"Do you want to change out of your boots, too?"

"Really?" I huffed a sharp laugh.

Did he need me in a well-coordinated outfit for this?

Arguing, however, would only prolong the whole thing.

"Fine." I kicked off my boots and rummaged in the long chest on the bottom of the clothing rack.

Finding shoes that would fit me wasn't as easy as the dress. Many had been worn by alien women with feet shaped differently than mine. Some were long and flared at the toes, some had been obviously made to fit over hooves. Finally, I fished out a pair of golden sandals with adjustable straps.

"Done." I straightened after fastening the straps over my feet and around my ankles.

The sooner this nightmare started, the sooner it would be over.

Chapter 6

His hand around Svetlana's arm, he steered her down the corridor and toward the mess hall. Crux and Nocc led the way. Trox, Wyck, and Lesh were at the back.

The dress she was wearing had no sleeves. The acute awareness of her bare skin under his palm was unnervingly distracting. He needed to keep his focus on the _errocks_, watching them as they watched everyone else. Yet his attention kept drifting back to that one warm spot of contact with her body.

The mess hall was the largest room they had on the Dark Anomaly. The layout of the living area had been changing over the years, with new ships crashing to the outer edge and the old ones compressing closer to the center. However, the changes were slow, and he had used this room for major gatherings for the entire seven years of his being the captain.

His crew already filled the space. Males sat on the chairs and tables that had been haphazardly arranged around the room. Some of the climbing species clung to the walls higher up. At least a dozen or two swung on the glowing ropes of light suspended from the ceiling.

Svetlana skipped a step, coming to a sudden stop at the entrance, her mouth agape, her dark eyes wide open.

He tried to see the scene through her eyes. The sweaty, mostly naked male bodies of all shapes, colors, and sizes. The musky scent of their combined anticipation hanging heavily in the air. Leering eyes. Smirking mouths. Bared teeth, dripping with saliva. All of this must be disconcerting to her—terrifying, judging by her expression.

"They won't touch you." He forced more reassurance into his voice than he felt.

The space was charged with lust and aggression, making him worry about his ability to keep his promise. Over the years, he had successfully dealt with his crew's rage, frustration, and aggression. However, he could not predict with any certainty what their combined arousal would do.

A rumble of growls, groans, and grunts rolled through the room when Svetlana finally took a tiny step in. It was followed by a shower of leers and screamed obscenities that he had no desire to focus on—as long as they weren't threats.

"This way." He walked Svetlana to the wall to the right.

Keeping his attention on the crowd, he made sure not to put anyone but his personal guard of *errocks* at his back. When he reached the spot he'd chosen for her performance, he edged the *errocks* out of the way, too, by stepping back to the wall until his tail touched it.

He moved Svetlana in front of him, turning her to face the room, her back to his chest. Her body trembled in his arms. He wrapped his hand around her neck, to check her vitals again. Through the sensors in his palm, he took a note of her pulse, body temperature, blood pressure, and rate of breathing—all significantly higher than what they had been in her room.

"Ready?"

"I never will be," she gritted through her teeth.

That was worrisome.

"I promised them some moans."

"Well, *you* can go ahead and moan then," she bit off.

He might not know much about women, but he assumed that to make Svetlana orgasm he'd need her co-operation.

"They're expecting to see and hear *you*." If she continued to stand there like that, tense and glaring at everyone, he suspected his crew would complain bitterly. Unfortunately, most of them complained aggressively. He'd need to kill many. They would want to kill him. And her. "You don't have a choice."

"And I hate you for that," she hissed.

Him?

The shock of surprise rushed through his brain, echoing deep in his chest.

Why would she hate *him* when every single thing he'd done from the moment she'd crashed here was to save her life? Her lack of gratitude for that had been puzzling.

Was she not glad to be alive?

It occurred to him that he had never asked her if she wanted to be saved. He'd assumed her species had similar self-preservation instincts to his. However, he'd read about some instances of individuals preferring death to pain or dishonor.

The situation didn't leave Svetlana much of a choice—either entertain his crew by disrobing and pleasuring herself for their entertainment, or risk being raped and eventually killed by them instead.

He could, however, offer her something else. Something he hadn't considered before.

"Would you rather die?" he asked earnestly.

Sliding his hand between them, he bared one of the blades he carried hidden on his body. He pressed the tip of the dagger below her left shoulder blade.

He could give her a clean, fast death—a luxury compared to the fate of any other female who had ever had the misfortune of landing on the Dark Anomaly.

"I'll make it quick," he promised. "And as painless as possible."

Deprived of their entertainment, his crew would most likely end up ripping him to pieces right after. That fact somehow wasn't at the front of his mind at the moment.

She stilled under his blade. The males in the room quieted down too, expectant. Some unfastened their pants, leaning back. Ready.

Her pulse beat faster under his palm. Her breathing turned to shallow, irregular gasps.

"No," she said softly, and he exhaled in relief.

For some unexplained reason, he wanted her to stay alive more than he had ever wanted anything else in his life.

"I'll do it." She yanked at the belt around her waist, untying it.

A roar of approval rolled through the mess hall.

He discreetly slid the dagger back into its sheath at his chest. His shoulders still ached from the strain and tension he'd felt while waiting for her answer.

Her hands trembling, Svetlana opened the front of her dress, revealing a pink harness underneath that holstered her breasts. Moving her hands behind her, she unhooked the closure at the back. The harness slacked around her chest.

Groans, wet sounds of approval, and clicking noises of unfastened clothes filled the room. Crux leaned back against the nearest table, whipping out both of his cocks. The *kreers* under the ceiling produced their genital clusters from the pouches on their segmented bellies. Crawling over each other, *yourlu* spread their tentacles open in a circle. Their undulating reproductive organs snaked out from the middle.

Svetlana staggered back, coming flush with his chest. "You do it..." Her throat bobbed with a swallow under his palm. "Please."

With a deep breath, he slid his other hand to her front, praying he'd get it right.

The sight of naked males groping themselves couldn't be helpful in getting her to relax, he assumed.

"Close your eyes." He tried to sound confident, hiding his inexperience.

She obeyed with a brief shuddered sigh.

Thinking back to everything he had read and watched during his recent research into female pleasure, he lifted his hand to her chest, cupping one full breast through her pink harness.

Her breasts were much larger than those of the *themul* female in the video. Heavy. He understood why Svetlana would need to strap them for support.

Her breathing hitched, and he moved his hand higher, sliding the dress and the straps of the harness from her shoulders. The dress slipped off, the voluminous skirt pooling at her feet. The harness followed.

He touched her bare breast, carefully. The images of the thrashing and growling female in the video came to mind again. Was that the way it had to be done? Was that how women liked it? Rough and furious?

"Don't hurt me," Svetlana had pleaded.

It didn't feel right to grab her by her hair.

Pushing the memories of the video aside, he followed his instincts instead. In addition, he kept one of his hands around her throat at all times, consulting the pattern of her erratic vitals.

Palming her naked breast, he found it surprisingly soft, her skin exceptionally smooth and silky. It wrinkled around the tip as the nipple hardened under his thumb. He marvelled at the change, rolling the tight bud between his fingers.

She exhaled sharply. A tiny sound vibrated in her throat.

An echo of a moan?

A sudden urge to taste her skin rose in him, like the male in the video had. Except that he couldn't do that here. His attention was already spread thin. He had to concentrate on his next move with her, continuously watching her reaction while also being mindful of everything happening around them—keeping track of the positions of everyone on his crew while gauging everyone's mood.

So far, they seemed to be enthralled, whether with lust or curiosity. The sight of a half-naked female was a novelty to many of them. However, not all would find her body alone appealing enough. The physical differences between humans and some of the species here were just too great.

They needed to see her thrash in the throngs of passion, to hear her moan, just as he had promised. Then, he hoped, their imagination would fill in the blanks to complete whatever image or fantasy each of them needed to achieve satisfaction.

He moved to fondle her other breast, while stroking the side of her neck with the thumb of his other hand. Not wanting to remove his hand from her throat, he reached with his tail. Wrapping it around her leg, he stroked the inside of her thigh with the tip.

She released a slight gasp at the caress of the fur of his tail.

He slid his hand lower, down her stomach and under the waistband of the short underpants she was wearing.

Several disgruntled growls came from the room, reminding him she had to be completely naked. He tugged her shorts down, past her hips and she wiggled her legs to make the underwear slide down to her ankles.

He discovered with surprise that she had fur between her legs. Short and springy, it differed from the long, silky hair on her head. He parted it with his fingers, finding by touch the small nub he had read would bring an orgasm to a *themul* female if stimulated. He hoped it would cause a pleasurable sensation in Svetlana, too.

He circled it with his finger, applying a little pressure while stroking her inner thigh with his tail.

Her breathing deepened, and she bent forward slightly, prompting him to finally remove his hand from her neck. Instead, he wrapped his arm around her chest, cupping one of her breasts as he continued to rub between her legs with his other hand.

She grabbed his hand on her breast, lacing her fingers with his. Her body relaxed into his arms, a small shiver running through her in response to his touch.

He blinked, amazed and thrilled by the reactions he was causing in her. It felt like a dance where he led, and she followed. The harmony that the two of them hadn't been able to achieve through conversation was suddenly happening wordlessly.

Tossing her head back on his shoulder, she whimpered softly.

He caught a glimpse of a new expression on her face. It conveyed both pleasure and ache. The same sweet torture he was experiencing that very moment as her backside pressed against his straining erection.

Then, he sensed her body tense. She circled his wrist with her fingers and yanked at his arm, shifting his hand away from the spot between her legs.

Whatever he had just ignited inside her, she forced it down, unwilling to let go.

"Pretend, if you must," he whispered.

She drew in some air then released a moan. Strong and loud, it was immediately echoed with grunts and groans from the males who rubbed, stroked, and fondled themselves.

She continued to thrash in his arms, making sounds that he now knew were fake.

A moment later, she stilled. Her eyes still closed, she appeared to be listening to the room, hugging his arms to her.

He glanced around the mess hall quickly, noting the slumped positions of the males. Most appeared satisfied. The rest were catching up. Crux reclined in a chair by the table, a limp cock draped over each of his thighs. A greenish puddle glistened on the floor between his feet.

"Are we done?" Svetlana asked in a hoarse whisper, letting go of his arms.

"Yes." Vrateus bent over quickly, picking up her dress. She grabbed it from him, wrapping it around herself, then snatched her underpants and her breast harness off the floor.

He spotted Wyck at the entrance. Lesh was nowhere around. The *errock* must have chained the animal somewhere to leave both his hands free for the event. Wyck's pants were on, however, with no green puddles around. The bulge in his pants seemed bigger than ever.

Vrateus couldn't concern himself with *everyone's* satisfaction. They all had their chance. If Wyck preferred to pleasure himself in the privacy of his own bed later, it was his choice.

He caught Wyck's eye, tipping his chin toward the exit. It was time to get out of here, and he needed at least someone from his guard for protection on the way back to Svetlana's room.

Wyck nodded, joining them. Vrateus wrapped his arm around Svetlana's shoulders, leading her out of the mess hall.

Chapter 7

MY KNEES SHOOK AND my hands trembled as I walked down the corridor back to my glass room. Then the whole-body shudders started, and I was grateful for the firm grip of Vrateus's arm around me.

I should not have opened my eyes until he had led me out of that hall. The sight of the sweaty males of various species now had been burnt into my brain. Glistening chests. Arm muscles straining as they stroked and jerked themselves off. Shoulders moving as hands pumped... Their mouths agape, fangs bared, hungry stares devouring me.

Even with my eyes closed, I had not escaped their grunts and groans, the sounds of flesh hitting flesh, the wet noises...

The smell of sweat...

The heavy, musky odor of semen rising into the air...

A shudder jerked my shoulders when Vrateus finally dragged me through the open doors and into my glass room.

"You did good."

The praise felt worse than a slap on the face would have. His words set off the explosion of rage, humiliation, and disgust inside me.

"Fuck you!" I snapped, shrugging his arm off me.

What was he praising? My performance during that grotesque show of mass masturbation?

Was I supposed to be proud of *that*? Did I need to strive to do *good*?

Centuries of civilization had just been stripped from me. All progress that humanity had made. The respect and equality I had earned because of my own work and the work of the women who had come before me. All of that meant absolutely nothing as tonight, I had been reduced to just a naked body to gawk at and be used for someone else's slobbering pleasure.

It was easy to hate them all, but it gave no satisfaction of revenge, since the rest of the males couldn't hear me curse at them.

It was Vrateus who'd had his hands on me. And at him, I directed my anger.

I hated him for ever coming up with this perverted idea. For somehow convincing me to agree to it.

Back in the hall, he had actually given me a choice worth considering. He had offered me a clean, quick death. By choosing to live, I had turned myself from a victim into a willing participant in what had happened.

I despised myself for that, too.

But most of all, I was angry that he'd made me *like* some parts of that horrible experience. Nothing about his actual touch had been revolting.

And I hated him for that the most.

SITTING ON MY SLEEPING pallet, hugging my knees, I couldn't stop the bouts of shakes that kept running through my body.

I didn't hear the doors open and close and had no idea when Vrateus had left my room.

When a small cluster of waxy yellow flowers slid into my view, I realized he had come back. Now, he was kneeling beside me, holding the translucent branch covered with tiny blossoms in his hand.

"What's this?" I gave him a sideway glare.

"*Irsen* flowers. Chew on them slowly, without swallowing. Their juice will help you fall asleep tonight." He put the branch into my hand and watched me as I mechanically shoved the entire thing into my mouth.

The bitter-sweet juice thickly coated my tongue when I started chewing. Then a fuzzy haze descended on my mind, warming my chest. My limbs grew heavy, and I sank back into the bedding of my pallet.

"Just this once," Vrateus murmured, tugging the covers over me.

He tucked me in as the feeling of soaring beyond the lights of the Anomaly swept me into a blissful delusion.

I did not hear when he left again.

I WOKE UP AT THIRTEEN minutes past nine the following morning. I knew the exact time because of the large, metal analogue clock left near my sleeping pallet.

Right away, I dashed to the bathroom to get rid of the nasty, sticky mess of chewed up flowers in my mouth. Spitting it out, I vigorously brushed my teeth, then took a quick cool shower, which brought me back to life.

Last night had drifted away, like nightmares always did in the morning. I had an amazing clarity of mind, and my body buzzed with energy. I didn't want to dwell on what had happened, I was ready to focus on the future.

Ripping a piece of cloth from one of the dresses on the rack that remained in my room, I wetted it and wiped down my bodysuit and undergarments. The self-cleaning material took care of the rest by absorbing the moisture and dissolving impurities into the air.

Fully dressed, with my hair brushed and put up in a ponytail, I sat down to eat my breakfast. It was a bowl of some grainy matter with the meaty taste of stew. Vrateus must have brought it earlier this morning, as it was still lukewarm.

Escaping this place appeared to be very executable today. Pieces of the plan turned in my head, like a puzzle about to be solved.

I could reasonably assume that my spacesuit had sustained only minimal damage during the crash. I knew the ship's fuel cells had been designed to fit on the suit, in case of an emergency. Their power would be enough to combat the gravity of a planet many times larger than the solid mass of the Dark Anomaly.

I had to make more accurate calculations, of course. For that I needed to know the exact combined mass of the metal wreckage of the Anomaly. I'd also have to get to my ship and the spacesuit somehow with enough time to assess it for any damages, fix them if necessary, then connect the fuel cells and program the trajectory.

Then, I would need to find my way out to the surface of the Anomaly disk.

To figure all of this out, I needed information that Vrateus must have. He was the captain of this place, after all. Which meant that as little as I wished to speak to him again, I would have to.

The door swished open as soon as I finished my breakfast, making me wonder if I had been watched.

"How are you?" Vrateus entered.

His appearance in my room jolted me with a shock of awareness through my system.

He must have just had a shower. The fur on his head, hands, and tail appeared damp. The faint scent of the same soap I used drifted my way. On him, it had the added flavor of male spice—his very own unique scent.

I had been apprehensive about seeing him this morning, but the effect was even stronger and somewhat different from what I had expected.

Was it because he had touched me? The phantom sensation of his hands on me glided over my body.

Hoping to escape his scent, I took a step back. My eyes however kept taking in the sight of his tall, well-build body, dressed in another one of his ridiculous, wide-sleeved, crispy-white shirts that he somehow made look appealing.

This must be some lingering side effect of the flowers.

Why else would I find anything about this man *appealing*?

His arms folded across his chest, he drummed the fingers of his right hand against his left bicep, waiting for my answer.

I made an enormous effort not to think about *where* those fingers had been last night when he held me so close to him.

"I'm fine." My voice came out husky, and I cleared my throat, schooling my expression into something hopefully neutral and casual. "I'm very good, actually. Feel free to show up here with a whole bouquet of those flowers next time."

"You can't have them often." He shook his head with a grim expression on his face. "If you give in to the craving, the juice of the *irsen* flowers would eventually rot your brain."

"Isn't that true about many kinds of cravings?" I muttered, blankly staring at his hand.

When was the last time I had a man make love to me? Definitely not while on the mission. Relationships didn't last long in the cramped environment of the research station. My parents had me during the one and only assignment they had ever worked on together in space. Neither of them had planned for me to happen, and neither wished to have anything to do with me or with each other when the project ended.

The last thing I wanted was to repeat their mistakes when they had treated me as the biggest mistake of their lives for as long as I remembered.

I no longer did relationships. The couple that I'd had, I'd made sure to end myself, leaving them before they left me. I knew way too well how much it hurt when people I loved left, and I refused to give the power to cause that kind of pain to me to anyone anymore.

Now, nearly a year of no physical contact whatsoever had made me suddenly ogle with appreciation the man who had publicly molested me just a few hours earlier.

Disgusting.

"Possibly." He reached for the empty bowl in my hands.

I blinked, snapping back to the task I had identified for myself. Information.

I needed him to tell me more about the Anomaly, to hopefully show me as much as possible of it, too.

"I'd like to go for a walk, please." I clasped my hands in front of me, giving him a friendly smile.

"A walk?" He stared at me as if I had just asked for something unreasonable, like going on a spacewalk in the nude.

"Yes. I've been here for two days now, but still haven't seen much of this place. You told me this is going to be my home now. I'd love to learn more about it. How do you operate things to ensure your survival? Where does the food come from? The layout of the entire habitable area. How large is it?"

"You want to leave the room?" he said slowly, as if struggling to grasp the concept of my simple request.

"Yes, please," I kept my voice light and friendly, almost imploring. "You can set a time limit if you wish, and I promise to return before it's up."

"It's not safe out there on your own."

As if I didn't know that. The amount of rude behaviour I'd encountered in the past two days by far exceeded anything I'd ever faced during my entire life prior.

"I'm well aware of that, and I'll be careful. I can go out at night when everyone is asleep. Or any other time of the day you'd suggest. I'll stay out of everyone's way. I won't talk to anyone..."

He shook his head, his sharp features hardening into a frown.

"It'd be too dangerous any time of the day. You *know* we have the worst kind of predators here."

"Predators?"

He arched a long, thick eyebrow. "Yes. I'm their captain."

Exactly. As their captain, shouldn't he have some control over them? Or he simply didn't want to exercise it on my behalf?

"Didn't your crew already get what they wanted?" I rolled my shoulders back, trying to hide my embracement at bringing up the last night. Unsuccessfully, it appeared, as I could already feel the blush creep up my neck. "You used me for their entertainment in exchange for my life and safety. That was the deal, wasn't it?"

"Yes. But only in exchange for your life. *Safety* is never guaranteed around here."

"That seems hardly fair." I bit my lip to prevent it from trembling. "I went along with..." I swallowed hard, unable to come up with an adequate name for the last night's depravity. "And none of that bought me even one safe passage through the corridors, deep at night, when everyone sleeps?"

He kept shaking his head, unyielding.

"You cannot leave this room. Definitely not on your own."

"Well...Can you come with me, then?" I'd rather have him for a company than not leave here at all.

"I'm busy," he bit off. "And I have no escort to give you, either. I don't trust anyone around here enough to leave you in their care."

I drew in some air, fighting dread and frustration. An argument would not be in my best interest right now. I needed his cooperation.

"You're not even trying to search for a better solution with me," I managed, calmly enough.

"I've already found the best solution there could be in this situation."

"Keeping me locked up? Around the clock?" My composure crumbled, and my voice leaped higher. "Why?"

"Because this is the safest place for you!" he snapped back. His own patience was obviously even shorter than mine. "Out there, someone will always want more from you than what is allowed."

"But that's not what has been negotiated. You said 'once a week' only, and I believed you..." My voice rang high and brittle to my ear. Frustration burned my eyelids with tears.

I'd gone through the most degrading experience in my life, and it bought me nothing. No safety, no freedom.

If I wasn't allowed to leave this room, my only chance for escape disappeared.

I could not stay here forever.

"You're their captain, aren't you?" I pleaded, already knowing he wouldn't listen. "Order them to leave me alone. That was the deal."

"I can't guarantee my orders will be followed, unless I personally supervise their execution."

"Sounds like something a micromanaging control freak would say," I couldn't hold back the snappy remark at his excuses.

He stretched his neck, his jaw tightened.

"You chose to live," he growled at me. "Your survival is now *my* responsibility. *I* decide how it can best be accomplished."

"And locking me in this room is the *only* solution?"

"Yes."

I groaned exasperated. "Forever?"

"Until the next week's session."

Session? Sounded so proper and legit, it made me want to puke.

"The jerk-off fest, you mean?" I called it what it was. "Is that all my life is now? You'll keep me locked up in here, like an animal in a cage? Letting me out only for that pathetic *entertainment* you've invented?"

He flinched at my words but recovered quickly.

"It's not my fault you crashed here." He kept his voice even, but a flush of color on his bronzed cheeks and the wild lashing of his tail against his legs betrayed his agitation. "Do you understand how much disruption your arrival has caused? I've spent years establishing the current order, and I have to work daily on maintaining it."

"Well, excuse me, for *choosing* to crash on your neat little freak fest and to wreak havoc with my arrival!" I no longer cared about preserving any kind of diplomacy, spurred by the frustration, shame, and desperation. And fear. The cold, brutal fear that I might be forced to remain here forever. That *this* would be the only life I'd ever know. "Do you think I wanted to come here? This shithole is the last place I want to be!"

He huffed, leaning toward my face and fully invading my personal space. The burnt orange of his irises lit up with barely contained rage. His hot scent wrapped all around me, making my breath hitch.

"I promised you a fast, clean death," he gritted through his teeth. "The offer still stands if you change your mind. Otherwise, you are to do what I say. Just like everyone else in this *shithole*."

This was an outright threat. The heat of it made my blood boil.

"If you think that I—" I started, not even sure yet how I was intending to finish the sentence but determined not to let him have the last word.

"You're staying here!" he bit off, his voice hard and cold like steel. "Locked in and safe."

Pivoting on his heel, he stormed out of the room, with an angry whip of his tail against the door frame.

Asshole!

I yelled in my head as the door closed, taking him out of the earshot.

Pervert.

And a brute. Despite all his fine shirts, embossed leather, and jewellery, he was no better than the last of his crew dressed in rags—a barbarian like the rest of them.

I paced the glass floor, raging inside.

I despised them all. However, the rest of the crew were mostly just one homogenous mass of sweaty bodies and leering eyes to me. Hellfire could come and burn them all en masse for all I cared.

Their captain, however, I yearned to strangle with my own hands. I wished to have *his* life in *my* control for a change, to see something else than that calm focus in his bright orange eyes.

Spotting the fiery glow of rage in them a minute earlier stirred something in me.

I was glad he'd left. Yet somewhere deep inside, I wondered what would have happened if he'd stayed.

He didn't matter.

I shook it off.

Even without his help, I would get to my ship. Sooner or later, I'd be out of here. And he could stay and rot in this place, along with his crew of degenerates.

Chapter 8

THE DAY DRAGGED ON. The hours between meals felt like weeks. Vrateus would bring my food and take back the empty dishes—all without saying a word, hardly throwing a glance my way.

Fine, be that way.

Sitting on the sleeping pallet, I watched the endless light show outside the glass during the brief few minutes he spent in my room each time.

The silence grew heavier with each of his visits and harder to bear. With no one to talk to, the loneliness grew. I had to speak with him to get some information, but more than that, I just wanted to *talk*—with anyone.

The next morning, I showered and dressed, unsure of why I even bothered. As far as anyone in this place was probably concerned, I could have stayed in bed for the next several days. As long as I showed up to excite them during their weekly public masturbation sessions, no one cared what I did the rest of the time.

"Good morning," I offered the greeting first when Vrateus brought my breakfast.

He froze, holding the tray with a huge metal bowl and an ornate metal cup on it. Narrowing his eyes, he gave me an assessing stare.

"Morning," he replied tentatively, still obviously sulking.

If he were expecting an apology from me, he would have to wait for a long time. I would not apologize for demanding to be treated as a free person with dignity, even as he had deprived me of both dignity and freedom.

I was not going to apologize this time. However, I couldn't bear to sit in silence, day after day, as years passed by in the outside world—the world where I belonged.

"I don't like this..." I waved my hand between us, gesturing at him and me, "This silent treatment thing."

"I am not enjoying it either." He placed the tray on the table but didn't leave immediately after, as he had done yesterday.

Instead, he took his usual wide stance, crossing his arms over his chest. The pose had a certain flare of arrogance, which suited him.

I stood in front of him, trying not to mimic his posture. "I would like to break this silence. Can we please talk again?"

"I would like that, too." He inclined his head as if he were accepting the apology I had never given.

In fact, shouldn't *he* be the one to apologize? After all, I was still the one destined to spend the rest of my life locked up.

I took a long breath in, reminding myself that getting into yet another argument would hinder my plans.

"So," I tried just one more time, as calmly and friendly as I could manage. "Are you absolutely positive that there is definitely no way for me to ever leave this room? Other than once a week, please?"

He dropped his hands to his sides with an exasperated sigh. "Svetlana."

There was something slightly indecent in the way he pronounced my name. It made me think of licking, for some reason.

He obviously wasn't thinking of *that,* judging by his frustrated expression.

"It wasn't a whim of mine, to keep you in here. Anywhere outside of this glass capsule is dangerous." He raked his claws through his fur. "Fuck," he groaned. "Even inside this room, I cannot guarantee your safety."

He frowned, peering past the glass into the dancing lights of the Anomaly.

"They'd drive you mad," he'd said to me once.

His wild expression made me wonder if he had already lost some of his sanity. After having spent who knew how much time in this place, I wouldn't blame him if he had. He definitely seemed to exhibit some signs of paranoia.

"You know your crew," I said, wishing to gauge the severity of the danger he had been talking about. How much of what he feared was a genuine threat? So far, they all seemed to listen to him and obey his orders, at least since the day he had shot one of them.

"I do. I have studied every species here in detail. I've also learned what motivates each individual, by watching them for years." A shadow drew over his features. "I killed ninety-seven of them the day I took over and declared myself their captain. Then I've shot another hundred and fifty-three, re-enforcing my rules and maintaining the order ever since."

He met my eyes, as if waiting for a reaction.

I didn't know what exactly he wanted me to say. That the killings he'd done must have been justified, considering the savage nature of his people? Or that I understood that it hurt him having to commit those murders?

"They are a wild, unrefined bunch of criminals," he continued as I kept silent. "Murderers, rapists, and cannibals. Anyone who had a conscience, manners, or honor had been exterminated long before I took power. Nothing good survives here, Svetlana. Nothing beautiful, delicate or feminine, either."

"Is that how you survived, then? By getting rid of your own conscience and honor?"

His jaw muscles flexed in obvious displeasure at my question. Yet his voice was calm when he replied, "I survived by making myself smarter than them. I've read, I've studied, and I've watched. Then, I've figured out how to overpower them and prevent them from rebelling against me."

Despite our mutual dislike for each other, I sensed some good inside him, buried deep under the hard exterior. Maybe it happened because he had stopped scowling and shouting, and was making an effort to finally explain things to me? For the first time ever, this felt more like a beginning of a real conversation rather than the usual argument.

I held back another snappy reply in response, and instead asked with a genuine interest,

"How, then?"

"Their minds and hands need to be occupied. I try to convert some of their aggression into productive results, by keeping them busy. There is always work to be done around here. My authority is absolute. I ruthlessly eradicate any doubt about that. But it does not go undisputed."

It occurred to me that it might be the only time Vrateus had ever talked to anyone this openly about himself. He was not only explaining *things* for me, he was explaining *himself* to me, as if he cared what I thought about him.

"You think all I need to do is to command and they will obey?" he continued. "Every order I give, I need to supervise to make sure it's executed the right way. I have to be physically present, everywhere at once. Because if I'm not there to check and reinforce, they slack off. Every one of them is just waiting for me to slip up and make a mistake."

He rubbed his face in the now familiar gesture. His exhaustion might be more noticeable by the end of the day but listening to him now, I realized he was *always* tired, no matter how much rest he got.

"Svetlana, I don't know what prior knowledge you have about the species of the Dark Anomaly. You seem to have come from a gentler, better place, where women feel safe on their own. But it's different here."

He held me with his gaze.

"Do you think a release once a week would take care of my crew's sexual frustration? It won't. *Dimos* come several times a day. And that's when they're single. If they catch a scent of a female, they can spend days doing nothing but having sex. Continuously."

He was no longer arguing or even trying to convince me of anything. He was simply stating facts, letting me do whatever I wanted with the information.

"*Errocks* have two cocks each, and they're only truly satisfied when they come from both. Simultaneously. *Ognats* chew the heads off their females during mating. *Kreers* have a birth rate of one male to ten females, because they mate in the water, often drowning the female during sex. Like *ognats*, they are cannibals. They eat everything they kill. *Everything.*"

He drew in a long breath, as if talking had exhausted him even more.

"Nothing would stop the monsters I call my crew from satisfying their basic instincts if they got within leaping distance from you while you were walking anywhere alone."

Faced with the horrific nature of the inhabitants of the Dark Anomaly, the argument died in me completely.

"Do you understand me?" he asked, peering at me intently. "Svetlana, do you believe me?"

I had many reasons to mistrust him, but I felt he was being sincere.

"Yes." My knees gave in, and I sank to the floor right where I stood.

Silently, he offered me the cup from the tray. Bejewelled and embossed, it appeared to have come straight from a storybook's pirate treasure. Except that no one here had come from a storybook—from a nightmare, maybe.

"I understand what you're saying." I took the cup from him mechanically. "What escapes me is *why* they are like that?"

"Some of it is in their blood. It's the characteristic of their species."

"No. That's not true." I shook my head. "All of them initially came from the same world I did. And I've never heard of any race being inherently brutal or violent like that. *Errocks* are an intelligent, civilized nation, for example. And that head-eating thing that you said *ognats* do..." I flinched, bringing it up. "It would not be tolerated anywhere in the modern world."

"Then it must be a better world out there now."

"What was it like when they got here?" I asked. "How long have you all been on the Dark Anomaly?"

"It depends. Malahki was the last sentient being to arrive here before you. That was about five years ago. I've been here for over two decades now. That's about six thousand universal years."

"What?" I stared at him, flabbergasted. "Six thousand years? That would be before the beginning of recorded human history!"

"Yours must be a very young race then. Many of the others have been here for much longer than that, twice or even three times as long as I have."

"That would be like traveling through time."

"Except that no one actually travels anywhere." He huffed a bitter laugh. "All of us are staying put."

I took a drink of tea, suddenly no longer feeling like talking.

All of what Vrateus had said was excruciatingly depressing.

He crouched in front of me.

"I have rearranged my schedule for tomorrow. Right after breakfast, I will have one hour to show you around. Crux, Wyck, and Nocc will come with us."

I snapped my gaze to his, shocked by his offer after the speech he had just given me.

"You *will* take me for a walk, after all?"

"With an adequate escort," he said with an emphasis. "You're never to step a foot outside of this room *alone*. Do you understand?"

I nodded, afraid to believe he was giving in.

"There are benefits to familiarizing yourself with the Dark Anomaly. You need to know your surroundings in case of an emergency."

"Thank you," I exhaled with relief and genuine gratitude.

He hovered his hand over my knee for a moment, before tentatively placing it on it. "You're welcome."

I covered his hand with mine, my fingers sinking into the soft fur on the back of his hand.

He blinked, slightly discomfited for once.

"Just, um... Make sure you stay close and do exactly as I say, Svetlana. Please, make it easier for me to keep you safe."

Chapter 9

IT WAS ONLY A WALK through the rumpled corridors of the junkyard of spaceships compacted together by the unexplained force field in space. Yet from the moment I woke up, I felt excited as if I were six again and my grandma was about to take me to the fair.

Being forced to stay in one room had made me eager to see *any-thing* outside of it.

"Morning," I greeted Vrateus the moment he walked in with breakfast. "I'll be quick." I grabbed the tray from him.

"Take your time. You have fifteen minutes for breakfast, then an entire hour for the walk."

His days seemed to comprise a string of time intervals, each with a specific task assigned to it.

For the next hour and fifteen minutes the task was me.

"Where are you taking me today?" I stuffed a spoonful of the watery stew into my mouth. The food on the Anomaly lacked not just taste but also variety. I'd had a slight variation of the same thing for every meal.

"We'll take a walk in the opposite direction from the mess hall."

"Oh, good." I wasn't too eager to see the mess hall again, anyway. "What's there?"

"The library and the gardens."

I was hoping for an airlock, the exit to the surface. However, seeing more of the layout of the habitable sector of the Dark Anomaly would still be beneficial. Besides, I might find some information I needed in the library.

"Sounds good."

"Today, we'll go to the library. The gardens will be next week. I also have a visit to the kitchen scheduled, two days from now."

"Really?" I exclaimed, surprised but even more excited now. It appeared I was about to see a lot of this place.

"This won't happen often." He toned down my enthusiasm. "I'll try to find time for more walks in the future, but I can't promise anything definite yet."

"I'd love to be able to walk as much as possible, please," I asked nicely. "Everybody needs regular exercise, right? How do *you* stay physically active?"

He sat down on the floor next to me, and I admired the thick muscles of his thighs, bulging against the dark-brown material of his pants.

"Physical labor." He blinked, following my gaze. "There is always a lot to be done around here."

I finished my stew in record time, drank the bitter-sweet, black tea just as fast, and got up.

"I'm ready."

The relaxed expression he had on his face while watching me eat disappeared at my words. Focus sharpened his features as he walked me to the door and placed his hand on the control panel.

The three members of his personal guard stood just outside the door. Wyck had the end of Lesh's chain wrapped around his wrist. The bizarre creature lowered all three of its heads, hissing at the doors as they slid open.

Neither of the *errocks* offered me a greeting, and I kept quiet, too, deciding it was best not to attract any extra attention.

Wrapping his hand around my upper arm, Vrateus gestured for Crux to lead. Wyck and Nocc flanked us, each about a step behind Vrateus and me.

I couldn't shake off the feeling of unease while walking down the corridors. This was not a relaxing stroll. The sensation of the *errocks* ogling me prickled my skin. The moist breathing of Wyck's pet heated my ankles.

I focused on where we were going, taking in the dented metal of the ceiling and the bent panels of the wall. Now and then, I spotted a thick round line of melted metal, crudely welded. It circled the corridor—floor, walls, and ceiling. Those must be the places where newly crashed ships were integrated into the Dark Anomaly, adding to the usable space of the metal disk.

I wondered what they'd use my spaceship for. Maybe a storage room, one among many.

"Have you stripped my ship?" I asked Vrateus.

"Yes. Everything we could use has now been taken off and put into storage," he replied, not taking his eyes off Crux's back in front of us.

"How about the spacesuit? And the spare fuel cells I had?"

"All in storage. Along with the other suits we have."

"You have more?"

I doubted any of the ones they had would rival the quality and power of mine. Considering the slower time on the Anomaly, everything Vrateus's people had at their disposal was severely outdated.

"We have several more suits. We wear them to go outside, to do any necessary repairs on the surface."

They *did* get out. There must be an airlock, then.

"What do you need to repair out there?" I asked.

Vrateus flicked his gaze to mine before returning it to the *errock* in front of us.

"Power generating panels. They convert the light of the Anomaly into useful energy."

"How about any antennae? Have you tried to send or receive communication signals from the surface?"

"No antennae. All signals get lost here."

"Yes. In *here*. But have you tried to send one from out there?" I insisted.

"Yes."

His brief answers weren't nearly enough. I wished to see some detailed data. Better yet, I wanted a chance to conduct some experiments myself. The mystery of the Anomaly was what drew me to sign up for the research mission in the first place. I was now inside it and still had so few answers.

Ironically, my main goal right now was to escape this place, not to study it.

"How often do you have to do the repairs?" I asked.

"As often as needed. With each new arrival, things often get banged up on the surface."

Arrival.

He'd made it sound as if they were scheduled—normal things to happen, not the catastrophic events they really were.

I wondered about the number and locations of the exits to the surface. Logic told me that at least one of them should be somewhere close to the storage room with the spacesuits, but I decided against asking him outright, at that moment. I didn't want to give him any more clues about my plans. The look he had given me was already suspicious.

At that moment, Vrateus stopped at the white single door on our left.

<u>*VRATEUS*</u>

He tapped the code into the door panel. Unlike the lock on his and Svetlana's rooms that had been programmed to open only with his palm print, the one at the library simply required a numeric code to enter. The number was not a secret. Anyone could access this place, though few of his crew ever bothered.

Unlike them, Vrateus had spent many hours here. However, this was the first time he had ever brought anyone along.

"Wow." Svetlana's eyes grew wider as she stepped inside, taking in the floor-to-ceiling shelf units arranged in parallel rows. The room was almost as large as the mess hall. The neatly placed slates of data glowed softly, illuminating the space with multi-colored light. "This is impressive."

Her reaction warmed his chest with pride and an odd sense of pleasure. The library has been one of the biggest accomplishments of his leadership, in his opinion. Sadly, it was also the least appreciated one.

Crux immediately bee-lined for the red-glowing section with sex videos of various species. The other two *errocks* followed him. With his personal guards now occupied by shifting through the data slates, Vrateus followed Svetlana deeper into the room.

"Did all these come from the shipwrecks?" she asked, trailing a finger along the hard edges of the slates that were glowing green. This section contained information on farming and agriculture.

"Yes. Most I've collected during my time as the captain, but some have survived from the prior years."

"They're all in the same format," she noted.

"I've converted everything to one format. It makes it easier to use." He gestured at a crate full of tablet frames. "You can have one if you want."

"Really?" She shot him a guarded glance.

"Sure." He selected a frame for her, in dark brown like her eyes. "What would you like to read or watch?"

"Well..." she rubbed her upper arm. "Since I'm to stay here for the rest of my life, it would be good to learn more about this place. What information do you have on the Dark Anomaly?"

It surprised him how relatively fast she seemed to have accepted the Anomaly as her future. It was good that she had, though, as it made things so much easier for both of them.

"The latest data on the energy field of the Dark Anomaly comes from your own ship." He moved over to the section of slates glowing in faint gray.

"Those would be the results of our research from the outside," she said. "I'd like to learn what I don't know yet. The actual structure where we are. How you've made it habitable and all the ways you keep maintaining it. As well as the information on all the species occupying this place."

"That might be too much for one visit, but I'll get you some to start with." He browsed the units with the gray shelves, selecting a few slates. "Nothing here is in any of the languages spoken on Earth, of course. Some newer articles can be read in the Universal language, though. Do you read Universal?"

She nodded.

"Good," he continued. "Many have an audio version, too, which your implant will translate for you." He then moved on to a much larger section that housed slates glowing in various shades of yellow—from the lightest, nearly white, to the darkest orange, almost brown. "These here contain information on the species, each is color-coded with its own shade."

He pulled out a few, making sure to include a documentary about the life of *themul* on Nofoi. For some reason, he wanted her to know more about his own species, even though he could hardly be considered part of Nofoi culture himself, having left the planet at a very young age.

"Thank you." She took a slate from him, turning it in her hands and examining it closely. "I've heard of this format before but have never held one in my hands until now."

"It must be considered an antique in the world out there by now?" He chuckled.

"Well, yes. It is a severely outdated technology," she admitted, then added quickly as though afraid to have hurt his feelings. "But it works, right? That's what matters."

"This one contains a fictional story from Hexol, the *errocks'* world." He pointed to the slate in her hands.

She'd mentioned she'd had a different opinion of *errocks* before her arrival on the Dark Anomaly. The group of them here were far from their home world, and not just geographically. He had accepted the fact that *errocks*, like all the other species here, had become the product of their environment. All of them have shed layers of civilization under the harsh conditions of life in the Anomaly.

The film he had chosen for Svetlana was a fictional story, but it contained hints of the raw violence he had witnessed in *errocks* over the years. The video would be possibly hard to watch for her at times, but he wanted Svetlana to have no illusions about what kind of people she now had to spend the rest of her life with. The more she knew, the more careful she would be, he hoped.

"Here are the documentaries on *yourlu, ognats, errocks*, and a few others. The largest groups we have here."

He glanced at the red shelves by the entrance.

Crux had taken a tablet frame and was now selecting slates to watch by ordering the other two *errocks* to pull them off the shelves for him, in no apparent order.

Vrateus made a mental note to reorganize that section after them when he had a minute to spare later. *Errocks* didn't know the *themul* alphabet to do it themselves. He doubted some of them knew any alphabet at all.

"Would you be interested in watching or reading about the mating habits of the various species?" he asked Svetlana, not entirely sure why.

Maybe, it would be good for her to know he hadn't been exaggerating when he told her about the various ways the species here had sex.

Or maybe, he hoped she'd watch the video of the *themul* couple, too.

Maybe, he would have loved to know her reaction to it.

"Mating habits?" She followed his gaze to the red shelf. The *errocks* were leaning over the tablet in Crux's hands. All three were snickering and elbowing each other. "No, thank you," she said quickly, a lovely shade of blush coloring her cheeks. "I think I've got enough here." She tipped her chin at the stack of slates in his arms. "Enough to tide me over until the next visit. We'll come here again, won't we?" She lifted her questioning gaze to his, undisguised hope in her eyes.

There was no reason for another visit to the library. The purpose of today's trip was to help her familiarize herself with the surroundings. Now, she knew the location of the library. He could exchange the slates for her, she didn't need to leave her room for that.

Yet he found himself unable to extinguish the hopeful expression in her eyes.

"Yes. We'll come here again if you want."

Besides, he couldn't deny himself the pleasure of having her here.

It was enjoyable to share this with someone like her, who appreciated the work he had done on the entire spectrum of the library, not just its red section.

Chapter 10

FOR A COUPLE OF DAYS after my visit to the library, I read and watched the info inserts.

Most of the species currently found on the Dark Anomaly came from the sections of the Galaxy farthest from Earth. They had travelled these parts during the early trading days of the Federation, and even before the Federation had been formed.

I found some clues on how they could have ended up here. After analyzing the data found on several ships of different species, I was beginning to believe that the gravity of the Anomaly lashed out, similar to a star's flares, randomly grabbing whatever spaceships might be passing by.

This discovery was eerie and disturbing, but it made sense. That would explain how I ended up sucked in here, too.

The Dark Anomaly spun through space like a giant squid hiding in the depths of the ocean. It shot out its tentacles of gravity to drag ships and their crew to their deaths.

Except that not all were dying on impact with the edge of its disk. I'd survived, as had many others. What killed some of them here was the hopelessness afterwards. Those who survived gave up on civilization, plunging the community into a dark savage state.

While examining the charts and diagrams of the structural improvements done on the body of the Anomaly, I realized that all of it had been done in the past seven years, the same amount of time as Vrateus had been these people's captain.

During this time, he had expanded the oxygen generating facility and improved the efficiency of the air filtration system, which allowed a much bigger portion of the Anomaly's disk to be populated.

Under his leadership, the wrecks of the ships, haphazardly squished together after the many crashes, had been stabilized and secured to create this segment of the Anomaly—rugged and dented, but safe.

A while back, a cargo ship had crashed here with a load of live *vasai*, hideous giant centipedes. Their meat was rich in protein and other nutrients. *Vasai* had escaped the cargo hold after the crash and spread through the numerous tunnels within the Anomaly, hunting and being hunted by others.

By now, most of them had been captured and farmed, their meat and eggs being the principal source of protein for the crew. That allowed Vrateus to outlaw cannibalism, which apparently had been rampant before that.

Cold prickled my spine when I thought about what this place must have been like before Vrateus had brought some modicum of law and order. As wild and crude as it seemed today, it must have been truly feral and brutal before he had come to power.

My sixth morning on the Anomaly was the time of my next trip outside of my room.

Just like the last time, we left after breakfast. Vrateus took me in the direction opposite from the library this time, toward the mess hall.

An uncomfortable feeling scratched inside me as we neared that room. It was very noisy here, with some aliens loitering in the corridor by the entrance. The noise was coming from inside the mess hall—screams, grunts, and dull thuds of flesh hitting flesh.

It sounded like a fight.

I tensed, determined not to look inside, but then couldn't help it and stole a glance as we walked by the entrance.

The mismatched chairs and tables had been shoved to the walls. The occupants of the Dark Anomaly gathered around the cleared space in the middle where two aliens fought. One was a burly humanoid with mottled purple skin and four arms that he sometimes used as legs, moving on all six of his limbs. He pounded with his ginormous fists through the air, occasionally landing a blow on his opponent, a giant black-and-yellow caterpillar with eight pairs of legs and a human-like head and torso.

Both appeared already severely beaten, with blood dripping from the cuts in the one's purple skin and the other's yellow-spotted black chitin.

Always on alert, Vrateus quickly scanned the room and its occupants. He then continued to walk by, not slowing his pace. My arm clamped in his hand, I hurriedly followed.

Crux threw a glance into the room over his shoulder.

"Krakhil will owe me a favor." He spit through his teeth with a crooked smirk on his face. "Remoid is winning."

"Have you made a bet?" I asked him. Despite my severe aversion to having Crux's attention directed at me again, I was curious about the nature of the fight. Vrateus's calm reaction to it told me he must have allowed it.

"I sure did." Crux gave me one of his sliding-down-my-body stares that made me feel like taking a shower right after. "And I'll collect on it tonight, it seems."

His winnings had nothing to do with me. He was talking about whatever deal he had made with Krakhil. Still, the unpleasant feeling inside my chest grew stronger. I vowed never to make any deals or bets with Crux, even if my life depended on it.

We continued down the corridor.

"You allow fights and bets?" I asked Vrateus, keeping my voice down so our conversation would remain private.

"Yes," he replied, looking straight ahead. "As long as they follow the rules."

"What are the rules?"

"No weapons of any kind. No hitting below the belt. No blows that would intentionally lead to crippling injuries. The first to scream for mercy loses and stops the fight. Both the winner and the loser stay alive."

"And they obey these rules?" I asked, sceptically.

He shrugged. "I keep all weapons locked away. They also know that if one of them is injured to the point he can't do his chores, the other one will have to pick up the slack until the first one recovers enough to return to work. If the loser dies, I'll punish the winner."

"What is the punishment?"

"Death."

"Is it always death?" Once again, I remembered him shooting one of his people for touching me on the day of my crash.

"Almost always. The threat of death is the most effective form of reinforcement I've found."

"What if they repent their choices and promise not to disobey? Would you consider their remorse?" I was curious about the way of life here, so different from what I was used to.

"No."

That sounded harsh.

"They don't repent," he explained. "There is never any genuine remorse."

"Ever?" I found this unbelievable.

"They only regret getting caught. If I let them go unpunished, they'd do it again, only more cunningly."

I contemplated his words for a moment as we walked around a bend in the corridor. A multicolored glow on the white paneling up ahead caught my eye. It was a reflection of the Anomaly lights, I realized. And it came from the window in the double-door on the outside wall.

An airlock.

My heart sped up with excitement.

Vrateus moved to turn into a hallway off the main corridor, but I stopped him.

"What is that way?" I gestured down the corridor, at the plain metal door past the glow on the wall.

"An equipment storage room. Beside it is the *vasai* farm, with the garbage sorting room at the back. Nothing of much interest. However, I'll try to find some time to show it to you later, just so you know where everything is. Come, now."

We turned into the short hallway to the right. It ended in a large arched entryway.

"Kitchen," he announced.

Since he hadn't released my arm, we walked in together.

This must be an older part of the Anomaly, an even more outdated ship. The walls here were made of weathered metal, their panels connected by double rows of rivets. The room was almost as large as the mess hall, with a higher ceiling that made it look even bigger. The semicircle of a metal countertop surrounded a huge flameless stove with two enormous pots bubbling hot on it.

About a dozen aliens mingled about, not appearing to be doing anything. It wasn't immediately clear who was in charge here or what exactly was going on.

"Captain." A male who looked like a bipedal cross between a rhino and a hippo covered by brick-colored plating, lifted one of his four giant hands in greeting. Some of the others in the room followed, making the same gesture. "The water is boiling."

"Taste it," Vrateus ordered.

Leading me to the counter, he finally let go of my arm but remained close. The rhino-hippo cross gave me a curious look that quickly turned into a leer.

I briefly considered if I should say anything in greeting but changed my mind, growing increasingly uncomfortable under his stare. It lingered on every part of my body without ever moving higher than my neck.

"Is she here to give us a show?" a smaller alien asked. Sitting on the counter top, he reached with one of his many tentacles into a large jar next to him then smeared the grease from the jar over the fuzzy tuft of hair on the very top of his head, slicking it down.

"No," Vrateus bit off, not glancing at the tentacled alien. "She is here to supervise the food preparation."

It was weird to hear them talk about me in the third person in my presence. However, the last thing I wanted to do was to bring any extra attention to myself. At the moment, I preferred to be invisible, so I kept silent.

"Is that going to be her task from now on?" the larger one asked, perking up.

"Today, it is." Vrateus tipped his chin at one of the pots. "Taste it, I said."

The big alien dipped a large metal spoon into the pot then swallowed its boiling-hot contents without flinching.

Vrateus met his questioning look with a nod.

"Good. Go ahead with the stew, now."

"What was that for?" I quietly asked Vrateus as he closely watched the rhino alien collect some roughly chopped things off the counter and toss them into the pot.

"I make sure no one adds *fuhnid* mushroom juice to the food. It's extremely poisonous."

"Why would anyone want to do it, then?"

"Mostly, to poison me," he replied calmly. "But some would gladly use the mushrooms against others who might have pissed them off during the day—not paid after losing a bet, or for anything, really. Life is cheap around here."

"Do many want to harm you?"

The thoughts about Vrateus suffering from paranoia came back to me. Surely, even these brutes could see how much he had improved life around here. Didn't they appreciate him taking all of this work upon himself? I saw no reason for his crew wanting to get rid of him.

"Most." He shrugged a shoulder. "Maybe all."

"But why?" It made no sense.

"My crew thrive in anarchy. They fiercely detest the order I've been imposing." He exhaled a brief, humorless laugh. "The only reason I've remained their captain for this long is because their dislike for any kind of organization prevents them from organizing against me."

The rhino alien took a blob of the substance from the same jar the tentacled one had used to slick down the fuzz on his head. He sniffed at it, then tossed it into the pot.

My stomach lurched at the sight. The earthy smell wafting from the pot was the same as the stew I'd eaten many times since my arrival.

"This is made for everyone?" I asked Vrateus. "It's the communal food, isn't it? Everyone eats the same?"

"Yes. The food is cooked once a day. Krakhil," he addressed the rhino chef. "Taste the second pot, now."

Krakhil unhurriedly obliged. Upon Vrateus's approval, he then tossed several ingredients into the second pot.

A loud screeching sound suddenly cut through the room. A group of males hauled in something large and terrifying from a side door.

It was a live creature. About six or seven feet long and probably at least a foot in diameter, it had several long skinny legs on each side of its body and a cluster of round eyes on the top of its flat head. With ear-splitting squeals, it struggled against the hold of four aliens, two of them dragging it by its claw-like mandibles.

I sucked in a breath in horror, leaning back against the counter.

"What is that?"

"*Vasai.*" Vrateus stepped forward as two of the males dragging the creature yanked at one mandible each, cracking the centipede's head in half. Its long body contracted with its last convulsions then dropped motionless to the floor, a milky substance gushing out of the wound.

"This is just..." I gripped my throat as my stomach churned with nausea.

Staring at the horrific scene in front of me, I hadn't noticed that something was slinking around my thigh, inching in between my legs.

Revulsion shot through me when I realized it was one of the tentacles of the greasy alien on the counter. He met my glare with a smirk. One of his other tentacles moved jerkily somewhere inside the cluster of the rest of them.

"Get away from me," I hissed, ripping the slimy tentacle off my leg, but not fast enough. Glancing over his shoulder, Vrateus saw what was happening. Not saying a word, he threw his right arm up, a gun sliding smoothly out of his sleeve.

The gunshot echoed through the room, the bright flash blinding me for a moment. When I opened my eyes, my offender dropped to the floor with a squishing wet sound. A round hole gaped in his head, the smirk frozen on his face.

"Oh God..." I stepped back, away from the purple liquid from his wound pooling on the floor. "You didn't need to do that..."

The group of males by the dead *vasai* centipede paused for a fraction of a moment at the sound of the shot. They then resumed butchering the dead creature by ripping its body to pieces with their teeth and claws. Krakhil threw the pieces they hurled his way into the pots.

"Can I toss Qen in the stew, too?" he pointed with his chin at his dead buddy, eyeing the tentacles sprawling on the floor.

"No." Vrateus sent his gun back into his sleeve. "Incinerate the body and take the ashes to Malahki for the garden."

Circling my arm with his long fingers, he then led me out of the room.

"SORRY ABOUT YOUR MAN," I said, still shaken by the incident in the kitchen as we returned to my room.

"Qen disobeyed my direct order. He was aware of the consequences," he replied grimly.

It was the second murder committed by Vrateus that I had witnessed. Both times, he acted swiftly and without reservations. Yet I could tell that killing his people was not easy for him.

"Why did Qen still do it then? If he knew you would kill him?"

Sliding the set of black claws out of the tips of his fingers, Vrateus raked them through his fur over the tattoos above his ears.

"Qen was hoping not to get caught," he explained.

"That wasn't very smart on his part."

Did Qen really hope I wouldn't notice him touching me? Or that I might let him fondle me between my legs while he rubbed himself inside the cluster of his tentacles?

A shudder of disgust ran through me at the memory of the slide of the tentacle, and I swiped at my thigh, trying to erase the phantom sensation.

"Obviously, he wasn't very bright," Vrateus agreed. "Most of them are all about the immediate gratification, not thinking past it."

"Could...um," I started, choosing my words carefully. "Do you think shooting him on the spot might have been a little too harsh?"

I sensed it hurt him to shoot his people and wondered if the murders could have been avoided. At the same time, I didn't want to sound as if I was criticizing his actions.

"Would a warning, or something else do in such cases?"

"No." He heaved a sigh. "I could give warnings until I lost my voice. They don't listen. The only things these males understand are actions. Qen knew no one was supposed to touch you but me. He broke the order. He has been shot. Now, the rest of them got a visual demonstration of what will happen if they break this order, too."

"Well, for what it's worth, thank you for protecting me," I said, meaning every word.

He nodded silently in response.

I was expecting him to leave now, but he took a couple of steps farther into the room.

"I shouldn't have taken you to the kitchen." His wide shoulders dropped as he rubbed his face. Again, the thought that he must be exhausted crossed my mind.

Most of the time, Vrateus was enclosed in a hard shell of intense focus and composure, projecting power and strength. Only here in my room with the doors closed had I seen him come out of that shell a little. Then, he always seemed fatigued.

It must be exhausting to run life on the Dark Anomaly. Especially, since he had to do it all on his own, with no help from anyone. Did he ever get enough sleep?

"I'm glad you showed the kitchen to me," I said. "It was good for me to see all of that. Even the disturbing parts."

I had been gaining a better understanding of my new reality. Vrateus's reasons for forbidding me to leave the room on my own also made more sense, now.

"If you think so," he conceded with a tilt of his head, then turned to the door. "I'll bring you dinner when it's ready."

"Thank you," I said, though the thought of the bubbling substance in the pot made my stomach roil.

I continued to stand in the middle of the room long after the doors had closed behind him.

The more I learned about the occupants of the Dark Anomaly, the more I appreciated that Vrateus was among them. He seemed to be the only one who could be reasoned with in this place. I was even beginning to feel respect for him for everything he had done around here and for what he did to protect me.

Except that I shouldn't allow myself to feel anything at all toward this man. I wasn't staying here. There was no way I could live here the way he did. I did not belong here, and I would do whatever it took to leave the Dark Anomaly as soon as possible.

Chapter 11

"GET READY," VRATEUS told me when he came to pick up my empty dishes after dinner.

As soon as the doors closed after him, I looked at the clothing rack. A week had passed since my last appearance in the mess hall. Tonight, I had to do it again.

A sinking feeling had been in my stomach since the moment I got up that day. The last thing I wanted was to face his wild crew again. Naked.

But that was the condition of my survival. And to escape, I needed to stay alive.

Soon, there would be an end to this.

I now knew where the entrance to the surface was located. By carefully asking just the right questions from Vrateus last night, I had also learned that the storage room next to the *vasai* farm contained my spacesuit. The spare batteries from my ship were stored in the same room, too.

Maybe, he was too tired and preoccupied with other things to question my interest in the spacesuit's location. Or maybe, he trusted me not to betray him.

In any case, I didn't see my escape as a betrayal. When I was finally back in the civilized world, I would send help for the Dark Anomaly's crew and their captain. Eventually, I would get them all out of here, give them a chance at having a better life, too.

I'd gone through the calculations many times. My knowledge, logic, and common sense told me that escape was possible.

All I needed now was to figure out how to get to the storage room with my suit without someone stopping me.

For that, I had to keep on surviving until the right moment came. I couldn't let any suspicions rise. I needed to make Vrateus believe that I'd accepted my fate and was willingly cooperating.

The thought of my future escape helped me approach the clothing rack now.

With a sigh, I slid aside some of the hangers with dresses.

The sooner it started, the sooner it ended.

Only now had I really noticed how exquisite the clothes on the rack were. The jewel-colored fabrics felt soft and luxurious under my fingers. Each dress was elaborately embroidered and encrusted with shimmering crystals. These couldn't have been made to be worn every day. They must be meant for special occasions.

The thought that the collection had been also assembled with care entered my mind. Having gotten to know more about the Dark Anomaly's crew, I knew that only their captain was capable of putting this wardrobe together.

I remembered him insisting on my changing out of my boots. He wanted me to look pretty. As if what I was about to do was indeed some special occasion.

Revulsion prickled my skin. That orgy last week was the biggest humiliation of my life. Even if I escaped the Dark Anomaly, I already knew I'd never escape reliving it in my nightmares.

How did Vrateus not see that him touching me in public brought nothing but shame to me?

How was he not ashamed of himself for what he'd done to me?

What was he thinking when his hands were on me?

What could it possibly bring to *him*?

Vrateus didn't pleasure himself in the mess hall as the rest of them did. That didn't mean he didn't do it later in his own bed, reliving every moment in his mind.

I knew he had an erection when he touched me. But did he do anything about it afterwards when he was alone?

Suddenly, I was trying to imagine him touching himself in the darkness of his room, wherever it was.

He'd always been exceptionally collected and in control. It didn't prove easy for me to visualize him completely relaxed, stroking himself, and coming undone. I wondered what noises he'd make when he came, would his chiselled jaw ever relax, would he melt into me afterwards if I were with him...

Had we met under different circumstances, what kind of lover would he be? Gentle, like his touch on my body? Or wild and unhinged, like the passion of rage I had glimpsed in his orange eyes?

Not that I'd ever find out.

Absentmindedly, I touched the turquoise-blue chiffon of one of dresses, my fingers sinking into the soft cloud of the many layers of its voluminous skirt.

Wrap style, the dress closed in the front with two bejewelled clasps at the waist, draping softly around the chest area. Two long slits on the back, embroidered with gold and pink, might be for the wings or fins the previous owner of the dress had.

What had happened to the woman whose dress it used to be?

Did she die in the crash when the Anomaly had claimed the ship she was traveling on? Or was she among those who were killed after?

Suddenly, I desperately hoped she hadn't been on any ship at all. That she had ordered the dress to be delivered from another planet, but it never made it to her. She had remained safely on her home world and had a long, happy life.

With a sigh, I took the dress off the hanger.

Slipping out of my bodysuit, I got out of my bra and panties, too. There was no need for them, anyway. The less I was wearing the faster it all went. That was one of the reasons I had chosen the turquoise dress. Fastened with only two clasps, it was quick and easy to remove.

The doors swished open a moment after I had closed the two clasps at the waist, and Vrateus came in.

I glanced up, catching him staring at me.

He paused, slowly rolling his gaze over me from head to toe.

"This is the most beautiful thing I've ever seen," he said softly.

It wasn't clear whether he meant the dress or *me* wearing it. My cheeks heated, nevertheless, as warmth of odd pleasure spread through my chest.

I hid my face from him by bending over to rummage through the shoe chest on the bottom of the rack. I caught myself searching for some that would go well with the dress.

Why?

I shook my head.

It almost appeared as if I was trying to please Vrateus by making myself pretty for him.

Ridiculous.

Annoyed, I grabbed the same pair of golden strappy sandals I'd had on the last week and shoved my feet into them.

"I'm ready," I said, straightening my back after fastening the straps.

He continued to stare at me for another moment. His lips parted as though he was going to say something. Then he nodded, taking my arm in his hand and opening the doors.

The *errocks* shuffled out of the way as we exited. Crux and Nocc bounced foot to foot, their eyes greedily undressing me already.

Bringing my shoulders back, I lifted my chin up and kept my gaze straight ahead, trying to ignore their ogling.

The mess hall was packed—filled with undulating, half-naked bodies. The large, brightly lit room buzzed with pent-up energy, lust, and excitement. I quickly focused my gaze at the white floor right in front of my feet, letting Vrateus maneuver me to the spot of his choosing.

He positioned us by the wall again, taking his place at my back. I tried to block the noise, ignore the lewd greetings and vulgar comments shouted at me from every direction. I needed to find something else—anything—to focus on for the next little while.

"Ready?" Vrateus whispered, sending a flash of irritation through me.

What a stupid question. How could I ever be ready for this? How could anyone?

"Are you?" I bit back.

"Yes," he replied earnestly, my sarcasm lost on him completely.

Letting go of my arm, he moved his hand to my throat again. The soft fur on the back of his hand and forearm tickled my underjaw. I stifled an uninvited giggle.

"Why are you holding my neck?" I brought my head down, getting rid of the tickle by rubbing my chin against his hand.

He shifted behind me, placing his other hand on my waist. "I have sensors in my palm, they enable me to monitor your vitals."

"To make sure I don't pass out before the end?" I made a grim attempt at a joke.

"To help me learn how you like to be touched."

He slipped his other hand into the deep neckline of my dress, pausing for a moment when he found my naked breast underneath. My not wearing a bra must have surprised him. Surely not as much as his words had surprised *me*.

Why did he care about my likes and dislikes?

"*I promised them your moans,*" he'd said a week ago.

Back then he had also told me to pretend, and I had. Why did he bother to learn how I enjoyed being touched? This was all for show, anyway. What did it matter if my moans were real or fake? His crew didn't seem that picky.

I ventured a quick glance around the room. Some males looked like they had already come once without me being even undressed yet. His yellow eyes on me, a sneer on his face, Crux sat on a chair nearby, holding his two humongous dicks, one in each hand.

I promptly closed my eyes, forcing my thoughts back to the only thing in this room that actually felt...nice—Vrateus's hand gently kneading my breast inside my dress.

I fell silent, not wanting him to speak either. This way, I could forget about everything, thinking only about his hands touching me, as if they didn't belong to him or to anyone else at all.

The hands and...that tail. I had almost forgotten about the tail. He snuck it under my skirt, sliding it up my leg, stroking the sensitive skin inside my thigh. The soft brush of his fur between my legs made anticipation tickle deep inside me.

Vrateus didn't open my dress, hadn't exposed me to the room yet, as if he first wanted to steal a moment with me for himself.

His hands moved with more confidence this time, igniting my body with excitement. Somehow, he'd figured out that plucking at my nipple the way he just had would send sparks of pleasure through my body. He must have known that dragging the tip of his tail between my legs would make my inner muscles spasm and my lower belly swell with liquid heat.

How did he learn so much about me so quickly?

He'd spent over twenty years on the Anomaly. Which must be his entire adult life.

Could I be the first woman Vrateus had ever touched, then?

What did all of this mean to *him*?

Suddenly, understanding filled me. For Vrateus, this *was* special.

As much as I detested the idea of what was happening in this room I believed I understood the tenderness—the reverence—of his touch.

For Vrateus, this was not a perversion as I had first thought. This might be the only intimacy with a woman he had ever experienced. This could even be the only physical contact with another person he'd had as an adult. Knowing his crew, he probably had been living without a hug or even a handshake from anyone during all these years.

Surrendering to his touch, I leaned back, relaxing against his strong body.

His hand slipping from my neck, he unclipped the clasps of my dress, finally baring me to everyone's eyes.

The cool air against my flushed skin was sobering, bringing the awareness of all those who must be ogling me.

Squeezing my eyes shut tighter, I forced my thoughts back to Vrateus. His arm under my chest, he slid his other hand between my legs where his tail had already spread the slick heat seeping out of me.

A genuine moan escaped my throat when he slipped his fingers between my heated folds.

I exhaled sharply, leaning my head back against his hard shoulder.

His chest moved with shallow, erratic breaths. It appeared that Vrateus's usual granite composure was finally cracking.

Suddenly, I wished it would crumble completely. I wanted him to unleash the fire I'd sensed inside him. I needed to see the passion burn in those vivid orange eyes of his.

He had been keeping not only his crew but also himself under a very strict control. And I wondered if Vrateus knew his own body as well as he had gotten to know mine.

A part of me wished I had a chance to explore it with him.

Reaching back, I searched for him with my hand. My fingers slid past the point of his ear and dipped into the hair on his nape. It felt soft and luxurious, like the fur of an arctic fox. A swirl of his fingers around the tight nub between my folds made me gasp from pleasure, and I fisted my hand in his fur.

A low rumble in his chest vibrated against my back.

He dipped his head. A puff of hot breath hit the side of my neck. Warm ripples ran down my skin as his sharp canines grazed my skin.

His arms flexed tighter around me. He rubbed harder between my legs, building up the tingling pressure that threatened to explode any minute, now.

The growls of approval and lustful groans reached me through the haze of blinding desire, but they only spurred my arousal.

I got caught up in the lustful frenzy of the room.

Arching my back, I thrust my hips forward, riding his hand. So close now...

A loud grunt came, just to the side of me.

Crux...

The noise yanked me out of the bliss of passion. I wanted to come, so badly. But I didn't want to share this moment with Crux.

This was not about *my* sexual pleasure, anyway.

Grabbing Vrateus's wrist, I discreetly jerked his hand off me.

This needed to end as soon as possible.

I moaned loudly, in a most believable manner I could muster. Digging my fingers into the fur on Vrateus's forearm, I kept his hand away, and he didn't fight me. Then, I ended it all in a few short fake groans and tremors.

Survival.

That was the point of this.

Survival was all that mattered on the Dark Anomaly. So, I did what I had to do to survive. I pretended to come. I faked the orgasm in a most dramatic fashion to satisfy a bunch of dirty aliens.

Vrateus held me from behind. My head down, I opened my eyes, staring at the huge ruby-red stone in one of the golden rings on his fingers.

His chest rose and fell against my back, his rugged breaths fanning across the skin above my ear and moving the fine hairs on my temple.

Our performance was not meant for either of us. Yet his reaction to it seemed to echo mine in its intensity. Uniting us somehow.

"Get me out of here," I whispered. "Please."

My words brought him into action. Shielding me with his shoulder, he quickly retrieved my dress from the floor then wrapped me in its skirts. He swaddled me in it just the way I was, my hands pressed to my chest.

"Come," he ordered, his voice clipped. His hard armour of control slid firmly back into place.

With my arms now buried under the many layers of chiffon, he led me with his hand on my waist—our only escort, Wyck and his pet.

Back in my room, I stopped near the entrance when the doors closed behind us. Vrateus moved to take his arm off me, but I grabbed it, pressing it to my waist.

More than anything in the world, I just wanted to be held at that moment. I sensed some slight fragile connection between Vrateus and me. It might have been forming for some time now, but I'd felt it most acutely in the mess hall tonight. I wanted to hold on to that while he held me in his arms for just a few seconds longer, without anyone else here.

He gazed at me with curiosity and some confusion.

"What?" I asked, not letting him go. "You don't hug?"

"Um...no." Tentatively, he wrapped his other arm around me. "I've had no chance for that."

With a long sigh, I relaxed against his chest, resting my head on his shoulder.

He smelled nice. He felt even better—big, strong, warm.

Safe.

It was wonderful to be held. The lingering sadness and anxiety melted away.

How did one survive for two decades without a hug?

Then, I realized, I hadn't been held like this for a very long time, either.

For a while, I'd had a boyfriend when I was at the Academy. I'd caught him kissing another woman at a party, and left, without ever speaking a word to him again. Months later, I had a number of intimate encounters with another man, but I made sure it never grew into anything more serious than that.

On the space station, I'd stayed away from men entirely. Random connections happened between the staff during missions. But since my parents had me like that, during the one and only project on which they'd both worked together, I avoided any sexual relationships on the station at all. In fact, I had avoided deep connections with people my entire life.

After my parents had left, each going their own way, my grandparents raised me. They were generally cold and distant people, not too pleased with having to raise a child during their retirement years.

My grandfather had been an astronomy professor most of his life. I'd sneak into his study when he wasn't around and pore over the charts on the walls, wishing to travel to the stars one day. My passion had always been exploring the unknown parts of space.

Consciously or not, I had been preparing myself for the same life as my parents. I knew from their experience that it would be a life unsuitable for long-term relationships or for having a family, which suited me just fine. I'd learned early on that the only way to avoid being hurt when people you loved left you was not to love anyone at all. If there were no strong connections, there was no pain in breaking them.

Now, was definitely not the time to think about any form of connection.

But I wasn't *thinking* about anything at all. For a few moments, I simply allowed myself to enjoy being held in a man's powerful arms, to let the feeling of comfort and safety take over me, even as neither was guaranteed around here.

The warmth of his body enveloped me, relaxing...and dangerous. For those few seconds, Vrateus made me forget that I *needed* to leave him. I had to get free from this place, and even more so from him.

"Vrateus," I said softly, prompted by our closeness to try again. "Please, help me leave here. I promise to organize a rescue mission."

If ever there was a person for me to talk sense into anyone here, it had to be him.

He jerked to attention, looking startled by my request.

"Leave?"

"I've done some detailed calculations," I hurried to explain. "I'm confident, it's possible—"

"No," he cut me off.

Instead of releasing me from his hug, he held tighter.

"Please. If you just let me, I could try—"

"No!"

I attempted to free myself from his arms, but he flexed them, forming a vise around me.

"Svetlana." He peered deep into my eyes. "*Trying* always leads to death. Do you understand? Every single attempt resulted in people and ships smashing against the edge of the disk of the Dark Anomaly." He gave me a firm shake, as if trying to get his words to sink into my head. "*Everyone* has died."

Words were not enough to convince me. I had been trained to test assumptions, not to blindly believe them.

"None of them had the most advanced technology, Vrateus," I argued. "Humans can now generate incredible amounts of energy from relatively small power sources. I'm confident it'd be enough to combat even the enormous gravitational field of the Anomaly."

His mouth pressed into a hard line, he combed the claws of one hand through the thick curl of fur hanging over his forehead.

"And what if not?"

I used the moment to twist myself out of his one-armed hug.

"Well, there is always a slight chance of failure in any test. I'm willing to take the risk—"

"Why?" He narrowed his eyes at me. "Why do you want to leave so much? Even risking your own life in the process?"

"Isn't it obvious?" I spread my arms aside, shaking my head in disbelief. "Out there I had the life I chose, the job I loved—"

He narrowed his eyes at me.

"Who is waiting for you there, Svetlana?"

I drew in a lungful of air and...released it, not finding it in me to confess that nobody waited for me out there. I had no one. My grandparents had passed away while I was still in the Academy. And my parents had never cared about where I was, anyway.

"That's not the point," I mumbled, breathing through a sudden tightness in my chest. "I'm not leaving for the sake of someone else. I want to come back to my old life. Don't *you* want to see what's out there, too?"

"No." He retreated to the exit. "Too much risk."

"But the chance of success is also there..." I moved after him.

"No," he repeated over and over, shaking his head, then resolutely slammed his hand on the panel, opening the doors.

"I want you alive," he said firmly before leaving.

The doors closed, shutting me in my room once again.

To live? Not like this.

How about what I *wanted?*

The thought burned through me with rising anger. His stubbornness was beyond exasperating. His curt manner of brushing me off—as if I were a child nagging at him with some trivial request, instead of a trained specialist offering him a chance at a better life out there in the world—was infuriating.

Maybe my earlier guess was right. Vrateus didn't want to be rescued—either out of fear of the unknown or unwillingness to relinquish the absolute control he had on the Anomaly. He might not want to leave behind everything he had accomplished here.

Why would he care how I felt about losing the life I had chosen? About having to play the role of a sex toy for the rest of my existence?

In the eight days I had spent here, over six years had already passed on Earth and my station. My mission contract had ended. Everyone I knew had grown that much older. And every day, every hour I spent here, the life out there kept moving at a much faster pace.

Obviously, Vrateus didn't feel my sense of urgency.

That had been my last attempt at trying to convince him to let me go. Now, I was certain I had to do it on my own.

Chapter 12

IT HAD BEEN ANOTHER week and another public "performance" in the mess hall before Vrateus finally allowed me another tour of the Anomaly.

This time, he was taking me to see the gardens. They were located past the library, along the same long and winding corridor that stretched through the entire habitable area of the Anomaly.

"*Damirian* technology allowed us to grow a variety of plants," Vrateus told me on the way there. "When Malahki arrived about five years ago, it helped me design and build our expansive gardens the way they are today. It's very knowledgeable about agriculture."

It?

"What is Malahki? A robot? AI?"

"No, it's a person."

"Didn't you just refer to him as *it*?" Or had I heard him wrong?

"That's what it is. Malahki is a *damirian*. Its species are born with no gender. They call it the 'neutral sex'. They are neither male nor female until they sexually mature."

That was new to me. Earth had been in contact with *damirians*. We had recently put a program in place, exchanging research findings between our planets. That didn't include an exchange of detailed information about the development of our species. Neither had I ever met a *damirian* in person.

"Referring to them as *he* or *she* before they mature is considered offensive," Vrateus added. "Inconsiderate."

"I'll keep that in mind," I assured him. "How long does it take for them to reach maturity?"

"There is no definitive age for that. Malahki is a full-grown adult. A *damirian* remains neutral gender until it meets the right person. They mate for life and choose the gender opposite of their partner."

"How does it work?" I asked, confused. "If two 'it-s' meet, both of neutral gender, who decides which one of them is to become a 'he' and which one a 'she'?"

"They know. Gender roles are clearly defined in their society. The neutral gender works in all levels of government due to their aptitude for diplomacy and their calm demeanour. The males are more aggressive and dominant, with the females being more playful, easy-going, and creative. After spending some time together, each half of a couple leans one way while the other one takes the opposing role. Then the physical differences form."

The concept sounded fascinating, and I made a note to get more information from the library.

"So, since you told me that Malahki is the only one of his species here, does it mean he...*it* is destined to remain *it* forever?"

"It's been five years since Malahki's arrival to the Dark Anomaly. I suspect if there was a suitable partner for it here, it would have chosen one already."

The fact that Malahki hadn't found a suitable life partner on the Anomaly did not surprise me. Though the fact that it might now be destined to remain alone for the rest of its days carried a certain sadness.

Walking to the gardens took some time. After several turns and curves in the uneven corridor, we finally came to a wide door of opaque glass that folded away to the sides, like an accordion.

The gardens had a very distinct look, different from everything else on the Dark Anomaly. Unlike the glaring white light everywhere else, here it was dimmer, with a yellow softness to it. Vines of every shade of green and purple covered the walls, making the already sizable space appear even bigger.

The air seemed cleaner, rich with moisture and scents of flowers and wet dirt.

"Malahki," Vrateus called out into the labyrinth of greens and purples that dominated the place.

"Yes, Captain," came a calm voice from behind the vines then a tall, lean figure slipped around them and headed our way.

"I want you to show Svetlana everything we have in here." Vrateus gestured for the *errocks* accompanying us to stay behind by the entrance.

"Welcome to the gardens, Svetlana," Malahki greeted me, which made the *damirian* immediately stand out from the rest of the Anomaly's crew, none of whom had ever shown any manners.

According to Vrateus, Malahki got here relatively recently. That might be why it still retained some shreds of civilization.

Tall, with toned muscles and shoulders slightly wider than the hips, Malahki's figure could have equally belonged to a slender male or an athletic female. Its beige skin was smooth and even, like a clean canvas. The same color as its skin, its waist-long hair was braided in plaits of different length and thickness and decorated with vines and flowers.

"It's nice to meet you." I gave Malahki a friendly smile.

At first, I thought the *damirian* was wearing a skin-colored bodysuit, then I realized it wore no clothes at all. Its chest was smooth, as was the area between its legs—no breasts, not even nipples, no distinct genitals, and no body hair.

"Follow me," it invited.

With all its politeness, Malahki's expression lacked emotion. There was no aggression or sneering that I was used to seeing from others here. But neither was there any genuine warmth or strong emotion—just a detached stoic calmness.

I understood what Vrateus meant by saying Malahki was of neutral gender. It truly was genderless, like a basic mold, waiting for the sculptor to add the finishing touches to be complete, both in physical appearance and personality.

We followed the *damirian* down the narrow passages between the long containers with dirt and plants.

"The gardens were completed four years ago," Malahki said, conducting the tour. "Soon thereafter, about ninety percent of the ground had been planted using the seeds and spores we were able to retrieve from the ships. Not all the varieties thrived right away. For the past three years, I have been increasing the yield by rotating crops and improving the soil quality."

The familiar scent of the soap used on the Anomaly wafted through the air as we approached a wide planter with gorgeous umbrella-like plants in it. Their tops were as wide as my hand, vivid burgundy with pink fuzzy lines. I slid the tip of my finger along one of the soft stripes.

"These are beautiful—"

"Don't!" With lightning speed, Vrateus yanked my hand away from the plant.

"Did she touch them?" Malahki hit a button on the side of the planter. A clear cover lowered over the entire container, securely enclosing the plants.

"She did." Vrateus held out my hand to the *damirian*.

It grabbed a bottle with some strong-smelling liquid from under the planter.

"Sorry. I've been fertilizing the soil and needed the cover raised." The *damirian* sprayed the liquid on my palm and fingers then rubbed my hand dry with a soft cloth, cleaning me as if I were a toddler who'd had a messy spaghetti dinner.

Confused and a little embarrassed, I asked, "Was I not supposed to touch these?"

"*Fuhnid* mushroom juice is poisonous," Malahki replied in his even tone. "If swallowed, it would put you to sleep, one you would never wake up from."

"Even touching them is dangerous?" I clenched my hands into fists, taking a big step away from the planter.

"If you touched your face right after or licked your fingers, it could still make you sick."

"Why plant them at all, then?" I asked.

Vrateus glanced over his shoulder at the *errocks*.

Nocc plucked small round berries off a bush, tossing them at Wyck, who laughed trying to dodge them. Standing by the same bush, Crux was stuffing his face with the berries.

"*Fuhnid* mushrooms have no taste or smell of their own," Vrateus said softly, leaning close to my ear. "When added to soap, they completely neutralize all body odors. *Errocks* have an acute sense of smell. They can trace a person by their scent up to an hour after they've passed by."

Malahki had moved ahead, meanwhile, seemingly expecting us to follow. However, I lingered by the planter with the mushrooms, confused by Vrateus's words.

"If they're odorless, what is this smell then?"

"You mean the scent of the soap?" He reached for the bush with white berries nearby, plucking one off it. "The soap is made with *chela* berries. They have a mild scent." He squished one between his fingers, showing me the gel-like substance inside it.

Grabbing his hand, I sniffed at the gel. "No, this smells much milder and different from the mushrooms."

"But mushrooms don't smell," he insisted.

Malahki had noticed that we weren't following and came back, now staring at me, too.

"What is this fragrance then?" I glanced at both of them in confusion, then leaned over the planter with the burgundy mushrooms.

Even the glass cover didn't completely stop the pleasant aroma from drifting around. "It's nice. Fruity, with a hint of some...baking spice. Can't you smell it?"

Both stared at me blankly, then exchanged puzzled looks with each other.

"You really can't smell it?" I asked them.

"No one can," Vrateus replied.

"Well, I can." I shrugged, "Must be a human thing, then."

"Must be..." He narrowed his eyes at me, then darted a glance at the mushrooms again. "Would you consider smelling our food every night?"

"Smelling it?" I frowned. "What do you mean by that? Like everyone's plates? Or those huge pots in the kitchen?"

I tried not to sound like I was mocking him, but his request seemed rather odd.

"No, not like that." He rolled his shoulders back.

My gaze slid behind Vrateus. Wyck and Nocc were still horsing around by the berry bushes, now trying to feed some berries to Lesh. Crux, however, was staring at us. The way his eyes glared from under the thick brow ridges made my spine prickle with unease.

Maybe Vrateus's request was not that out of place, after all.

"You want to make sure the food isn't poisoned?" I asked, and he nodded in reply. "How would you like me to do it?" I pretended not to pay attention to Crux anymore, though I could still feel his heavy stare on us.

With the considerable distance between us, he couldn't possibly hear what we were talking about. *Errocks'* hearing wasn't as acute as their sense of smell. Despite that, Vrateus and I both spoke in lowered voices.

"I normally eat in my room," Vrateus said. "After everyone else has had their dinner, including you. From now on, I want to feed you first. If you notice this smell in your food, I'll order the entire pot dumped."

"All right," I agreed. "But what are the chances of anyone poisoning the food? What's the point of killing everyone? No one could survive here on their own. People are needed to run and maintain things."

He rubbed the back of his neck. "It would be just another precaution."

"Okay." I conceded. "I'll do it if it makes you feel better."

"Thank you."

After that, Malahki showed us a variety of edible plants the *damirian* had been cultivating, including some grains and greens.

"Are any of these used in meals," I asked, trying one of the juicy strings from the cluster he had given me. It tasted a little like a banana but with the texture of a watermelon.

"Some." Malahki pressed its mouth into a thin line, displaying obvious displeasure. "Other than grains, the crew prefers meat to plants. And now that they have a whole farm of *vasai*, they can have as much meat as their digestive systems can handle."

The savage scene of butchering the giant centipede came unbidden to my mind.

"The *vasai* also lay clusters of eggs," Vrateus commented. "Which are highly nutritious."

In the meantime, we had circled the gardens, our tour coming to an end. Vrateus stepped aside, talking with Crux about something. I lingered by the last bed with ridged, dark-green spheres that reminded me of a cactus, though they had no needles or spikes.

Idly, I walked around the planter, admiring the round fruit. I wasn't in a hurry to return to the room that felt more like a prison cell with each passing day.

"Watch your step," Malahki warned me.

"Oh. What is this?" I skipped over a pile of dry branches on the ground behind the planter.

"Just some garden waste. I was going to send it to the garbage sorting room." Malahki lifted an armload of the twigs then kicked aside a piece of loose paneling on the wall.

It revealed an opening, large enough for me to fit through. A wide, ribbed strip moved inside it, like a conveyor belt. The *damirian* shoved the branches inside. With rustling and thumping, they moved down, pushed by the belt.

"Is it like a garbage chute?" I asked. "Where does it lead to?"

"To the waste sorting room, near the *vasai* farm. They use these for bedding for the centipedes."

"Does all garbage end up being sent to the same location?" I asked.

"I believe so."

That might mean there were more garbage tunnels accessible by openings in the walls.

"The system isn't perfect," Malahki complained. "You might have seen dead grass and leaves in the corridor not far from your room. There is a kink in the tunnel and debris is often blown out through the wall. I have to sweep the floor there, every time I get rid of garden waste." It shook its head, dumping the rest of the dry branches into the chute.

"Are they steep? The tunnels?"

"In some places they are. But they need to be even steeper, as some garbage, especially the garden waste, ends up getting stuck. I go down the tunnel now and then, to clean or to fix the conveyor belt when it gets stuck. But it's still more convenient to have the tunnels than to carry every armload to the farm myself."

Vrateus returned to us. He took hold of my arm again, signaling it was time to leave. The now-familiar sensation of his large hand firmly circling my upper arm spread with warmth through the rest of my body. I couldn't resist drawing in a long breath, savoring his scent as it filled my lungs.

What was I doing?

I might have just discovered a way to finally escape the Dark Anomaly. Now, was definitely not the time to get distracted by its captain. If anything, I absolutely needed to get out of here rather sooner than later, before whatever it was that kept pulsing hot and cold inside of me in his presence would get out of control.

I no longer felt sad for Malahki possibly having to remain a gender neutral forever. Now, I was envious of the *damirian's* morose serenity. Wouldn't it be a blessing? Not to be affected by hormones at the most inconvenient of times?

As we walked down the corridor, I watched the floor under my feet carefully. A short distance before my room, I spotted a dusting of dirt and some tiny twigs stuck in the cracks between the floor tiles. Passing by, I took a closer look at the wall in that area, noting a gap where a loose panel covered another entrance into the tunnel.

That must be the kink that Malahki had talked about. From here on, the tunnel went to the waste sorting room by the farm, to the air-lock near it, and to the storage room with my spacesuit.

I now had the way to freedom figured out.

What I still needed was a chance to get out of my room.

Alone.

Chapter 13

AS SOON AS VRATEUS left after breakfast the next morning, I spent the entire time until lunch studying the door panel.

Using the breakfast utensil, I pried the top cover open but couldn't figure out how to change the program to add my palm print. The technology differed from what I was used to. It was much older too.

At lunchtime, I quickly put the cover back on, then dashed to the bed that Vrateus had found somewhere to replace my sleeping pallet. It was large and comfortable, and aside from the clothing rack and a small table, it was the only furniture I had in this room. I sat on the bed, while Vrateus carried my lunch in and exchanged a few sentences with me.

The moment he left, I continued to work on the panel.

By dinnertime, I'd only figured out the way to disable it, unlocking the door. Before Vrateus returned, I quickly re-attached the cover.

The confirmation light went on and the signal sounded when Vrateus touched the panel outside. However, the lock was no longer functioning. Thankfully, Vrateus didn't notice that, as the doors slid open the way they always did. As he entered my room, his focus was on the two plates of food in his hands.

"This was cooked this afternoon." He handed me a plate. "Can you smell any trace of *fuhnid* mushrooms here?"

I took the plate from him, bringing it to my nose and inhaling deeply. It smelled of wet earth and grease. Not appetizing, at all.

For a moment, I wondered if I should volunteer to make a decent meal for them. Although I wasn't the greatest cook, I was sure I could still whip up something more appealing than this. I would use some plants from Malahki's garden as herbs. Maybe experiment with different grains—try to soak them and the meat in water for a while, to get rid of that musty earthy smell.

The thought of having to cook in that kitchen, though, immediately turned me off the idea. Even if I stayed on the Dark Anomaly for the rest of my life, I'd rather eat the gray, dirt-smelling stew than spend any time in the company of Krakhil and whatever helpers he had there.

"No smell of mushrooms here." I gave Vrateus the plate back then sniffed the second plate. "Or here. Just the usual, meat and grains."

The pleasant aroma of the deadly mushrooms would have actually improved that smell.

"Thank you." Vrateus left one plate on the table, taking the second one back to the door. "Enjoy your dinner."

I stared at his wide back as he departed, noting his posture relax a little after my confirmation. The weight this man had to carry on his shoulders to keep this place from falling apart was enormous.

Having gotten to know the Dark Anomaly and its inhabitants by now, I understood much better the gargantuan task Vrateus had undertaken. I marvelled at his resolve and his ability to keep order here. I even felt sympathy for him, too. He was doing it all alone, saving the people who didn't even realize they were being saved. None of them appreciated his efforts. No one cared or truly helped, either.

Taking a seat on the floor by the door, I propped the big round clock in front of me, watching the time. Guessing that the dinner should be done soon, I calculated the approximate time when life on the Anomaly would finally quiet down. The crew and their captain should settle down for the night at some point.

Then, I would sneak out, down the waste disposal tunnel, and to the spacesuit storage room.

After I had finished the thick stew on my plate, I waited until a significant amount of time had passed.

When I could reasonably assume that most of the crew had gone to bed, I stole to the door and placed my ear to it, listening carefully for any noise. When no sound came, I quietly pushed the door aside. Sticking my head out, I made sure no one was out there.

The corridor seemed deserted. Though, its bright lights remained on. For a moment, I wondered where Vrateus's room was and whether he would be asleep, too. Even the captain needed to rest sometimes.

Once out of my room, I slid the door closed behind me. Unfortunately, with the panel in my room being disabled, I could no longer lock the door from the outside.

With any luck, my disappearance wouldn't be discovered until tomorrow morning when Vrateus would come by with breakfast. By then, I should be far away from here, in another place and even another time.

I ran to the part of the corridor where I'd seen the dust and twigs from the garden on the floor earlier. Tapping along the panels on the wall, I found the one with the tunnel behind it. A ribbed, rubbery strip ran along it on the bottom, moving noiselessly as a conveyor belt.

Quickly, I slid into the tunnel. Lying down with my back on the belt, I let it carry me along.

The space was rather narrow. I pressed my arms to my sides to make sure I didn't get accidently stuck along the way. Malahki had spoken about going down here, occasionally. The *damirian* was tall but slender, only a little wider in the shoulders than me. I doubted Vrateus would fit through here, though. Definitely none of the *errocks* would.

That was good. Even if anyone discovered how I had escaped and where I was heading, they would have to use the corridor to catch up with me, which should take them considerably longer.

A faint murmur of voices came from up ahead, making me realize I must be nearing the waste processing room. I had hoped no one would be there at this hour. Now, I scrambled for a way to slow myself down. Falling out of the chute in front of the undersexed aliens who had used me as a visual stimulus for self-pleasuring for the past three weeks would be a disaster.

Pressing my arms and feet into the walls of the narrow tunnel, I lifted my body off the conveyor belt. The rubbery material of the soles of my boots connected well with the uneven surface of the walls, allowing me to control my climb down this slanted section of the tunnel.

The voices grew louder as I progressed. Several of Vrateus's crew members were there in the room, yelling and arguing by the sound of it.

Keeping my eyes on the tunnel up ahead, I stopped moving as soon as a brightly lit opening came into view.

Judging by the voices, there must be at least four of them out there, but it could be more than that. Not all the males in this place were vocal. Some, like Qen, the tentacled alien who got shot in the kitchen, acted without saying a word.

Even four was too many. I had no weapons to fight them with.

Flexing the muscles in my arms and legs, I hovered inside the tunnel. Suspended over the conveyor belt, I knew I wouldn't last long. Eventually, my legs would give out, and the belt would propel me out into the room.

Although the arguing grew louder, I failed to understand what the four were fighting over. Only a few words reached me in the tunnel, most of them were curses.

My legs felt numb and my arms shook. I prayed no garbage would come from behind and push me out of the tunnel.

A fifth voice joined the group in the room, yelling at the rest to get the fuck out. After that, all went quiet.

Afraid to move, I remained in the tunnel a bit longer, waiting for any noise from the outside. When none came, I relaxed my muscles, letting myself fall back onto the conveyor belt. It took me into the room, dumping me onto a pile of dirt and twigs.

I exhaled with relief, finding the room empty. Picking up a thicker stick from those lying around, I was glad to have at least some kind of weapon.

The room was filled with crates stacked along the walls. Piles of garbage littered the floor. Stepping around them on my way to the exit, I realized that what seemed to be aimless littering must have had a system. The contents of the crates were sorted by the type of material. Unsorted waste piled up on the floor, to be processed next.

The arched doors to the room remained open, and I quietly snuck closer, listening for any voices or footsteps. When none came, I carefully poked my head out.

The small corridor outside the door was empty. It led me to a larger, dimly lit room. Here, there were plenty of noises, but they didn't come from the crew.

Huge cages stood in rows on the floor and along the walls. The giant centipedes crawled inside them. Their hissing and the rustling of their chitin covered bodies filled the air.

This was the Dark Anomaly's *vasai* farm.

Holding my stick in front of me, I carefully made my way between the cages, taking care not to come too close to any of them.

The *vasai* hissed and screeched as I approached. Some lunged at the cage walls, their massive mandibles closing over the thick rusty bars with loud clanking noises.

Heavy clusters of black spheres—each about the size of my fist—hung in some of the cages. These must be the *vasai* eggs Vrateus had spoken about.

A shudder ran across my shoulders when I thought about the horrific centipedes crawling free around the Anomaly, years ago. Vrateus had said that *most* had been captured. Did that mean that some might still be out there, possibly even in the tunnel I had just come from?

Relieved to leave the farm, I exited into the main corridor. My back to the wall, the stick clutched in my sweaty hands, I moved toward the storage room as fast as I dared while making as little noise as possible.

The door across from the entrance to the storage room with my spacesuit had a large glass insert. Behind it was another one, also with glass in it. The brilliant lights of the Anomaly swirled in their timeless dance beyond them.

As I had guessed, this was the exit to the outside, leading to my freedom. There were even bright markings on the wall, from the storage room to the glass doors, to show the way to a person wearing a spacesuit, I assumed. The helmets of some of the older suits limited visibility for the one wearing them, making the markings useful.

The door to the storage room was locked, as could have been expected. I knocked the cover of the door panel off, using my stick. This one turned out to be much easier to tamper with than the one in my room. Instead of a palm print, it was the old primitive technology that required a numeric code to enter. I quickly disabled the lock, bypassing the code.

The suits were neatly arranged along the walls inside the storage room. Some pieces hung off the hooks, some had been laid out on the shelves. My suit stood to the right, its rigid construction supporting it in the upright position.

Tossing the stick aside, I searched for the spare fuel cells that had been taken off my ship. I found them nearby then attached them to the back of the suit, connecting its power supply system to the batteries.

Opening the hatch in the front, I climbed into the suit. Large and clunky with all its systems off, the suit was a self-contained, flexible, and powerful unit when it was fully functioning.

First, I turned the life support system on, quickly checking the performance of the other systems, too. Running the diagnostics, I was relieved to discover that the suit was in a perfect working order. Only the outside sound receptors were malfunctioning, which I didn't need for the escape anyway.

I programmed the trajectory I'd been calculating and re-calculating for days.

It'd been nearly three weeks since my crash. That meant more than sixteen years had passed outside of the Anomaly. The term of my mission had long ended. My team must have reported me as dead, lost in space without a trace.

Most likely, the station was no longer orbiting the Omphi planet. But there might be another station in its place, now. Either way, one of the spacecraft travelling along the trade routes by the water world could intercept my distress signal.

But first, I had to get off the Dark Anomaly.

Unlike most celestial bodies, the gravity of the Anomaly was erratic, making orbiting it impossible. If I didn't gain enough momentum from the start, I risked being sucked back in again. At take-off, the suit's thrusters needed to be at full power to propel me well beyond the gravitational force of the Anomaly.

Powering up the exoskeleton of the suit, I moved out of the room, no longer concerned about anyone seeing or hearing me. Inside the suit, I was unreachable, protected, and stronger than anyone on the Anomaly.

Out in the corridor, I sensed vibrations through the floor. With the suit's noise sensors malfunctioning, I couldn't hear any sound from the outside, but I assumed the vibrations came from the foot-falls of someone running my way.

My escape must have been discovered.

I was safe in the suit, though. There was no need to panic.

As I approached the door with the glass insert that led to the air-lock, the panel on the wall next to it lit up. The suit's glove glowed the same color as the panel. Vrateus must have programmed it for his use. I placed my hand on the panel, and the door slid open. I moved into the chamber, quickly closing the door to the corridor behind me.

Inside the airlock chamber, I shuffled toward the identical panel on the opposite wall. All I had to do now was to activate the panel for the outside door to open.

I was almost free.

Something hard slammed into my back with enough force to make me stagger, even inside the powered suit. Startled, I took an-other step forward. It proved difficult, as if something or someone held me from behind.

I activated the three-hundred-sixty vision inside my helmet, to see if the suit had gotten caught on something that was holding me back.

Instead, I came face to face with Vrateus.

Both hands wrapped around the connection of the fuel cell, he held on to me. His expression furious, he yelled something I couldn't hear.

He was the only one in the airlock with me. Holding on to the suit, he couldn't even use any of his weapons. They would probably be useless against the material of the suit anyway, even without me engaging the defense shield.

Despite his significant physical strength, Vrateus was no match for the suit's thrusters. All I had to do was to engage them, open the outer door, and be on my way.

If the emissions of the suit engines didn't burn Vrateus to death on the spot, he would die, blown out into open space with me.

Surely, he understood that. Yet he wouldn't let go.

The man wasn't stupid, but right now he was acting suicidal.

Dammit!

I hit the microphone button inside the suit, hoping it worked even as the sound receptors didn't.

"Let me go," I said loud and clear.

"*No,*" he shook his head. Judging by his expression, he yelled it, too, though I couldn't hear him.

"I will get help," I said, sincerely meaning it.

He shouted back. Unable to hear the words, I could still read his fury as he held on to the suit that would incinerate him at the press of a button. The skin on his sharp cheekbones flushed red. Anger burned in his intense orange eyes, and something else was there, too.

Fear.

Raw terror.

"Please, Vrateus. Please. Let go of me." I was not giving up now, being this close to my escape, with nothing but this stubborn man between me and my freedom. "Go back inside in the corridor or you will die."

"*So be it,*" his hard expression told me.

His determination shocked me.

I realized he wouldn't let go, dead set to keep me here in this vile place.

At that moment, I hated him more than ever.

Then the hatred turned inwards. I loathed myself for being unable to push that damn button. I couldn't send Vrateus to the certain death, even if the success of my escape depended on it.

I couldn't.

His life for my freedom turned out to be the price I couldn't pay.

Self-loathing, I lowered my hand, away from the door panel. Quickly moving to my front, he opened the hatch of the suit then reached inside it to drag me out.

"I hate you!" I spat in his face.

Without a word, he crushed me to his chest in a wild embrace that squeezed the air out of me. I wiggled one arm free, slapping him across his cheek, hard.

Silently, he caught my hand in his, stopping me from hitting him again. Not a muscle moved on his face. It looked like it was set in stone.

"I hate you," I hissed again, anger burning me from inside like acid, stronger than despair or fear.

"You would have died," he finally said, his voice hoarse and repressed.

"I would've been free!" I yelled, struggling against his hold and wishing I could strangle him with my bare hands.

Yet I couldn't kill him just a moment earlier when my freedom had been at stake.

So stupid!

I groaned, hating myself even more than I hated him.

"You would have been dead," he repeated quietly.

"That's what *you* think!" I struggled in his arms. "Your stubbornness, your stupid ignorance has ruined my life."

Something dangerous flashed in his eyes. Keeping an arm around my waist, he shoved me toward the suit.

"Initiate the launch sequence, just like you intended."

For one tiny moment, I believed he was setting me free. Then I realized, he only wanted me to send the empty suit into space.

"Set a one-minute delay," he added.

He was getting rid of my only means of escape.

Swallowing the hard lump in my throat, sorrow threatening to suffocate me, I did what he said. Except that I also secretly added the coordinates of the starting location. Now, if the suit were found, they would know where it came from. Someone would match its serial number to my mission and, hopefully, figure out I was trapped here.

"Come." Vrateus dragged me out of the room after I was done.

A group of *errocks* waited for us in the corridor, along with a few members of other species who were awake. Anything out of the ordinary passed for entertainment around here. Apparently, watching the recapture of the only female on the Dark Anomaly after her failed escape attempt was worth staying up for.

"Watch." Vrateus pushed me against the door, the glass insert positioned right in front of my face.

The thrusters went off the moment the outside door opened. The empty suit launched toward the dancing lights beyond.

Without me.

It grew smaller and smaller the farther it went—a dark, humanoid silhouette against the vivid light show.

My chest hurt watching it go, taking my last hope with it.

Before going completely out of sight, the suit jerked suddenly, sharply changing its trajectory. Swirling off course, it headed back to us, moving exponentially faster than when it had departed.

That was *not* in the program I had inputted.

With a strangled noise of shock, I watched it propel through the distance between us. My hands splayed on the door, I sensed the faint vibration of its impact against the outer hull.

"See this?" Vrateus yanked me from the window to the screen by the door. Punching into it, he brought up images of the outer edge of the metal body of the Anomaly that must have come from cameras they had installed outside.

My spacesuit—made using the latest experimental technology, tested in the bottomless ocean of Olphi, proven to withstand the unimaginable—was smashed against the wreckage of a ship. Its arms and legs bent, its torso twisted in a way that allowed for zero doubt, I would have had no chance of survival had I remained inside. The entire thing squished and dented by the unbeatable gravity of the Dark Anomaly.

I stared unblinking at what would have been my death had Vrateus not dragged me out of the suit just minutes earlier.

I could not accept that all hope was now truly gone.

"My body weight would have made a difference, were I inside," I kept arguing in my head, knowing that it would not, at least not enough to change the outcome. I might have crashed at a slightly different spot, but I still would have crashed.

And died.

My hands trembled, the shakes spreading to the rest of me, as the realization of what this crash really meant descended on me.

I was truly, completely, inescapably trapped on the Dark Anomaly.

For the rest of my life.

Chapter 14

STILL IN SHOCK AND overwhelmed by despair, I was only half-aware of Vrateus dragging me through the corridors of the Anomaly, back to my room.

A group of aliens had gathered in front of it, watching as we approached. They gawked at me and made jokes, mocking my failed escape attempt.

His expression grave, Vrateus hit the panel, opening my door. When he shoved me in, I sensed his hands shake.

"Wine, Captain?" One of his males offered a metal canteen to him.

Vrateus grabbed it from him. Keeping his eyes on me, he took a huge swig from the canteen.

I staggered into the room. The lights of the Anomaly no longer seemed beautiful or mesmerizing. They were mocking me, destined to spend the rest of my life in this inescapable glass prison. I felt like a moth trapped inside a lantern, only with the light being outside of the glass—teasing, enticing, and deadly.

The slam of Vrateus's hand against the door panel was followed by the swishing sound of the doors closing. I idly wondered if he had discovered that I'd disabled the locks. The doors might be closed, but they weren't locked unless he'd fixed the panel, which I didn't think he had.

Suddenly, he grabbed me by my neck, swinging me to the wall and pressing my back against it.

He leaned into me, his face coming close to mine, feral rage distorting his hard features. The orange eyes aglow, his lips stained blood-red by the wine, any shred of his usual composure was blown away. I wondered in an oddly detached way if he would kill me right then and there.

"You could've died," he gritted through his teeth. A flash of unguarded vulnerability flickered through his eyes.

Fear.

For me?

Something clenched painfully in my heart in response. Something I didn't want to feel for anyone.

Terrified of the flames of passion burning higher and higher in his eyes, I searched them for the traces of furry, begging him in my mind, *"Hit me. Hurt me. Give me another reason to hate you."*

The hate for him and this place had been fueling me with energy all this time. The resentment that I cultivated inside me with more fervour that Malahki worked in his garden was dissipating, slipping between my fingers, no matter how hard I tried to hold on to it. Another feeling, just as passionate as hate but so much more dangerous, was taking its place.

Was it lust?

Please let it be just lust.

"You would have been dead if I didn't stop you," he kept saying as if struggling to comprehend that fact.

"*You* would've died, too, had I pushed that button," I bit out.

"Why didn't you?" The fury in his stare settled down as something deeper and darker moved in.

"I couldn't..." I drew in a shuddered breath. The adrenaline receded, leaving deep sorrow behind. "Then we both would have been dead," I said softly. "Not sure about you, but for me... For me, it might have been for the best."

His thick eyebrows drew together, intensity sharpening his gaze.

"You've chosen to live," he reminded me.

I swallowed against his hand on my throat, his hold firm but not oppressive.

"Because I had hope, Vrateus. Hope to get out of here, eventually. There is no point, now. What kind of life do I have ahead of me? Being locked up in this room? Used as your sex toy?"

"My toy?" he sounded confused. "From what I know about sex toys, they're used solely for one's sexual satisfaction."

"Exactly."

"That's not what you are to me." His eyes flickered between mine, something warm and intense brewing behind them. "Svetlana, do you dislike me touching you so much that you would rather risk dying than continue with it?" he asked suddenly.

I wished I could lie about that, but his touch was the one thing I enjoyed. As much as I detested being brought into the mess hall on those nights, I started looking forward to the moment when his hands connected with my skin.

Even thinking about it now sent a ripple of pleasure through my chest. Its warmth melted the sorrow away.

"It's not your touching that I dislike, Vrateus..."

How could he not understand that I found being paraded naked in front of hundreds of slobbering, masturbating men degrading?

But then I believed I knew how. Having grown up in the savage environment of the Dark Anomaly, Vrateus simply wouldn't know all the moral implications of some actions.

Only now, after having been immersed in life on the Anomaly for some time, could I see it from his perspective: I was not physically hurt, and his crew was satisfied. As far as he was concerned, he kept me alive and safe by doing what he had to.

He wouldn't know *why* I resented it because I had never really explained the reasons. I had mistakenly assumed he would have the same understanding of morals and values I had. It could never be the same, though, as his background was so different from mine.

Obviously, he believed he had saved me and had been protecting me ever since.

"I like it when you touch me," I confessed. I knew I shouldn't have, but couldn't bring myself to care about the reasons why.

What did it matter now if he knew the truth?

Nothing seemed to matter anymore.

"Like?" My words seemed to send a charge through his body.

I sensed his shudder as he pressed himself closer to me. Another wave of warmth rushed over me, sending tingles over my skin.

Lust. Strong and invigorating desire for a man, for him. Like a powerful drug, it killed the pain of defeat. Completely, even if temporarily.

Needing more of the rush, I pressed my hands to the hard planes of his chest.

"You, Vrateus, turned out to be the most unexpected surprise of the Anomaly, for me," I muttered.

His eyes flashed with heat. His arms shook with strain as he struggled to keep whatever distance still remained between us.

"I don't understand this...what I feel for you, Svetlana" he groaned. "Why are you in my thoughts? Constantly. When you're not around, I need to see you. And when you're near me, I feel like touching you." He slid his gaze to my lips, his thumb stroking my neck. "It's never enough. No matter how close I get, I wish to be closer." His heart thundered wildly against my chest. Sliding his hand up my neck, he cupped my jaw, brushing his thumb along my bottom lip. "And when I touch you, I want to taste you," he whispered, bringing his mouth closer, so close, his breath warmed my face.

I drew in brief, shallow breaths. My body heated under his stare. Desire flooded me. It was so much better than misery.

I focused on the awareness of his hand on my face, his large warm body pressed to mine. My future was dark but distant. This very moment was different—Vrateus was here. The heated gaze of his orange eyes set me on fire.

"Go ahead, then." I slid my hand to the back of his neck. "Taste me..."

Determination flared in his eyes. He wrapped one arm around me, moving the other to the back of my head.

Instead of the brutal kiss I had expected, the brush of his lips on mine was barely there. Truly only a taste, not a kiss. Forever in control, he tentatively slid the tip of his tongue along my lip then peppered my skin with tiny nibbles along my jaw line.

It hit me that Vrateus had never kissed anyone before, never even had the chance. What he was doing to me right now was all him, unskilled but raw and real.

His tenderness melted my heart.

"Vrateus," I whispered.

Taking his face between my hands, I peered deep into his eyes. His pupils, usually in the shape of narrow vertical slits, now widened and rounded, nearly replacing the burnt orange of his irises.

He breathed hard. His lips parted.

"Come here." I took his bottom lip between both of mine, swallowing his sharp exhale.

He tasted of berry wine—tart and heady—with a hint of something fruity and of his very own spice.

He tasted like the only pleasant thing left for me in this life, and I drank him in, never wanting to stop.

I slid my tongue deeper, feeling the muscles in his neck stiffen for a moment. How would a man who had never been kissed react to the tongue of a woman exploring his mouth?

Was he shocked?

Disgusted?

Definitely not the latter, I realized with relief, as he groaned softly then met my tongue with his. He moved one of his hands to my breast, palming my backside with the other. There was confidence in his touch as he kneaded my breast through the material of my suit.

He knew exactly how to touch me.

But there was also some frantic urgency, as if he wanted to caress every part of me he'd never had the chance to lay his hands on before. As if he wished to touch everything, now that it was just he and I, with no one else watching.

The hard ridge of his erection pressed against my hip. Fisting my hand in the fur on the back of his neck, I snaked the other through the opening of his shirt, my fingers skimming the dagger sheath strapped to his chest.

His skin felt flushed, feverishly hot. The fruity flavor of wine on my tongue nagged at my memory, distracting me from the kiss.

I pulled back a little, tearing my lips from his.

"Svetlana..." he panted, reaching after me.

His warm breath fanned across my face. I recognized the fragrance of the soap I used every day.

Fuhnid mushrooms...

"Vrateus?" I grabbed his face between my hands.

His pupils were fully dilated, his eyes glistened dark and wild. From lust?

Or from the poison?

"Do you normally add *fuhnid* mushrooms to the berry wine?"

"What?" He blinked, unfocused. His body still intertwined with mine, he wouldn't let go of me. "No. Mushrooms are poison."

He ducked his head down again, reaching for another kiss, but I shoved my hands against his shoulders.

My mind flashed back to the flask of wine the male outside the door had offered to him. Too upset by my escape attempt, Vrateus hadn't questioned the offering.

He had drunk it.

The one time he had his guard down, his worst suspicions came true.

He'd been poisoned.

Dread prickled with icy needles down my spine.

"Vrateus. The wine you drank was laced with *fuhnid* juice."

His features settled into a frown, focus returning to his gaze. "Are you sure?"

I nodded. "I can smell it."

He raised his hand to his lips.

"How are you feeling?" I asked, cautiously.

"Lightheaded." He rubbed his temple. "My mind is...hazy. But it always is when you're nearby." He gazed at me. "It's hard to focus when you're this close."

"Where do you keep the antidote?" My hands on each side of his face, I directed his attention to my question.

"There is no antidote."

His words exploded through my brain, freezing my insides with fear. I might have been willing to kill him with my own hands a short while ago, but I was not ready for him to die.

Swaying on his feet, he pressed both hands into the glass above my shoulders.

"What happens next?" I asked, my voice shaking. "How long do we have?"

"Next? Dizziness. Muscle weakness. Lethargy..." He closed his eyes for a moment, obviously struggling to collect his thoughts. "By morning, I'll be dead."

"No, you won't," I said stubbornly, having no good reason to make this statement other than the denial of the obvious.

"Svetlana..." He shook his head, as if attempting to shake off whatever fog was clouding his awareness.

The gesture cost him his balance. He stumbled to the side, then slid down the wall to the floor.

"Careful." I grabbed him under his arm, steadying him. "Stay sitting, don't lie down. I'll be right back."

I ran to the bathroom, filling the crystal tumbler left from my dinner with water from the tap.

Back in the room, I shoved the glass to Vrateus. "Drink it. The whole thing."

He obeyed, emptying it in a few big gulps.

"Now come to the bathroom with me." Both hands under his arms, I tried to pull him up, but he proved to be too large and heavy for me to manhandle. "Help me, please. Can you try to get up?"

With a groan through his clenched teeth, he heaved himself up, letting me lead him to the bathroom. I held him around his waist as he lowered himself in front of the toilet.

"Drink this too." I gave him another cupful of water. "Then try to make yourself vomit."

"Vomit?"

"You need to get whatever is left of the poison out of your stomach."

Kneeling by the toilet, he propped his hands on his thighs. "Leave," he growled, glancing from under his eyebrows at me.

I rolled my eyes.

"Fine. Just do it, please. And quickly." I exited the bathroom but didn't close the door behind me, afraid to leave him completely on his own.

Pacing the glass floor, I nervously clenched and unclenched my fists, thinking through everything I knew about poisoning.

"There is no antidote."

Recalling his words paralyzed me with fear, bringing my thought process to a halt.

He couldn't die.

I couldn't let him die.

He had said he wanted me to live. Well, I wanted *him* to live, too.

Besides, what would happen to me here, without him? I *needed* him alive.

Rinse out his stomach. I started to build a list in my mind. *Find charcoal. If they don't have anything like it here, find some hardwood to burn to make some...*

That would take way too much time!

I groaned in frustration.

"I'll be dead by morning."

Time was something we didn't have.

There must be something that would neutralize the poison of the mushrooms. If only I knew exactly what type of poison it was. I had no time to do any tests to determine that, either.

Why would Vrateus allow this stuff to be grown here? Without searching for the antidote? He was always so cautious, so smart about everything.

I was angry at him now, which was nothing new. What *was* unusual was that I felt also terrified for him.

I couldn't let him die.

As soon as I heard Vrateus finish in the bathroom, I rushed back to him.

Resting his forehead on his hand, he crouched on the floor.

"Come." I helped him to get up again. I wanted him to move, afraid that if I left him alone, he'd fall asleep...and not wake up again.

Back in the room, however, he sank to the floor again.

"Tell me what I can do." Grabbing him by the shoulders, I gave him a firm shake as his head started to drop. "Is there anything in the medical kit that would help? Do you even have a medical kit somewhere? How about some charcoal pills? Activated charcoal? Is there anything like that around here?"

With another shake from me, he lifted his head. His gaze focused on me after a moment.

"Svetlana..." he drew out my name, a delirious smile tugging at his lips. "You drive me mad, you know that? And for some reason I love it."

"Vrateus, where can I get help?" I asked firmly, giving him one last chance to point me in the right direction. Time was running out. I needed to do something. With or without his instructions.

"Help?" He blinked, then tightly shut his eyes before opening them again. "When I die, you must go to Malahki," he said quickly, as if rushing it out before his mind plunged into a toxic fog. "Malahki is the only one around here who is not interested in either eating or fucking you." He lifted his hand to my face. "Svetlana...I *need* you to be safe. When I'm no longer here to protect you—"

"Malahki!" I jumped to my feet, filled with sudden hope.

The genderless alien was the one cultivating the damn mushrooms. If there was anyone who knew what to do, it would be the *damirian*.

"Give me a weapon." I knelt in front of Vrateus again.

"To defend yourself," he said, in a distant voice.

"Right. I need something to defend myself if I'm attacked out there."

He shifted, shaking his head. "You can't go out there. Not on your own."

"Well, I'm not staying here, waiting for you to turn into a corpse, either." I slid my hand into his shirt, finding the dagger strapped there.

Before I could pull it out, he trapped my hand, covering it with his. His hold remained encouragingly firm.

"You are the most infuriating being," he said, gazing at me with his eerie, glossy eyes. "The most fascinating and beautiful one, too. I'm glad I lived long enough to meet you."

Was that a goodbye?

I bit my lip, willing my voice not to shake. "You'll live longer than that. I will get help, Vrateus." I wrapped my fingers around the handle of the dagger at his chest.

"I can't stop you." It wasn't a question, more like stating of fact to himself.

"I need to go. I need to do something."

"Here." He allowed me to take out the dagger. From the holster at his thigh, he then took out a device that reminded me of a laser gun I had seen in old movies. "Take this, too. Shoot from a distance, don't let them get too close."

"Thank you." I tucked the dagger into my boot, keeping the gun in my hand. "I'll be right back."

"No." He shook his head several times, as if unable to stop it after just once. "Don't come back here. Tell Malahki to hide you. There are lots of spaces to hide around here. I used them when I was a child. Tunnels, cracks in the hulls, gaps between the walls..."

Sitting on the floor, he tilted to the side as his voice trailed off.

"Vrateus!" I shook him again, sitting him upright. "Stay awake."

I grabbed the tablet he had given me. Finding a video with the most obnoxious music of the last species I had studied, I set it to play in a loop, then turned the volume all the way up.

"Wait for me!" I shouted over the noise. "Please. I'll come back. I promise.

He swayed, his head nodding. There was no way of telling whether it was involuntary or in reply to my request.

With no time to lose, I dashed to the door.

Thankfully, the corridor behind it was empty. Keeping my back to the wall and the gun in my hand ready, I ran toward the gardens, praying that Malahki was there and that it was able and willing to help me.

Chapter 15

ALL SEEMED EERILY QUIET in the gardens when I arrived. Creeping between the planters, I peered through the vines and branches, hoping to glimpse the lithe shape of Malahki nearby. I was also watching out for any trouble, hoping that everyone else would have gone to their beds by now.

Most likely, Malahki would be also asleep at this hour. I hoped that it slept nearby somewhere and that I could find it and wake it up.

I heard nothing but the soft rustling of leaves and the quiet trickling of water from the irrigation system. Then a hand covered my mouth as someone grabbed me from behind, pressing both of my arms to my body.

"What are you doing here?" Malahki's calm voice sounded above my ear. Next, the *damirian* slid its hand to my gun, taking it from me.

I jerked my head to the side, freeing my mouth. "I need your help."

Malahki lifted the gun into my line of sight. "And *this* is to persuade me in case I refuse?"

"No. The gun is to protect me from anyone I may run into on my way here and back."

The *damirian* let go of me, inspecting the gun in its hand. "Probably wouldn't have helped you anyway, human. Most of the males around here would let you shoot their eye out for a chance to fuck a female. A gun wouldn't stop them from trying."

I paid little attention to its words. Right now, I had no time for fear.

"I need your help," I said again. "And I need it quickly. What can I use to neutralize the effects of the *fuhnid* mushroom poison?"

"Nothing." Malahki pressed its colorless lips into a thin line. "There is no antidote." It turned to leave.

"There has to be something," I said, with nothing much but blind faith to keep pushing. "How did you find out the mushrooms were poisonous in the first place?"

"We obtained that information from the ship that delivered the spores."

Delivered. As if it was an order, voluntarily fulfilled.

"Has anyone poisoned themselves with their juice before?"

"Yes." Malahki walked away, and I rushed after it.

"Has anyone died?"

"Also, yes."

I grabbed its arm, yanking the *damirian* to a stop.

"He can't die."

"Who is *he*?" Malahki didn't sound annoyed at my insisting. Though its detached tone of voice didn't offer much hope for help, either.

"Vrateus has been poisoned. I need to counteract the effects before it's too late."

If it wasn't too late already...

I shoved the terrifying thought away. Losing all hope and my mind along with it wouldn't help anyone.

"Make him retch," Malahki suggested with the same calm aloofness that proved extremely irritating right now.

"I did. Would that be enough to save him?"

"No."

Now, I really felt like punching the *damirian*, to knock off its serene composure.

"I need something more effective," I insisted, grabbing its arm again.

Malahki glanced at me, worrying its bottom lip with its teeth, as if hesitating.

"There *is* something, isn't there?" I stepped in front of it. Hope and determination vibrated through me, making my hands shake. "I know you have nothing in common with the savages out there. You don't participate in the fights. I haven't seen you in the mess hall, either. How do you spend your time? Pruning and seeding, sure, but there must be something else. Unlike all of them here, you've been raised and educated outside of the Dark Anomaly. You're smart. Mushrooms would present a challenge for your mind. Please tell me you've experimented with their fascinating qualities. For medicinal purposes, if nothing else?"

The *damirian* remained silent, looking like it was about to turn away from me again.

"Malahki, please," I exhaled a whispered plea.

"Knowledge is the only asset, the only advantage I have over 'the savages out there,'" it replied, flexing its jaw. "I work hard to gain it, and I'm not obligated to share it with anyone. No one cares about me here. Why should I care about anyone?"

"Do you think *I* care about this place, about any of them? I don't care about Vrateus, either." Something pinched uneasily inside me at these words, but I kept going, "But I don't want him to die. What do you think will happen if he dies? To you? And to me?"

"Someone else will take his place."

"Who? You are a smart—" I stopped myself before saying "man." "You're a smart individual, Malahki. Surely, you can see that there is no one even remotely as capable as Vrateus to keep this place going the way he has. If he dies, anarchy will prevail. Neither you, nor I will be safe."

"Most of the species here respond to female pheromones in their lust. They have been leaving me alone." It shrugged.

"So, you'll be okay with *me* potentially being raped, without Vrateus's protection?" I fisted my hands at my side, stopping myself from saying more. As outraged as I was by the *damirian's* indifference, I knew that an argument with this person would bring me nothing.

"No, of course not." It frowned.

"Then help me, please," I begged. "Besides, it wouldn't be just rape that we would have to worry about. If Vrateus is gone, none of his laws will stay. The cannibalism will return. Your genderlessness won't protect you from being eaten. Neither you nor I are strong enough to fight them."

Malahki's chest rose with a sigh. "That is true. I am not strong enough to fight any one of them." Its facial muscles twitched. "What will I get if I save the captain's life?" it asked, narrowing its eyes at me calculatingly.

I suppressed a breath of relief. This wasn't over yet.

"What do you want?"

Malahki gave me a long, measuring look. It was unnerving in its intensity, as if the *damirian* had just truly *seen* me for the first time. "I'll need a favor from the captain."

"We'll have to hurry," I snapped, losing my patience. "Otherwise, there won't be a captain to grant a favor."

"Fine," it relented. "I want you to promise the captain will hear me out once he is well and able."

"*If* he is well and able." I bounced on my heels. "Hurry, please."

Malahki demonstratively folded its arms across its chest. "I'm waiting for your promise."

"I promise," I rushed the words out. "I will tell him you saved his life and asked for a favor in return."

Malahki seemed satisfied by my words. Waving me to follow, it headed to the tall planter with the bright *fuhnid* mushrooms.

Raising the clear cover, the *damirian* plucking one out of the dirt. It then squished it between its palms, letting the vivid pink juice drip back into the ground. He then sprayed the now flat-like-crêpe mushroom from the bottle under the planter.

"Here." Malahki ripped a wide round leaf from a vine nearby, wrapping the flattened mushroom he'd rolled into a tube. "Feed this to the captain, with a glass of water. Just one cup of water, though, no more. Wait for ten minutes, then make him throw it all up again."

I stared at the dark green package in its hands.

"Are you saying to neutralize the poison that is killing him, I need to give him more of it?" I asked sceptically.

"Isn't that how many poisons work?"

"No." I shook my head. "A sip of wine, laced with *fuhnid* juice, is about to kill Vrateus. How is feeding him an entire freaking mushroom supposed to help?"

"By drawing the poison out," Malahki replied calmly. Shoving the leaf-wrapped mushroom into my hands, it took the spray bottle again and cleaned its hands, then sprayed my hands holding the package, too. "I squeezed the toxic juice out of the mushroom. If the captain eats it now, it will soak up whatever *fuhnid* juice there is in his body. He would have to get it out of his stomach afterwards, so the poison doesn't seep back into his digestive system and bloodstream."

"Are you confident it will work?" I stared at the package in my hands, afraid to hope. "Has anyone ever tried this?"

"I have. Myself."

That was a relief to hear.

"Only I've had more time for 'experimenting' as you've named it," Malahki added. "I completely dehydrated the mushroom and grounded it into powder first."

"Powder?" I huffed in frustration. "That is very different from what you've just given me. Do you have any of the actual powder left?"

"No. Unfortunately, I don't." The *damirian* pursed its lips. "And *you* don't have the luxury of time to be picky."

That was true.

"Well, thanks for this." I pressed the bundle to my chest.

"Where is Vrateus?" Malahki asked, handing me back my gun. "How far do you have to go, now?"

"He is in my room."

"It's next to his, then."

"Is it?"

"His is the second glass capsule. There are two, side by side."

I had seen the second bubble next to mine, but it had always been dark, and I assumed it was empty. Vrateus had never told me it was his room. Not that I'd ever asked.

"Don't use the corridor to go back," Malahki said. "Take the garbage tunnel from here. It's safer. Just make sure you get out in time. There is an opening in the wall, not far from your room."

I knew about the opening. I'd already used it during my failed escape.

"Thanks. I'll take the tunnel."

Chapter 16

LYING ON MY BELLY ON the conveyor belt inside the tunnel, I travelled feet first toward my room. Afraid to miss the spot where I needed to get out, I kept my hand on the wall, trailing my fingers in search of the loose panel. When it moved as I passed, I quickly crawled back to it, ready to climb out.

The distant tromping of footsteps suddenly reached me from the corridor, making me pause. I spread my arms and legs wide, removing them from the belt and pressing them into the walls of the tunnel, then froze in place, listening as the footsteps approached.

"We didn't find his weapon storage." I recognized Wyck's voice.

"He hides it somewhere," Crux growled in reply.

The sound of their voices made my knees shake from fear. Nothing good would come if the *errocks* found me here, alone and pretty much helpless. Straining to stay off the conveyor belt, I couldn't even free a hand to use the laser gun tucked into one of the pockets of my bodysuit.

I desperately hoped Lesh wasn't out there with them. Or if he were, that he wouldn't be able to catch my scent. The soap I used made me undetectable to the *errocks'* acute sense of smell, but no one mentioned if it worked the same for Wyck's terrifying pet.

"No matter. He won't be able to do much now, anyway," Crux kept on talking. "Use whatever we have for weapons. Get everyone in the mess hall. Kick them out of beds if you have to. They've got a new captain, now." He guffawed, his voice thick with satisfaction.

My heart dropped.

Was Crux behind Vrateus's poisoning? He sounded as if he was at least aware of his captain's current condition.

No. Crux had just called *himself* the captain. He already thought Vrateus gone.

If Crux was in charge now, I stood no chance. Vrateus was right, the best course of action for me would be to get back to the gardens. I harbored no illusions, Malahki wouldn't go out of its way to protect me. But Crux was cruel and unpredictable. No one could be safe with him in charge. Maybe, I could convince Malahki to be my survival partner. We'd find a place to hide and watch each other's backs.

Meanwhile, the sound of the footsteps faded into the distance.

Carefully inching toward the opening, I peeked into the corridor, making sure it was empty in both directions. Climbing out, I threw a glance back toward the gardens.

I knew Crux would come for me as soon as he had established his full dominance over the Dark Anomaly or even sooner. The way he always stared at me, I knew he meant danger—probably torture and death.

My instincts told me to run straight to the gardens and hide before it was too late.

Yet I couldn't leave Vrateus to his fate. Against all common sense, I ran back to my room.

The doors remained closed but unlocked, just the way I had left them. Icy fear spread down my back when I thought *errocks* could have easily found Vrateus here, weak and unprotected, had they but checked the doors while passing by.

Slipping into the room, I closed the doors, then pulled the cover off the lock panel and slid the part I'd loosened back in to engage the lock from the inside.

The music still blared from the tablet, but Vrateus was no longer sitting upright. His arms tucked under his torso, his legs spread wide, he lay on his stomach, motionless.

"Oh, God, Vrateus..." I rushed to him, praying I was not too late.

He felt cool to the touch, his fur slicked with sweat over his forehead, his eyes closed.

"Vrateus!" I shook him, everything inside me frozen with fear.

Placing my hand on his neck, I found a barely detectable pulse. Weak and uneven, it was still there, easing my horror. Dashing to the bathroom, I filled the crystal tumbler with water then ran back to him.

"Can you hear me?"

I hit the *off* button on the tablet, plunging the room into silence, eerie and ominous after the deafening noise of music.

"You need to wake up. Now!" Rolling him to his back, I slapped his cheek, making his head loll to the side. "Captain!" Straining my muscles, I tried to heave him up into a sitting position. "Your crew won't survive without you. They need you..." His large body, a heavy, solid mass of muscle, was nearly impossible for me to maneuver. Still, I propped him into a reclining position by wedging my shoulder under his. "Fuck it, Vrateus! *I* need you."

His head rolled to his shoulder, with a muffled groan escaping from his throat.

"Vrateus?" I scooted on the glass floor, sliding behind him. My leg on each side of him, I leaned his back to my chest, propping his head with my shoulder. "You need to eat this right now." I yanked the bundle with the flattened mushroom out of the pocket at my hip, then unwrapped it, bringing the mushroom to his mouth. "Dammit, Vrateus. I swear I'll hit you again if you don't wake up, right now!"

Dropping the mushroom into his lap, I grabbed the glass instead. Pressing it to his lips, I tipped it, letting the cold water spill over his mouth and down his bare chest into the opening of his shirt. He winced with a gasp, and I quickly poured some water into his open mouth, making him sputter and cough.

"Good," I murmured. "Now that you're awake, eat this." I ripped a piece of the dry mushroom and shoved it into his mouth. "Chew it." I cupped his jaw. "Or don't chew it. Whatever, just swallow it, please."

Not waiting for him to react, I ripped another piece off, bringing it up to his face. "Here you go," I said when he swallowed, then I quickly shoved more pieces into this mouth. "That's a good boy," I cooed as if he were a baby eating his first solid foods, not a grown man nearly twice my size, dying from poison.

The last piece of mushroom stayed in his mouth when his head dropped to his chest again.

"Vrateus!" I slapped his cheek again. Hard.

"Guh..." he groaned. "That hurt."

"Drink this." I pressed the edge of the glass to his lips. "Or I'll do it again."

I watched his throat bob with each swallow as he emptied the glass. I hoped and prayed that Malahki hadn't misled me, that I hadn't made a colossal mistake by trusting the *damirian* and feeding more poison to our captain.

"You're not only infuriating, you're also brutal and terrifying," he muttered, dropping his head back on my shoulder as if drinking had completely exhausted him.

"Oh, you have no idea how scary I can be," I assured him, trying not to think about how frightened I felt. "Just try dying on me, see how angry I'd get."

His chuckle came out with a cough.

I remembered Malahki had said to wait for ten minutes. The clock was still by the door, but thanks to its huge dial, I could make out the time even from a distance.

Ten minutes.

I wasn't sure if I should try to keep Vrateus awake. Would it be better to let him rest for a few minutes while we waited for the results?

I reined in my fear, letting hope into my heart. Holding Vrateus to me with my arm across his chest, I rested my cheek against his head. The many golden hoops in his pointy ear pressed into my skin.

"Please stay with me, Vrateus," I whispered, not sure if he could hear or comprehend what I was saying. "You said you wanted me to live. Well, I need you to stay alive, too. I'm still not sure if this life is worth living, but it definitely would be so much worse without you." I patted his chest through the soft material of his shirt, feeling the straps and the sheath of the dagger underneath. "I know things haven't always been great between us, but I don't hate you as much as I thought I did." With a sigh, I nuzzled his high cheekbone. "In fact, there are many things I like and respect about you. I hope we can be friends."

What if we could be more *than friends?*

The thought alarmed me, and I chased away the memories of the kiss we'd shared.

Not that it mattered now. Nothing would matter if he were to die in my arms.

A sudden convulsion ran through his body, sending me to my feet.

"Are you okay?" Fear and worry spiked in me. I tried to focus. "You'll need to throw up, now." I attempted to get him up, to lead him back into the bathroom. With no cooperation from him this time though, it proved impossible. He was just too heavy for me to lift on my own.

Bending to the side, he retched on the floor. I stared in horror at the black tar-like contents of his stomach on the glass as the pleasant aroma of the loathed mushrooms rose into the air.

"This is good," I forced the words out. "At least this shit is out of you, now."

Fetching some water from the bathroom, I cleaned up after him, forced another cupful of water into him, then cleaned whatever came out again.

When the shudders of dry heaving stopped wracking his body, I brought the pillow and blanket from the bed.

"Rest now." I tucked the pillow under his head, hoping that everything I had just put him through would be worth it.

I unbuckled the straps around his chest, loosening them to ease his breathing. When I pulled his tall boots off, two knives dropped out of them, clanking to the floor. I also found guns in some elaborate mechanical holders strapped around each of his forearms and concealed by the wide sleeves of his shirt. Those looked too complicated to remove, and I left them, taking off the holsters around his thighs instead.

"You're just like a walking munitions storage," I muttered, tucking the blanket around him.

Vrateus had always seemed tense and alert, always ready to pull the trigger. He acted like a cocked gun himself, ready to strike at any minute.

"It couldn't be easy to go through life while constantly having to look over your shoulder," I said, sitting on the floor next to him.

He didn't respond, didn't even appear to hear me at all. But talking felt so much better than sitting in silence, listening to his labored breathing, and watching the glow of the Anomaly lights reflecting off his white shirt.

"Being alert didn't help you, Vrateus. They still got you." Heaving a sigh, I lay on the floor next to him. "I know it's all my fault. With my escape attempt, I've knocked you off balance when nothing else ever did. When you're better—because you *have* to get better—I promise I'll make it up to you. You know I could be useful if you let me. I am a well-educated, highly trained specialist. I scored in the top ten percent of my graduating class. And I could most definitely cook a better meal than Krakhil. You can also trust me to never add these freaking mushrooms to any of your food or drink."

I didn't tell him I was feeling scared and insignificant, uncertain if I could prevent his possible death, or what to do about *errocks* taking over at this very moment.

Through all of this, a long-forgotten ache grew in my chest—the mixture of warmth, pleasure, and worry for him so intense it brought pain. I hadn't allowed myself to feel any of that for so long, I'd begun to think I was no longer capable of these feelings—caring, attachments. For me, sooner or later, they all unfailingly resulted in the agony of heartbreak.

Lately, I'd trained myself to run from the people who'd stirred any shadow of affection inside me. Was that at least a part of the reason why I'd tried so desperately to escape this place? I'd sensed I'd have to escape this man before he'd wreaked havoc in my heart?

Even now, my mind urged me to run. To hide before it was too late from him as much as from his crew. It was just a matter of time before they came for me.

Yet I only moved closer to him, unable to leave him to face his treacherous crew alone.

"There's no escaping you, Vrateus. Somehow, you've managed to get a hold of me as strong as that of the Anomaly. And I haven't even noticed when and how it happened."

Laying at his side, I draped my arm around his middle.

"Just get better, please." I buried my face in the voluminous fabric of the sleeve over his bicep. "That's the only thing that matters."

Chapter 17

VRATEUS

Every part of his body hurt, as if he had been slammed against the hard edge of the Dark Anomaly without the protection of a spaceship around him.

He tried to move, shifting his legs. A groan tore from his sore throat, hurting on its way out.

Something held his arm down. He rolled his head over, finding Svetlana clinging to his side. She was asleep, and he took a minute watching her, momentarily forgetting about the pain.

With her eyes closed, the frown she often had when she looked at him wasn't there. She appeared relaxed and peaceful, almost childish in her vulnerability. A wavy strand of tea-colored hair had fallen over her face, and he couldn't help himself. He picked it up between two fingers and moved it aside.

She stirred. Her slim dark eyebrows moved together, the usual worry wrinkle forming between them.

"Vrateus?" Letting go of his arm, she patted his chest while blinking her eyes open. "You're up? Awake?" Questions rushed out of her mouth as she jerked herself into a sitting position. "How are you?"

"Um...not sure." He rose on his elbows, and she leaned over him.

"You're alive," she breathed out, pushing the curl of fur over his face back and letting her hand linger on the side of his head.

The caress was unexpected, even more so was the warmth in her dark-brown eyes directed at him and the shy smile on her lips.

"Are you really happy about that?" he asked, skeptically.

"Of course I am." She straightened under his stare, removing her hand from him. He immediately missed the contact. "With you dead, they could've made someone with tentacles or pincers, or lobster claws touch me weekly." Her voices sounded light, cheerful even. "I'd rather it'd be you, with your hands—claws and all."

"So, you like my hands on you?" A smile tugged up a corner of his mouth.

"That was *absolutely* not what I just said." A lovely blush spread on her cheeks in response. He fought the urge to cup her face.

What *did* she say?

He tried to concentrate, but his thoughts remained cloudy. Pushing off the floor, he hauled himself into a sitting position. His head swam with dizziness, his muscles ached, and his throat hurt with each swallow.

"How are you feeling?" She peered at him intently. "Can I get you anything?"

"Water?"

She jumped to her feet, rushing to the bathroom with a glass, then returned, crouching in front of him.

The cold water soothed his parched throat, settling in his stomach with a fresh cooling sensation.

"What exactly happened?" he asked, wishing he could rinse the fog out of his brain the way he had just gotten rid of the thirst. The only thing that remained clear was Svetlana's face in front of him.

"You don't remember?" Her eyes widened with worry.

"I do. Parts. I just need some help organizing them."

She nodded, drawing in a breath.

"Okay. So. You took a sip of wine, from the canteen of someone who looked like a, um... He is lanky, with six arms and a sectional tail that curves up." She swung her arm backwards then over her head. "Like this."

"Tunkrox." The description jolted his memory.

"Right. The wine had been laced with *fuhnid* mushroom juice. It made you sick. You also told me there was no antidote and that I should run and hide in the gardens because you were about to die."

"You didn't run," he stated. Some of what she was saying he already knew. The rest was filling in the blanks as his memory cleared.

"No. Well I did, but I came back. I went to the gardens, found Malahki, and convinced it to help me save you."

"You saved me. How?"

"Malahki told me to feed you a dehydrated mushroom, to draw the poison out. There was also some drinking of water and puking involved, but that's a messy part not worth mentioning. That's pretty much it—about the sick part. Though I do need to talk to you about something else, now."

"There was also a kiss, wasn't there?" The memory of it flooded his mind. He'd seen people bringing their mouths together in videos. Some kissing was friendly, some sexual. When Svetlana had kissed him, though, it was more than anything he could've expected. "I couldn't have dreamed that. I simply wouldn't be able to conjure *that* on my own."

The pink on her cheeks deepened. It went well with the sweet smile that curved her lips.

"It was pretty amazing, wasn't it?" She dropped her gaze to his chest, then slowly raised it back to his face.

He pondered the best way to tell her how he felt but couldn't come up with anything smooth or romantic.

"I want to do that again," he said simply, choosing the most direct route to get his point across. "The kissing. And more. I want to have sex with you, too. Real sex."

Maybe he should have thought about it longer before blurting it out. Something about his words or his tone must have been wrong because Svetlana's expression changed from the sweet and unguarded back to her usual frown.

"Hold your horses, Romeo." She pushed to her feet. "You've just come back from the dead. Plus, there are a lot of other issues."

Not all of what she'd said made sense to him, but the essence was clear. There'd be no sex right now.

"What issues?"

"Crux is taking over your ship as we speak."

"Crux?"

"Yes. I overheard him speaking with Wyck about it. I have a suspicion he's behind the wine poisoning, too."

"Most likely."

He tried to get up. His head swam violently, sending him down to his knees.

"Careful." She grabbed his arm, steadying him. "You need some time to recuperate, get better, and come up with a plan while Crux thinks you're dead and out of the picture."

She was right. He was still too weak. If Crux thought him dead, it could be used to their advantage.

"One thing I'd love to do as soon as possible is to get out of this room." Holding on to his arm, she rubbed her forehead with her other hand. "I have a feeling they'll be coming for me any minute."

"Right." Svetlana was the bounty Crux wouldn't wait long to claim. "We need to leave."

"Your room might be better," she suggested. "If they think you're dead, they may leave you alone for a while. Especially since Crux is not fond of places made entirely of glass and has no interest in taking your room for himself."

"Not the room, but he'd want to get to my weapon storage, eventually."

"You store weapons in your bedroom?" she asked, then slid her gaze to his chest. "That shouldn't surprise me since you store a lot of them on your body, too."

He patted his chest, remembering giving her the dagger and the gun. "You went out there on your own."

"Yes. That's why you're still alive." She brought his boots over, placing them in front of him. "Get ready."

He hadn't even realized he had his boots off. The blanket he was standing on with his knees had been draped over his legs when he woke up.

"Did you...take my boots off?" He stared at them. The only time he'd ever had them off was when he removed them himself. He only ever had a blanket over him when he remembered to cover himself before falling asleep. "No one has ever done things like that for me before..."

"Like what? Looking after you while you're sick?" She gave him her arm for support as he put his boots back on. "Someone had to. I'm glad I was around." She picked up the blanket, taking it back to the bed.

Regret suddenly tugged at his heart. He would have liked to be awake and aware when she had been tucking that blanket around him. For the first time, someone had taken care of him, and he was too out of it to even know what it felt like.

"I'm...um, grateful." He raked his claws through the fur on his nape. "Thank you—"

A screeching noise suddenly came from the door, as if someone scraped it with a metal blade. Or a tool.

Svetlana jerked her head toward the sound, color draining from her face.

"Here they are," she said.

Chapter 18

A SICKENING FEELING of déjà vu churned in my stomach. The noise of the tool digging into the door, followed by the sparks of fire and the smell of melted metal, made my mind flash back to the day of my crash on the Dark Anomaly. Only now I knew for sure that nothing good waited for me on the other side.

"Stand back." Vrateus moved to the doors, still unsteady on his feet.

Flicking his wrists, he made both of his guns slide out from his sleeves. I searched around, finding my laser gun on the floor.

Not waiting for those in the corridor to cut through the doors, Vrateus hit the panel, opening the doors himself.

The males, about a dozen of them, stared at him in astonishment, either surprised at finding him still in my room or shocked at seeing him alive, or both.

They recovered quickly.

"Get him!"

Four of them rushed Vrateus.

Lifting his guns, he fired, immediately killing two. Before the rest rushed the room, he leaped into the corridor then hit the panel on the other side, closing the door in my face.

He must have done it instinctively. Because if he *really* thought about it, his going alone against all of them could easily result in him being killed, especially in his condition. And with him dead, it wouldn't take them long to finish what they'd started and break through the door. Locking me in did not save me, but it deprived me of the possibility of helping him.

I huffed in frustration. His protectiveness would get both of us killed.

Vrateus had been doing everything on his own, all his life. Having someone on his side, ready to help, must be new to him.

Hadn't I made it clear I was on his side? Or did he still have doubts about trusting me?

Luckily, since I had tampered with the panel before, he could no longer lock the doors from the outside. All I had to do now was to slide them open, which I did.

About half of the aliens lay on the floor, dead. The other half, however, were swarming Vrateus.

Shoved by one, he fell on his back. A burly alien, with a crown of horns growing on his head and a row of them rising from his spine, lifted the tool they had used to cut through the door.

With the rest of them holding Vrateus down, the one with the tool leaned over him, clearly intending to use the device to cut their captain's throat.

I swallowed a cry of horror, quickly raising my gun.

Aiming at a spot between the horns on the male's head, I pulled the trigger. With a flash of the laser, the alien staggered back, dropping the tool. Vrateus jerked to the side, letting the blade embed in the floor instead of his flesh.

Steadying my trembling hand, I fired again. This time, I aimed at one of the aliens holding him down. Two of them let go of him to rush me. I promptly retreated into the room, taking cover behind the wall. Peeking out, I shot them one by one while Vrateus made quick work of the others.

The last one glanced at me then at the approaching Vrateus, then took off down the corridor.

"Stop!" Vrateus shouted, shooting at the back of the escaping male. He skidded to a stop before tumbling down to the floor, face first.

"Are you okay?" Vrateus hurried to me. Grabbing my shoulders, he spun me around. Patting down my arms, back, and sides, he inspected me for injuries.

"I'm fine," I assured him. "Are *you* okay?"

He nodded.

"No more shutting the doors in my face," I said, grimly.

"Sorry. That was reflex." He had the decency to look remorseful.

"From now on, please, try to treat me as an asset rather than a liability."

He stared at me for a moment. "That will be an adjustment for me. It'll take a while getting used to having someone I can fully trust. I've never had that."

At least he realized he could trust me.

"Well, I got your back." I stared at the floor littered with dead aliens. "We have to get out of here."

He grabbed the nearest dead body by the legs. "We need to lock them all in here. Without the bodies, it will take some time for Crux to figure out what happened."

I shook my head.

"Sorry. I've tampered with the panel. You can't lock the doors from the outside anymore."

Vrateus dropped the legs of the dead alien down again.

"What else have you done?" He stared at me with a mix of shock and admiration.

"Nothing else. Promise. And, Vrateus," I added, desperately wishing to keep his newly found trust. "I will not do anything behind your back, anymore. Okay? From now on, you'll be a part of everything I do."

He gave me a long look, then a brief nod, before retrieving the cutting tool from the floor.

I slid the doors closed, even if they couldn't be locked anymore.

"Come." He took my hand in his, tugging me down the corridor. "We'll need to get more weapons."

More weapons?

I'd say we needed to come up with a plan of action. But sure, why not start by arming ourselves to the teeth?

"SO, THIS IS YOUR ROOM?" I took in the capsule's interior, identical to mine in size, but vastly different in décor.

The floor was bare, just like mine, but he'd plastered his walls with maps and charts. Papers, scrolls, and tablet inserts were piled on every piece of furniture, including the narrow metal bed.

"I had no idea you stayed this close to me." I glanced toward the glass capsule next door. In the lights of the Anomaly, I could clearly see the clothing rack and my bed. "No idea that I was living in a fishbowl all this time, either." I turned to face him. "Have you been watching me?"

His own capsule appeared completely dark from my room—the glass too opaque to see through.

"Yes," he said, obviously not finding anything wrong with that.

"All the time?" I couldn't recall every embarrassing thing I might have done while thinking I was alone, but that was not the point anyway. I thought I'd had privacy, when in fact I had none.

"I watched you whenever I could." He went to the door identical to my bathroom door.

"Why?"

"I had to make sure you were safe."

I folded my arms across my chest. Irritation and embarrassment stirred inside me, but I forced them down. Getting angry with him wouldn't accomplish anything when he clearly didn't understand my take on it. Just like with the weekly sessions in the mess hall, he believed he was doing the right thing.

"The only reason I made it to the airlock in time last night," he added, "was because I noticed you weren't in your room when I was going to bed."

I tried to see this through his eyes. At the same time, I wished he would understand my feelings as well.

"You should have told me I was being watched."

He stopped in front of the bathroom door.

"Why?"

"So, that I knew." How would one explain the concept of privacy to someone obviously unfamiliar with it? "I'm sure I did things I didn't want you to see. Maybe even some embarrassing things. I would have acted differently had I known you were watching me."

"You did nothing embarrassing." He waved me off.

"I'm pretty sure I've walked around naked a few times."

"You have. But you have nothing to be embarrassed about. You look good naked."

Now, my face warmed with blush. It heated even more when I started thinking about *him* possibly walking around naked too, in this very room...

"It's not about that. It's just that..." I rubbed my face, forgetting what I was going to say. "Anyway, spying on people is wrong. Watching them undress when they are not aware of being watched is also wrong. Okay?"

"Okay. So, next time I'm watching you, I'd have to tell you about it first. Would that make it better?"

Well, it was better than nothing.

"Ideally you wouldn't watch me at all. But if you must, yes, at least let me know what you're doing."

He nodded, moving to the wall with charts. "We need to get going, now."

I stepped away from the glass, glad to change the subject.

"Where to?"

"Out of here. Eventually, Crux will send more people to investigate what happened to those who were supposed to retrieve you. If he's been looking for weapons, he may order to search my room, too."

"Where will we go?"

"Here." He ripped one of the large drawings off the wall. "This is the latest map of the inhabited segment of the Dark Anomaly." He pointed at the section along the arch in the drawing. "Here is the kitchen. The mess hall. This is the main corridor. And we are here. See? These shaded areas are the cavities inside the crashed ships. Some formed between the hulls when two or more spacecraft crashed onto each other."

"How often does that happen? The crashes?"

"We get a few a year, all around the outer edge of the Anomaly's disk. As soon as the crash happens in our section, we cut through the hull then weld the new ship solid with the rest. If it's a large spacecraft, I order the oxygen supply and ventilation system expanded into it. If it's a smaller one, like yours, we just cut openings in a way that ensures the best air circulation inside it."

"What happens to those that crash outside of your sector?"

"We use the spacesuits to travel along the outer edge of the Anomaly and collect whatever we can salvage from them."

"So, the gravity doesn't squish you on the outside?"

"Not if you're on the surface, no. Only if you build up some distance from it, it reins you back in with a vengeance."

"Do you know exactly what distance that is?" Even if I never fully explained the mystery of the Anomaly, I couldn't stop trying to solve it. I kept collecting every bit of information I could find.

"I believe there is no exact distance."

"What do you mean?"

"From the data we have from the crashed ships, not all of them travelled at the same distance from the Anomaly when they got sucked in. Some were fairly far away."

"I know I was." I believed I was safe even as the crash happened.

"Right. The Anomaly's gravity acts in a similar way to a star's energy, with flares that reach out into space at irregular intervals."

I'd had the same idea myself. Which meant the reach of the Anomaly's gravity field was even wider than my research team thought.

"So, this...mass is sitting there, like a giant squid deep in the ocean, and it throws out tentacles to capture unsuspecting travellers."

"Not exactly a squid, more like a whirlpool in space," Vrateus said. "It spins, drawing the spacecraft in, compacting them into a disk in the center of its force field. The ships crash along the edge. They then get compressed closer together over time. See?" Vrateus placed the paper in his hands over another similar drawing on the wall. "This one was made by one of the earlier dwellers of the Dark Anomaly, someone who died way before my ship crashed here." I could see the older drawing through the paper of the newest one, backlit by the Anomaly's lights. Vrateus circled a few shaded sections with his finger. "The cavities within the ships have been getting smaller with time." He moved his finger along the radius down to the peak of the segment on the map. "Closer to the center of the Anomaly, all spaces between the walls eventually disappear completely. The ships end up being squished together with no cavities left inside or in between."

He glanced my way.

"I suspect the middle of the disk is compressed so hard that all materials merge. Particles of all substances squeeze between each other, creating a homogenous mass of a high-density material which may be in a liquid state."

"Have you ever gone that way? To the center?"

"Not too far. But when I was little, I climbed through the cavities inside the ships and between them as far as I could squeeze through. At some point, I remember hearing the metal groan, as the Dark

Anomaly crushed and compressed the ships deep inside it. I felt the vibrations through the walls, too."

I stared at him, imagining the little boy wiggling his way through the metal body of the Anomaly. It was a miracle he didn't get trapped somewhere.

"And on the surface?" I asked.

"When we go outside, we only travel along the edge."

"You've never explored the rest of the surface of the disk? To see if you could travel to the center from the outside?"

"No. You can see from the edge that the middle is not flat like the rest of the Anomaly. The center of it is bulging out like a sphere. If the material there is liquid, it could also be hot and dangerous. Life around here is all about survival. I can't afford to send people exploring just for the sake of exploration."

"I understand."

He ripped all drawings off the wall. "We better take them all with us, no need to leave Crux a map on how to follow us."

He rolled the drawings together then took a tablet frame and gathered a few opaque inserts from the desk and the bed.

"These, too." He retrieved a long leather bag from a trunk by the wall, packing everything in it, then added a coil of thin rope and a change of clothes. "I'll get us some water."

With two canteens in his hands, Vrateus went to the bathroom.

"Can you grab some blankets, please?" he shouted over the noise of running water.

"Sure." I looked around in search of them.

The fur spread on his bed was soft and luxuriously decadent. Its red color changed to bright orange and yellow in my hands when I picked it up. Despite being thick and fluffy, it took little space when I rolled it into a bundle and stuffed it into the bag.

"You like pretty things," I observed when Vrateus walked out of the bathroom.

"As long as they're also functional." He handed me the filled canteens to put in the bag. "Come."

Taking the bag from me, he picked up the metal-cutting tool then headed back to the bathroom.

"That way?" I asked, confused.

"We need to get more weapons, remember?"

"In the bathroom?"

"Not exactly." He lifted a piece of wall paneling, revealing a hidden door behind it.

"Is that where your weapon storage is?" I gasped. "Crux would love to know that."

"He might still figure it out." Vrateus entered the hidden room, gesturing for me to follow. "Maybe."

The room behind the door was at least ten times larger than the bathroom. Shelves lined the walls, displaying a collection of weapons that would make any museum proud. The earliest models Vrateus had might have been millennia old. Though I couldn't date them accurately, as many seemed entirely unfamiliar.

I recognized a toolbox from my ship standing in a corner.

Vrateus locked the door behind us.

"Let's see." He took a leather belt with holsters from a peg on the wall then turned to me. "This should fit you."

Leaning over, he wrapped the belt around my waist then buckled it in the front. "These go here." He slid a small gun into the holster on my left then put a slim knife into the sheath on the right. "And this will go here." He took a cluster of narrower belts with a sheath. Getting down on one knee, he wrapped the belts around my right thigh.

"I'm not sure how to use any of these."

"You did pretty good out there." He tipped his head toward the corridor that must still be littered with dead aliens. I had shot some of them. The reality of me being a murderer still hadn't settled in. "This gun is similar to the one you've used." He took the small weapon out of its holster on my belt then showed me how to use it, explaining its parts. "Shoot from a distance," he added. "Aim for their face, neck or stomach. Most of the species have thinner skin, smaller scales or a finer chitin layer in those areas."

He placed the gun back into its holster. Sliding his fingers around my leg, he adjusted the straps of the dagger sheath around my thigh next.

The sudden awareness of his hands skimming the inside of my thigh sent a warm shiver up my body. He must have sensed it too, as his fingers stilled on the strap.

His hand splayed on the back of my thigh, he released a shuddered breath, letting his head drop between his shoulders.

"Is everything okay?" I asked, my voice unintentionally breathy.

"Now, more than ever, I need to be fully alert. But you're such a distraction, Svetlana," he groaned.

It didn't come out as an accusation. Still, I felt a pang of guilt. The image of him chugging the poisoned wine after my failed escape attempt rose in my mind.

"I've been wreaking havoc on your world, haven't I?"

"You have no idea," he growled.

"I'm really sorry about how it all happened. I didn't know that Crux would use my escape attempt as a distraction and strike against you."

"I'm not blaming you for *my* lapse in caution."

"For what then?"

He lifted his gaze, meeting mine.

"For everything that has been happening *inside* me." A storm was churning in his vivid eyes.

"What would you have me do to change that?" I asked quietly.

"I don't want to change a thing, Svetlana. From the moment you arrived, you've scrambled my thoughts, deprived me of focus, and wreaked havoc on my body." He remained on one knee in front of me, his hands splayed on my thigh. "There is a pleasure in this torture, though. I don't understand it, but I don't want it to end. In fact, I crave more of it."

I stared down at his face, confusion visible in his hard features. His physical reactions weren't surprising. If I was the first woman he had ever encountered, some surge of hormones, pheromones, or physical desire on his part could be expected.

What was shocking to me were my own feelings for him. The initial resentment had disappeared, slowly replaced by desire. Now, the genuine attraction was growing strong inside me. It scared me. At the same time, I craved more of him, too.

He slid his hand down, to the back of my knee. My skin inside my suit tingled from the warmth of his palm. Suddenly, I knew what about his touch was so incredible—the gentle reverence with which he treated my body—even when he had touched me for the entertainment of others. I always sensed that, for *him,* every moment with me was special. He had made it intimate, even when we'd been surrounded by hundreds of sex-starved males.

I hovered my hand next to his face then gently placed it on his shoulder instead.

"I like you, Vrateus," I confessed. "I tried not to. I didn't believe it was right for me to have any kind of sympathy or attraction for you. But I ended up having both."

With a long exhale, he pressed his forehead to my belly.

"You can't imagine how good it feels to hear that from you. I've sensed your animosity with my skin."

"It wasn't for *you,* Vrateus, but for this entire situation. I dislike being put on display for your crew. For me, the intimate touch between two people is not supposed to be shared with anyone else. If the intimacy is real, it shouldn't be for the entertainment of others. That was probably why it felt so exceptionally wrong—because with you, it did feel *real.*"

"You should have told me that sooner." He gazed up at me.

"I'm afraid I couldn't have properly explained it before."

"It won't happen again." Determination flashed in his eyes.

"But it has to." I cupped his face, gently tracing the sharp ridge of his cheekbone with my thumb. "I understand now why you did it. It's survival, Vrateus. We both need to do what we have to do to survive."

Chapter 19

INSTEAD OF GOING BACK through the doors, Vrateus used the tool to cut out an opening in the back wall of his weapon storage room. We exited into a narrow tunnel behind it then climbed through the crumpled bowels of the Anomaly.

I held up a piece of the thin rope he'd cut from the coil in the bag. As soon as he'd cut it off, the piece glowed bright blue, lighting our way.

Using the tool and consulting the map from time to time, Vrateus cut through the walls that blocked our way, opening a section of a ship or a sealed tunnel between two hulls, allowing us to keep going.

"We should be close," he muttered under his breath, setting the tool down and taking the bag off his shoulder.

"Close to where?" I asked since he still hadn't shared our final destination with me. The habit of being on his own and doing everything alone obviously wasn't that easy to shake off for him.

He pointed at the map. "I slept in this space often when I was younger. It's just behind the library. We'll need to turn here."

He folded the map, then picked up the bag and the cutting tool.

After another turn, we squeezed between two wall panels into a small room with no doors or windows.

No one must have used it since Vrateus. It was empty and clean of any garbage.

"You've slept here?"

"Sometimes." He tossed the tool aside then took the blanket out of the bag. "There was no library back then. Just a storage room full of stuff looted from ships. Right behind here." He splayed his hand on one of the walls.

"How old were you?"

"Eight, when I first got to the Dark Anomaly."

"That small?" My breath caught in my throat. "What happened to the rest of those who were on your ship? Did anyone else survive the crash?"

"Some. But not for long." His jaw flexed. "I'll need to go out, now," he changed the subject. "You'll wait here—"

"Wait, what?" I grabbed his arm. "You want me to stay here, while you're out there alone? Facing hundreds of hostile aliens?"

He widened his stance.

"The *aliens* you're talking about are my crew."

"Doesn't mean they aren't hostile. Didn't some of them nearly cut your head off back there?" I gestured toward my room. "Listen, let me come with you. After all, why dress me up?" I gestured at the weapon holsters strapped to my waist and thigh. "If I don't even get to use these?"

"The weapons are for your protection," he replied, somberly. "In case someone finds their way here."

"Come on, I can be useful, Vrateus." The thought of him going out there on his own filled me with dread. "You never know, you may even enjoy having someone watch your back."

"I..." He raked his claws through the soft curl of fur over his head, pushing it back only for it to fall back down again as soon as he released it. "If you come with me, I'd be terrified for you. It'd distract me, risking possibly getting both of us killed."

His expression was pleading, making me ease off with my demand.

"What are you planning to do out there?" I asked.

"Just a brief reconnaissance trip. I need to know how things are out there before coming up with a plan."

"Promise not to start a war all by yourself."

My words made him smile. "I'm not even planning to show my face to anyone, yet. Promise, no war."

"Good." I nodded, clasping my hands in front of me. "How are you getting out of here?"

Crouching by the bag, he opened the map again, pointing at the place a couple turns back.

"I'll retrace our steps to this spot here. See this corner? Where the hulls of two ships smashed together? If I cut an opening here, this part would hide it from view of anyone in the corridor."

I stared at the map, already silently praying for his safe return.

He picked up the tool again, heading to the tunnel.

"Vrateus..." I stopped him with my hand on his sleeve.

He looked over his shoulder.

Rising on my tiptoes, I placed a quick kiss on the ridge of his cheekbone. "Please be careful."

His eyes glistened fiery orange in the blue light of the string.

"I will."

ACCORDING TO THE TABLET Vrateus and I had brought with us, it'd been only twenty minutes since he'd left, but it felt like hours.

Sitting in the small room, lit only by the short string of glowing blue light, I cuddled into his soft fur blanket. All seemed to be quiet out there. Unnervingly silent. The growling of the Anomaly compressing the wreckage that Vrateus had told me about didn't reach this far. It must be getting lost in the layers of insulation and paneling, never making it to the outer segments of the disk. Still, sitting alone in this tiny windowless room made me feel claustrophobic and...lonely.

The rustling noise of someone moving inside the tunnel Vrateus had left through sent me to my feet. My heart raced with hope that it was him returning, and fear that it might be someone or something else.

I quickly tossed the glowing string on the floor by the tunnel, illuminating the entrance, it allowed me to hide in the shadows. Grabbing the laser gun from the holster on my thigh, I held it up, ready.

The noise came closer. Then the blue glow fell on the white material of Vrateus's shirt as he entered.

"You..." I lowered the gun. Relief spread through me in a calming wave.

"Has anyone told you that you look fierce with a gun?" A corner of his mouth lifted in an unexpected smile.

"No." I holstered the weapon. "Probably because I've never handled one before."

He entered the small space, immediately filling it with his presence. I stepped back to the wall, though everything inside me urged me to come closer.

"You're a natural, then." His tone was light.

His words brought back the images of the males I'd killed. I hadn't thought twice about pulling the trigger, then. I would have done it again, under the same circumstances. The images of the smoldering holes in the dead bodies, however, stayed in my memory.

"Hungry?"

Only now had I noticed a grease-stained, paper-wrapped bundle in his hands. The smell of cooked meat wafted from it. It wasn't the most appetizing aroma, but my mouth watered. It had been nearly twenty-four hours since I'd last eaten.

"How is everything out there?" I asked, after we both had settled on the blanket, our backs to the wall.

"As I should have expected. Total chaos." Vrateus shook his head, his mouth tightening into a thin line of disapproval. "They are guzzling unmeasurable amounts of berry wine and butchering a month's supply of *vasai*."

"Are they celebrating?"

"Yes. Crux has declared himself the captain and cancelled all my restrictions."

He sounded less upset about the loss of his position than about his crew needlessly wasting supplies and resources.

"Here." He handed me a bone with meat on it. It appeared to be an entire leg of *vasai,* with a meaty chunk at the very top.

I was too hungry to decline.

"Thank you." I peeled a strip of meat off then chewed on it, slowly. "Where did you get it? And how?"

"I stole it from the kitchen. It wasn't hard." He bit a chunk of meat off another bone he had taken out of the paper bundle. "No one is paying attention to anything. Crux has lifted my limits on wine. They're getting drunk out of their minds."

"Sounds like a perfect time to show up and restore the order," I suggested.

"No. Not yet. It's best for us to wait. Alcohol has different effects on different species. *Ognats* have a strong allergy to the berry wine. It doesn't stop them from drinking as much as they can fit in their bellies, though. Most of the *ognats* will die before morning."

"That's awful," I gasped. "They're willingly killing themselves?"

"One of the many reasons I imposed strict limits on alcohol, in the first place." He shook his head. "Those without the allergy have been getting into fights and scuffles. It's not going to end well. *Dimos,* for example, get extremely aggressive when they're drunk. They'll fight anything that moves. When plunged in a killing frenzy, they continue fighting even if their heads get cut off."

"Well." I rubbed my forehead. "It's quite a crew you've got there."

"They are what they are." He shrugged.

"Don't at least some of them come from civilized worlds?"

"All of them came from planets with some form of government. It's just that many had been on the fringes of society even before they crashed here. Most of what we have here now used to be pirates, smugglers, and criminals on the run."

"Those couldn't be the only space travelers in the area."

"Many were," he replied. "Regular trade routes steered clear of the Dark Anomaly. The criminals took risks, by coming closer than they should, to evade being detected or captured. But you're right, not *all* who crashed here were on the wrong side of the law. Some were law-abiding citizens. Most of them didn't survive, though. One needs to be tough and ruthless to make it here."

"Was your family among those who didn't make it?" I asked carefully.

Finishing his meat, Vrateus took the water bottles out of the bag, handing one to me.

"My family were merchants," he said quietly. "Although they didn't shy away from some illegal smuggling here and there as I've learned while examining their log books."

"Do you remember any of them?"

"Vaguely. Everything that happened before the crash is like a dream—foggy and fragmented. The strongest memory is that of my mother patting me here..." Staring straight ahead, he lifted his hand to his temple, touching the tattoos above his ear. "While she sang me to sleep at night, she would trail her fingers here. It felt soothing..." He dropped his hand to his thigh.

"Do your tattoos have meaning?" I asked softly.

He nodded. Sliding his finger along the ornamental lines, without even being able to see them, he named them all, "My name, the name of my clan, the name of our ship, and its home port on our planet. The tattoos tell where I belong... Where I was *supposed* to belong."

Bending his legs, he rested his forearms on his knees.

"*Themuls* live in clans," he continued. "The crew of our ship comprised twenty-eight people, all of them related, either by blood or by marriage. My parents, their siblings and their families. My aunts, uncles, cousins..."

"You said not all of them died in the crash."

He'd mentioned they didn't live long after. That he had survived the cruel world of the Dark Anomaly alone seemed a miracle to me.

"Most died. I was strapped in bed, sleeping, when it happened. The beds with my cousins were crushed, killing them. Mine ended up wedged under theirs with enough space to keep me alive."

He ran both hands over his face.

"By the time I climbed out, the *ognats* and *kreers* had already made their way onto the ship. The killings of the survivors had started. Then *errocks* and *yourlu* joined them, with *dimos* and the others. That was when the rapes began..."

"Did no one see you?"

"In the chaos that followed, I crawled under wreckage and snuck out."

"You were only eight years old, Vrateus. How on earth did you survive here alone?"

"I hid. Smaller than anyone, I could fit in tiny places no one would bother to look. As a child, I had the same advantage Malahki has. I had neither the scent of a female to excite lust nor the size or attitude of a male to ignite aggression."

"Many would still eat you if they caught you." Even after all my time on the Dark Anomaly, I still couldn't fully imagine the horrors he had lived through.

"True, food was scarce. As was air and water. Without one interconnected air supply system, we relied on the oxygen production equipment of individual ships. The air was thin and poorly distributed. Cannibalism was rampant and widely accepted in those times. The strongest routinely killed and ate the weakest."

"Oh God...It's just awful." I winced, rubbing the pain out of my tightening throat. "What did *you* eat?"

"Whatever I could steal from the others when they were asleep or intoxicated and passed out. A few years later, the ship with *vasai* crashed here. The centipedes got loose, spreading through the body of the Anomaly. By then, I had grown big enough and learned to hunt them. I would corner one, separating it from the rest, then kill it. After a while, I had enough meat to sustain myself and even to trade for things I needed."

"When did you decide to become the captain?"

"Well before that." A crooked smile appeared on his hardened face. "I knew right after the crash that I would kill Raex, one day. The *errock* boasted he'd raped my mother. He was the unofficial leader. I decided when I was big enough, I would take his place to lead them all. Unlike him, I wanted to do it right."

"Did you kill him?"

He nodded. "I knew I needed to be patient, and I was. Biding my time, I learned everything I could about the species populating the Dark Anomaly. Their strengths and their weaknesses. What motivated each of them. I used to sneak onto the newly crashed ships. While everyone else looted them for food and weapons, I'd search for data storage devices. Then I brought them all here." He tipped his chin toward the wall separating us from the library. "I studied everything there was to learn about the world outside and the people we had in here. There was no order back then. But Raex was the leader. I challenged him seven years ago and won that fight."

"You killed him," I exhaled.

"Just as I'd promised myself." An expression of grim satisfaction settled over his face.

"How did the rest of *errocks* take it? Did they defend one of their own?" I drank more water from my bottle, listening to him intently.

"Back on their planet, *errocks* live in tribes. The leader of a tribe can be challenged in one-on-one combat for leadership. I defeated Raex in an honest fight. Not all of them liked it, but they've accepted it."

"Is that what you're planning to do, now?" I asked tentatively, unsure if I'd like the answer. "Are you going to challenge Crux?"

"I'll give him a chance to surrender first." He stuffed his canteen back into the bag.

"Do you see him taking that chance?"

He drew in a long breath. "Probably not. But I want to use any possibility to avoid more violence. Our population will already be drastically reduced when all of this is over. No need to court another rampage."

"Are you planning to talk to Crux?" I cleared my throat, breathing deeply as worry tightened my chest. "When?"

"By tomorrow morning, many of them will have drunk themselves unconscious. Some will be dead. Others hangover. I'll try to talk with Crux then."

"*We'll* try," I corrected him.

He glanced my way.

"Svetlana, it would be best if you stayed here."

"Again?" I stared at him.

He remained silent, shifting his eyes from mine.

I exhaled sharply, calling on my patience. "Listen, I'm not saying I should be out there, slaying men and kicking ass. All I'm asking for is for you *not* to dismiss my ability and willingness to help. If there is any chance for me to be useful, please, include me in your plans."

He reached over and moved a strand of my hair away from my face.

"If there was an absolutely safe place anywhere on the Anomaly to hide you, I would," he admitted. "You have become my dearest treasure, Svetlana. I feel this powerful urge to lock you away and keep you safe."

I blinked at his confession, uncertain how to take it, though something warm and pleasant glowed inside of me from the tenderness in his tone.

"I know that crashing here was a disaster for you," he continued. "But for me, your arrival turned out to be the best thing in my life. From the very first moment, I couldn't get you out of my thoughts. Though, there were some frustration and annoyance too, at the beginning." He smiled.

"*Frustration and annoyance* still sound milder than the emotions I had for you." I chuckled. "I hated you then."

He tilted his head. "How about now?"

The half-grin remained on his face, slightly teasing. However, the intensity in his eyes betrayed how important my answer was to him. He seemed to halt his breath, waiting for it.

"I've already told you, Vrateus, I like you. I just..."

"What is it?" He frowned.

A flicker of enduring hope in his gaze pinched my heart with ache. Vrateus longed for affection, even as he hardly could remember what that feeling was.

Was it specifically *my* affection that he wished for, though?

I was literally the first woman Vrateus had met who wasn't family. Would he have cared just as much about any female who'd crashed here instead of me?

Would he leave if another female came along?

The thought zigzagged with pain along the scars of my previously broken heart.

I crashed here first, I saw him first. He was now all mine to take. And I wanted him so badly.

Could I still stop this, whatever it was between us, from growing any stronger? Could this simply remain all about lust?

"What is it, Svetlana?" he prompted, carefully.

"Nothing." I gave him a smile to mask my thoughts and took his hand in mine.

The soft fur on the top of his hand reached up to his knuckles, leaving his fingers bare. I circled the green stone of one of the huge rings he wore.

"Why don't I believe you?" he insisted, his eyes searching mine.

Because you see through me? You see *me.*

Over the past weeks, he'd learn not just my body, he'd learned to read *me*.

"You've made me feel so many things, Vrateus," I squeezed his hand, afraid to say too much but unable to say nothing at all. "From hate, to rage, to...attraction." And so much more. All the feelings that now bubbled hot inside me, scaring me with their intensity. "No one else has ever made me feel the way you do."

Clasping my fingers in his hand, he shifted closer.

"What are you feeling right now, Svetlana?"

"Now?" I slid my gaze to his mouth. Often pressed into a firm line in focus, anger or disapproval, his lips were slightly parted. Inviting and enticing.

"This very moment...I just want to kiss you again." The words came out, taking my breath with them.

His eyes flashed with heat as he leaned closer.

"Kiss me then," he whispered, his lips brushing over mine. "Use the moment, Svetlana, because on the Dark Anomaly that's all there is. Just this very moment."

Chapter 20

He claimed her lips. Remembering everything from their previous kiss, he mirrored her actions. His execution was far from precise. His thoughts were on everything at once as he tried to take her in with all his senses.

Listening and touching.

Tasting and feeling...

She gasped softly into his mouth. Her body stilled, then seemed to come back to life with his touch. Wrapping her arms around his neck, she shifted closer, sliding into his lap. Her scent wrapped around him, and he happily allowed himself to drown in it.

Just like she had, he slipped his tongue deeper, searching for hers. A soft moan vibrated deep in her throat.

Desire jolted through his body like lightning, crushing his self-control.

Letting go of her mouth, he trailed his lips down on the side of her neck, instead. Inhaling deeply, he filled his lungs with her scent, breathing her in. She gasped as his canines grazed her skin. The sound went straight to his cock, making it hard as steel.

Fervently moving his hands, he searched for a way to get under her suit, needing to feel her naked body. His claws sprang from the tips of his fingers, raking along the indestructible material of her suit.

"Here..." She whispered breathlessly, yanking at something in the front. The suit opened from her neck down to her navel.

The claws didn't disappear all the way as he palmed her breasts through her pink harness. She hissed at the prick of the claws, her nipples tightened and hardened under his thumbs.

"Oh God, yes…" she moaned, riding the hard ridge of his throbbing erection through his pants.

Pressing her breasts into his hands, she grabbed fistfuls of fur on his scruff. Intense pleasure coursed down his back from the sting at the roots, making him growl.

More blood rushed to his groin. His cock pulsed hot with need. Hands under her backside, he flipped her down on the fur blanket, grinding himself against her.

Lost in her scent, the feel of her, and her taste, he felt nothing else. Everything ceased to exist. There was just her warm, writhing body under him.

The unbearable, all-consuming need was building up, threatening to explode and tear him apart.

A feral roar vibrated deep in his chest somewhere.

Ecstasy spiked.

Delirious, he bit down on her shoulder, just below her neck, and growled through his teeth as a mind-blowing climax rocked through him.

Again and again.

Brutal pleasure shook his body, rolling through him in waves. He couldn't breathe, couldn't think. When the last spurt of his release burst out of him, he no longer knew his own name.

Spent, he released her from the grip of his teeth, gasping for air and rolling off her into the fur blanket.

"Vrateus?" Svetlana's hand stroked his heaving chest. "Are you okay, sweetheart?"

The tender concern in her voice made him want to cry.

Then, worry chilled the sweat on his back.

"Svetlana…" He jerked his head up, searching for her eyes, afraid of what he might find in them. "I did it all wrong, didn't I?"

For a few blissful moments, he had lost himself to her, forgetting about *her* pleasure.

Her dark eyes glistened in the bluish glow of the light string as she rose on her elbow at his side.

"Not wrong." She gazed at him with a warm excitement. "This was…intense." Her hand went to touch the bite mark on her shoulder. "I knew it would be wild if you let go." She leaned in, cupping his face. "I've seen it in you," she murmured, with a soft kiss on the corner of his mouth. "We haven't even done the whole thing yet, but was it good for you?"

Good?

He still felt like a part of his soul was floating out there among the lights of the Anomaly. He didn't think it would ever come back to reunite with his body. Not when she was stroking his head like that, combing through his fur with her delicate little fingers.

"But I wanted it to be good for you, too," he groaned.

She breathed out a soft laugh.

"It still can be."

Arching her back, she clicked open her breast harness.

Leaning over her, he rolled her onto her back, then pushed the pink material up to her chin. Freed, her breasts spilled out, round and full, tipped with dark pink. The sight of them made his cock throb all over again, but he ignored his own arousal, this time.

"Tell me if you like this." He lowered his head, dragging his long tongue across one of Svetlana's nipples.

Soft and silky, her skin quickly wrinkled around the tip which got hard like a small, perky button.

"I do…" She smiled at his questioning glance, her chest rising faster. "Do you like doing it?"

"I've wanted to taste every part of you for such a long time," he rasped, sucking the nipple into his mouth.

She moaned, stretching under him.

He moved his mouth to the other nipple while stroking the one he had just released with his fingers. Carefully, he slid out the very tip of the claw on his thumb.

She whimpered when he lightly scraped across her skin with it, circling the tip of her breast.

"More...please," she panted.

Releasing all his claws on that hand, he gently dragged their tips over her skin. A shudder ran through her body with her long, shuddered exhale.

"That is so good, Vrateus..."

Good.

The word gave him encouragement. He wrapped his hand around her throat quickly, just to check what he already knew—she was aroused and ready.

He slowly trailed the tips of his claws down her belly, then sheathed them completely before slipping his hand inside the waistband of her shorts.

Touching her there felt familiar. He'd done it several times, now. Except that this time, it was just for the two of them. There were no others.

She gasped, the same way she always did when he circled that spot between her legs.

Rising on his elbow at her side, he watched her face, noting every change in her expression.

She gazed at him with a small, happy smile. Then her eyelids dropped. The smile melted off her face. Her lips parted, letting out a soft moan.

Just for him.

"Faster, Vrateus..." she begged. "Just a little harder...Oh, yes right there..."

Then, she stopped talking completely. Her breathing hitched. Her body tensed; she fisted her hands above her head.

With a long groan, she released her breath that broke into a series of gasps and moans a moment after. Her hips jerked, and she trembled.

He removed his fingers from her. Instead, he cupped his hand between her legs and gently massaged her there, curious how many little shudders he could reap out of her.

Finally, her expression melted into a blissful one. With a sweet, delightful moan, she opened her eyes, meeting his.

"All *these* moans were real," he whispered, happy to see her smile.

"Of course, they were..." She released a shuddered breath, the smile slipped off her face. "This is so not just about lust, is it?"

The sudden fearful expression in her dark-brown eyes made his heart flip.

"No, it's not." He gathered her into his arms. "It's never been just about that, sweetheart."

She closed her eyes tightly, hungrily drawing in another breath.

"Which means it'd hurt that much more if you leave," she whispered, barely audible.

"Leave?" He exhaled a laugh, confused. "Where? There is no leaving here, you know it yourself now."

"People can physically be in the same room, Vrateus, but so far away from each other emotionally, as though galaxies apart."

He took in her beautiful face—the dark eyebrows curved tragically, the bottom lip worried between her teeth. Those eyes—the color of the dark, bitter tea he brought for her with breakfast every morning—glossy with emotion.

"Are you scared that what we have will end before it's begun?" he asked. "Have I given you any reason to feel that way?"

"Not you." She lifted her hand to his face, obvious in her need to touch him. He leaned into it, needing her touch, too. "People don't tend to stick around me. Everyone I've ever loved left, Vrateus."

"Even your family?"

A shadow or hurt crossed her lovely face, making her look younger and vulnerable. Then the words started pouring out, as if they had been piling up inside of her for so long, they couldn't wait to get out.

"I've hardly ever had a family. I lost my parents when I was still a baby. Only they weren't taken from me the way yours were." She stroked his cheekbone gently. "They left on their own and never came back. My grandparents died when I was in the Academy, but emotionally, they'd left me to my own devices long before that. They weren't easy people to love, but still I tried. They were all I had, and I cared for them. My grandmother gave me a hug and a kiss here..." she tapped her cheek, her eyes staring past him somewhere, "every year on my birthday. And my grandfather would shake my hand and pat my shoulder when I brought home a good report card at the end of my school year." A faint smile ghosted her lips. "I tried so hard to have the best grades in my class. And sometimes I wonder if that was because I simply wanted that handshake so badly."

Her chest rose as she heaved a sigh. Her words resonated with his own feelings from his distant past. He had no handshakes and no kisses growing up, but he recognized the longing in her eyes.

"None of my relationships with men have worked out," she continued, dropping her hands in her lap. "And that may be my fault, because after the first one failed, I've never given it my all again. My work has always been there for me, and it's become my one true passion. Until you..." She met his gaze with hers again, and her eyes spoke even more than her words.

"Svetlana..." he half-whispered, afraid to break this moment and the connection that had stretched between them. Only it couldn't be broken that easily, he realized. There was nothing he wouldn't do for her. All he needed in return was for her to be at his side. Always.

"There're so many reasons for me to be afraid right now, Vrateus," she said softly. "There's real danger out there. But right now, my biggest fear is that this..." she waved her hand between them, "is just another heartache waiting to happen. I want to open my heart to you, all the way, but I'm afraid what will be left of it once you're gone..."

"Svetlana," he said again, stretching her name on his tongue like the sweetest of treats. "I'd never touched a woman before you. I'd never held anyone in my arms like this before. The only physical contact I knew was the one aimed to hurt or to kill. I have no idea what I'm doing and how it all works, but I know one thing, there is no *me* without *you* anymore." He tightened his hold on her, feeling every word he said in his heart. "What I feel for you is new, exciting, and unsettling. It's like every nerve in me is exposed, ready to be hurt or experience the highest of pleasure, or both."

"Are you scared, too?" she murmured, raising her large, lustrous eyes to his.

"Terrified," he confessed. Having her in his life made him feel like a part of him now existed outside of his body, beyond his control, extremely vulnerable and painfully precious. "But I want it all. Everything. From now on, there is no parting from you for me."

HIS WORDS AND EXPRESSION floored me. There was so much tenderness in his eyes, open and unguarded. And there was faith, unshakable faith in *us*.

I breathed deeply, soaking in his words and his strength. It was scary to let him into my heart, but I had no control over it. He'd already made his way under my skin, and I liked having him close way too much to push him away. In fact, I needed him even closer.

Cupping his face in my hands, I kissed him again. Slowly and tenderly, I took his bottom lip between mine then slid my tongue in to meet his, using my kiss to tell him all the things I couldn't put into words right now.

Despite the many horrible things Vrateus had lived through—things that had hardened him, made him strong and uncompromising—he remained innocent in so many ways.

I had the unstoppable urge to kiss and cuddle him.

He welcomed my affection, soaking it in like a desert absorbed the first rain of the season. I realized that all of it was new to him. Every single thing that had happened between us—each touch, kiss, caress, and whisper—was something he had never experienced before with anyone else.

And I wanted to give it all to him—everything he'd missed, stranded in this place with no one capable of any feelings.

I wished to give him my all, but I hadn't expected how much he would be giving back.

With Vrateus, I felt not just wanted, but *needed*, desperately. His strong arms around me made me feel safe in this place filled with danger.

Rolling to his back, he drew me over his chest. I broke the kiss, rising over him on my arms.

He gazed up at me, making me warm with pleasure from the glow of affection in his bright orange eyes. "You make me happy, Svetlana. When I should be stressed and terrified."

"With you, I'm not scared of anything," I confessed. The fear, the dread of what was to come were still there. But all of that seemed manageable as long as he was with me. "Together, we'll be okay, Vrateus. You and me."

Together.

For once, I truly believed it was possible for me to be no longer alone.

Chapter 21

"HERE, TAKE THIS, TOO," Vrateus said, taking a ruby ring off his pinky and putting it on the ring finger of my right hand.

"A promise ring?" I attempted a joke with a nervous giggle to combat the dreadful anxiety of the looming uncertainty.

This morning, he had taken me to the functioning bathroom on one of the ships near the gardens. Then, we'd had some berries and fruit for breakfast. We had taken care to stay out of sight. However, the gardens appeared deserted. Even Malahki seemed to be gone.

Back in the room behind the library, Vrateus was now getting ready to confront Crux.

"If you press the button here..." He lifted my hand, pointing at a small bead in the setting of the ring. "A needle will slide out. It's soaked in a concentrated *fuhnid* juice."

"It is?" I took a closer look at the tiny button he had indicated.

"Very potent." He nodded. "The needle is too fine to penetrate the skin of every species on the Dark Anomaly, though. If anyone gets too close, aim for the eyelids or lips if you can. It should kill a large male within seconds."

"Wow." I admired the ring with newly found appreciation. "I see what you meant when you said you liked things that are pretty *and* functional."

He checked all my weapons, as if I were the one going out there to face the wild crowd, not staying in the small room behind the library, waiting for his return.

He cupped the side of my face for a moment, then slid his hand down my arm, lacing his fingers with mine.

"I'll come for you in an hour or two."

I squeezed his hand, wishing I didn't have to let go.

"Be careful, please. I need you to come back."

"I will *always* come back to you." He held my gaze. "You understand what you've done to me, Svetlana? It's no longer just about survival for me. You've shown me how to *live*. If I lost you now, I wouldn't know how to go on."

ONCE AGAIN, I WAS SITTING in the dark, waiting. My eyes on the glowing screen of the tablet, I tracked every passing second, counting down the minutes until Vrateus's return.

An hour passed, then another crawled by, and he still wasn't back.

I strained my hearing, listening to every little noise out in the tunnel, but none of them were the sounds of him returning.

At lunch time, I ate some fruit Vrateus and I had brought from the gardens. Unable to sit, I paced in the small space.

Something must have happened. I couldn't shake the dread.

I had no doubt Vrateus would have come for me as soon as he was able. *If* he was able.

Something bad must have happened to him, and I couldn't stay here, not knowing what it was or if I could help.

Adjusting the weapons strapped to my body, I slipped out of the room and into the tunnel, then made a turn to the gardens, the way Vrateus had shown me that morning.

From there, I travelled via the conveyor belt inside the garbage tunnel.

My plan was simple. Stay out of sight, learn what had happened, figure out how to help Vrateus if he needed help.

Keeping my hand on the wall, I felt the loose panel that covered the opening into the corridor not far from my old room. Getting off the conveyor belt, my hands and feet pushed into the walls of the tunnel, I crawled up, then peeked out into the corridor.

No one was here. From what Vrateus had told me, Crux and the crew would either still be celebrating, or recovering after last night's party. Either way, most of them would congregate around the mess hall and the kitchen where the food and the wine were.

Getting back down on the conveyor belt, I kept going in the direction of the waste sorting room.

My destination shouldn't be far now.

I got ready to stop if necessary, listening for any noise up ahead.

Instead, a rattling sound came from behind me.

Was it some large debris going down the tunnel?

It sounded big and heavy enough to push me out into the waste processing room. I had no way of knowing if anyone was out there, and I would get no chance to stop myself before falling out.

I braced my arms and feet into the walls. Maybe, I could at least try to slow down my tumbling out of the tunnel by stopping the debris with my shoulders?

The next moment, the thing behind me rushed down with a sound of a rumbling log. It painfully hit my shoulder, narrowly missing my head, then wedged between the wall and my body.

My stomach lurched with terror when I realized what it was.

A full-grown *vasai* centipede!

It hissed, thrashing violently against me. Its jaws clanked somewhere just above my head.

I shoved at its chitin-covered body as its many legs scraped at my bodysuit. Horror and disgust exploded in my chest. I couldn't scream. My throat closed in terror, choking me.

Tumbling together with the centipede, my limbs tangled with its countless legs, we both flew out of the garbage shoot, landing in a pile of trash below.

The *vasai* seemed really pissed. Sinking its mandibles into my shoulder, it shook its flat head like a fighting dog. It seemed determined to let go only with a piece of my flesh in its mouth.

Rolling down the garbage pile with the nightmarish insect, I frantically patted my side in search of the gun holster. As soon as my fingers brushed by the smooth handle, I yanked the gun out and fired.

I had no time to aim properly. The laser ray grazed the creature's side, not harming it much but enraging it even more. Kicking me with all its legs, it shoved me to my back, knocking the gun out of my hand.

Two brick-brown hands suddenly gripped the centipede's head, twisting it out of its body. A stream of milky-white goo gushed out of the wound, foul and steaming.

My stomach roiled. Then, a fresh wave of terror chilled my spine at the sight of my "rescuer". The burly *dimo* lifted the severed head of the centipede to his mouth, sucking on the dangling tissue and torn vessels.

"God, it's so gross," I groaned, scrambling for my gun.

He tossed the *vasai* head aside, kicking the gun out of my reach.

"Huh!" A *kreer* peeked at me over the *dimo's* shoulder. "Crux's female is here."

Both aliens appeared to be fresh out of a fight. One of the *kreer's* arms hung motionless. The *dimo's* side was covered in blood, his or the *kreer's,* it was hard to tell.

Two more *dimos* were lying by the wall, either death or passed out.

"Go, get Crux," the *dimo* ordered.

"Why me?" the *kreer* whined, his bloodshot eyes fixed on me. "You'll have all the fun with her while I'm gone."

"Go," the *dimo* roared. "Tell him we found her. Crux may let you have her after he's done, for bringing him the good news."

"But you'll have her now—"

"Go, I said!" The *dimo* shoved the *kreer* toward the exit, so hard, the male nearly lost its balance. Spurred into action, the *kreer* jumped to all his feet and ran to the short hallway that led to the *vasai* farm and the main corridor.

At the same moment, the *dimo* lunged for me.

Scurrying around him on all fours, I leaped to my feet and dashed after the *kreer*. This was the only way out of the room besides the tunnel I'd arrived in.

It was quieter inside the *vasai* farm this time. I ran between the cages, many of them empty, their doors open. The clusters of eggs in those were squashed, with the clear contents smeared all over the floor, mixed with the creatures' spilled blood.

My feet slipped in the gore. The heavy footfalls of the *dimo* sounded close at my back.

I sprinted for the entrance.

The sound of other footsteps came from the corridor, then the *kreer* rushed back into the farm, with Crux on his heels.

"Where is she?"

I skidded to a stop, nearly crashing into them. My feet slid in the mess on the floor, and I grabbed on to the bars of the nearest cage to stop myself from falling.

Then the heavy hand of the *dimo* fisted in my hair.

"Finally." Crux smirked, a black flash in his yellow eyes promised nothing good for me.

Fear paralyzed my mind and my body.

The lanky alien, Vrateus had called Tunkrox, staggered unsteadily through the entrance into the farm.

"Hey, Crux..." he hiccupped. "The captain escaped—"

Crux span on his heel, glaring at Tunkrox. "*I am* the captain! You idiot."

"Okay." Tunkrox shrugged, swaying on his feet. "He is still gone, though…"

"How?" Crux roared, hands fisting at his sides. "Lock her in the cage," he threw over his shoulder to the *dimo*. "Fuck! How did he get out? Who was supposed to be watching him? Do I have to be everywhere at once? A bunch of idiots!" he raged, stomping out of the farm.

Unperturbed, Tunkrox stumbled out of the room, following his new captain.

"The cage can wait," the *dimo* growled, flipping me to face him.

Snapping out of the stupor, I punched him in the jaw. The blow didn't seem to affect him, but definitely hurt my knuckles.

He smirked.

"Crux said to lock her up." The *kreer* bounced on the balls of his feet by the entrance to the farm.

"I will," the *dimo* growled, pressing himself against me. "In a minute…"

Glancing out into the corridor then back at the *dimo* assaulting me, the *kreer* seemed to be torn between joining in the fun with the *dimo* or running to rat him out to Crux.

Finally, the fear of the new captain must have won, as the *kreer* ran out the way Crux had left.

Trapping my legs between his, the *dimo* gripped my waist with the two short arms he had growing from each side of his abdomen. He then caught my wrists with the second pair of hands of the arms that grew from his shoulders.

"Now what are you going to do?" He sneered, licking his lips with a wide, meaty tongue, the centipede's body fluids still glistening on his face.

"I guess I'll just let you have me," I said, trying hard not to grimace in revulsion. "If you're good to me, I can be good to you, too."

"I don't need you to be *good*." He dragged his tongue along the side of my face. The stale stench of alcohol assaulted my nostrils. "I don't even care if you're alive." He guffawed as if he'd just made a funny joke.

"Oh, but you don't know how much more fun I can be alive," I attempted a flirtatious murmur, though it came out more like a strangled croak, as terror pressed the air out of my chest. "Just let me use one hand." I wiggled the fingers of my right hand, playfully. "And I'll show you."

"Just one?"

"Mhm." I nodded, biting my lower lip seductively.

He released his grip on my wrist. "If you try anything funny, I'll make sure it hurts more when I fuck you," he warned.

"Don't worry." I brought my hand up to his cheek. "There is definitely nothing *funny* about this."

Hard plating covered the *dimo's* skull and most of his face. He had no eyelids, his eyes mere slits under the thick brow ridge. His lips seemed just as hard as the rest of him.

"Shove your tongue down my throat," I moaned breathily, trailing the back of my hand down his jaw line.

With an intrigued growl, he stuck his thick tongue out. It descended toward my mouth.

Pressing the small protrusion on Vrateus's ring, I released the sharp needle and stabbed his tongue with it.

He roared in pain then slapped me across my face with his free hand. My head slammed into a cage bar. The blow rang through my head, disorienting me for a moment.

"I want you dead, after all," he snarled, putting his huge hands around my neck.

His enormous body suddenly shuddered. The hands choking me relaxed, allowing me to twist my neck free from his grip.

With gurgling noises coming from his mouth, he collapsed at my feet, thrashing in convulsions.

The *dimo's* tongue had quickly swollen to the size of my forearm, completely blocking his mouth. A pair of his hands clawed at his throat as he struggled for air, the other pair scratching at his chest.

"What did you do?" the *kreer* yelled from the entrance.

He was followed by a group of others. Crux might have sent them to make sure the *dimo* complied with his order of locking me up.

"Get her! Now!"

All of them rushed me.

Jumping over the *dimo's* writhing body, I dashed back to the waste sorting room—there was nowhere else to run.

Swiping my gun off the floor, I shot at the two males who came the closest.

Spinning on my heel, I climbed up the garbage pile, back to the chute. The belt inside moved down when I needed to go up. I'd have to climb up the walls inside the tunnel, careful to stay off the belt. It wouldn't be easy, but I had no other choice.

"Get her!" Someone shouted drunkenly behind me. My stomach dropped with dread. My heart beat so fast, it was hard to breathe.

More of them rushed in.

Frantically, I scrambled into the tunnel. Bracing my boots and my arms against the wall, I climbed up.

Screams and growls reverberated through the room behind me. Then, the sounds of clawing and slamming at the wall began.

Someone must have yanked at the belt with enough force to rip it because it slackened then started moving much faster. The males were pulling it out of the tunnel, probably hoping to get me out this way. They would succeed at that, too, if my arms or feet slipped, and I fell onto the belt.

I clung harder to the walls, afraid to think about what would happen if I fell. The shoulder that the centipede had mauled ached. The mandibles of the creature hadn't been able to pierce through the reinforced material of my suit, but it still hurt.

Something wrapped around my thigh—one of the long, segmented tails of a *kreer*. My heart leaped into my throat. Shoving the loose belt aside, I propped my hand on the floor of the tunnel, then used the other hand to get the knife out of the sheath on my belt.

"Get off me," I hissed through my teeth, slicing the tail off my thigh.

A screeching sound of pain came from outside of the tunnel as the tail limply fell away from me. Clenching the knife between my teeth, I kept moving up the tunnel, eager to get out of reach of all their tails, feelers, tentacles, and other appendages.

My arms and legs shook uncontrollably when I finally came upon the loose piece of paneling in the wall, up the corridor from my old room. There was no way I could make it all the way to the garden by crawling up the tunnel like this. Making sure there was no one around, I climbed out into the corridor, instead.

Like a woman possessed, I ran back to the gardens, and from there, to the small room behind the library.

Chapter 22

MY HEART POUNDED HARD when I made it back to the room. Disappointment, worry, and fear filled me at finding it empty.

Vrateus wasn't there.

From the few words exchanged between Crux and the others, I understood that Vrateus had been captured and escaped. The question remained—had he kept his freedom or had he been re-captured?

Part of me wished I'd immediately run back out there in search of him. The other part held me back out of caution. I was much more useful to Vrateus free and alive, than captured and potentially dead or used as a pawn by his enemies.

Pacing the tiny space, I listened to every small noise while trying to decide what to do next.

A screeching noise outside the wall shared with the library startled me. Sparks flew, and a line formed in the paneling, with melting plastic dripping on each side. Someone was cutting through the wall from the outside.

I darted for the tunnel to hide.

"Svetlana." Vrateus kicked in the piece of the wall he had just cut out.

"You!" Relief spread through me, making me weak in the knees.

He tossed the cutting tool aside and shoved a shelf in the library over, to cover the opening he'd just made.

I threw myself at him, and he caught me in his arms.

"Why cut the wall?" I asked, between the frantic, messy kisses I showered his face with. "Why didn't you use the tunnel?"

"I couldn't get to that section of the corridor," he replied, looking somewhat stunned by my wild affection. "Someone was there, I didn't want to lead them to the tunnel."

"You're alive. Are you okay? I can't believe you're free." I grabbed his shoulders, touched his neck then cupped his face, all the while kissing him wherever my lips would land. "I was so scared for you. What happened?" I slid my hands inside his shirt, needing to feel more of him. "They caught you?"

"Blocked me off, in a dead-end hallway..." He walked me backwards until my back pressed against the opposite wall. "They barricaded me in. I used the laser of the gun to cut through the wall paneling and escaped in the gap behind it. You..." Holding me tight, he blinked and smiled as I kept showering him with kisses. "Did you miss me?"

Missed him? That was the understatement of the century.

Taking his face between my palms, I stared into his bright eyes.

"Vrateus. You are my treasure too, you know? You turned out to be the best surprise of the Anomaly, and I can't let you go."

With a groan, he pressed his body to mine. Digging my fingers into his back, I drew him even closer.

His kiss was hot and frantic. I yanked my bodysuit open, wishing to climb out of it completely. I yearned to feel all of him with every inch of my skin.

We had no time, and it was the wrong place. So much about this situation might be wrong, but I didn't care. Being with him felt right.

He was here, with me, and that was all that mattered.

The glide of his hands over my skin filled me with life. I yanked at the waistband of his pants, and he opened the fasteners for me.

Sliding my hand in, I found his hot, straining erection. Under my fingers, thick grooves swelled and pulsed along his shaft. He hissed under his breath as I stroked the ridges.

"Does it hurt?"

"No, my treasure," he rasped. "But it's a different kind of torture." He lifted my leg to his hip, sliding his hand inside my panties. "There is no way I can stop this now."

"Don't," I replied breathlessly. "Please, don't stop."

I needed this badly. The adrenaline still coursed high inside me. The lingering fear of losing him urged me closer to him. I rocked my hips against his hand between my legs, letting the rush of desire wash away the worry and fear.

"Let me see you," he demanded, leaning back.

One hand on my neck, the other rubbing between my legs, he kept his gaze on my face. I stared back at him, losing myself in the vivid orange of his eyes, until the tide of approaching orgasm made me drop my eyelids.

"Oh, I want you...Vrateus," I panted.

Before the pleasure crested, he entered me, sliding in firmly, in one smooth thrust.

A shudder rolled through his body, resonating through me with another wave of sweet heat.

"Better than I could've ever imagined," he groaned.

His arms pressed into the wall above my head, he moved his hips slowly. The thick ridges on his shaft tugged at my opening, pulsing through my core with pleasure.

I moaned, rolling my head along the wall. My temple touched his arm, and I sensed his body tremble.

"Let it go, honey," I whispered. "Don't hold back."

Even in the frenzy of passion, I trusted him not to hurt me more than I would enjoy.

With a deep growl, he shifted his hand behind my head, grabbing my ponytail. Hiking my leg higher, he brought us closer, plunging deeper.

I slid my hands behind his neck, gripping the fur on his nape. He drew in a sharp breath as my hands fisted tight. A guttural moan came from deep inside his throat.

His thrusts grew faster, more urgent, desperate.

The achy pressure building up inside me threatened to explode any minute.

Yanking my ponytail back, he latched onto the side of my neck, his teeth scraping my skin, without breaking it. The brief pain of his bite skittered with pleasure down to my chest and lower belly, setting off an explosive orgasm.

With a muffled, tortured growl against my neck, he came, taking me with him. Ecstasy rocked me in swells as I clung to him, letting the pleasure consume me.

Our bodies fused together, we remained at the wall, coming down from our climax together.

"You're mine," he murmured into my hair. "I want all of you, Svetlana. Just for me, alone."

"Yours," I echoed, feeling it in the deepest places of my heart.

"Every moan of yours is mine." He licked over the bite on my neck, then hugged me closer, kissing the side of my face. "I'm not sharing your pleasure with anyone else ever again. I'm keeping you all to myself. I don't know how I'll do it, but I *will* make it happen."

VRATEUS GAVE ME A LONG, penetrating stare.

"You're coming with me?" He obviously struggled with the idea of me going out in the open.

Since Crux had been unwilling to negotiate, Vrateus was now going to openly challenge him to a fight.

"Well, I have gone out on my own once already, searching for you." True to my word to share everything with him, I'd told him about my trip to the waste processing room. I'd tried not to get into the gruesome details, but Vrateus was still horrified. "Instead of sitting here alone, dying with worry, I'd rather be out there with you."

"You almost got caught."

"So did you."

His expression grim, he drew in some air to argue with me.

"Listen," I didn't give him the chance to respond. "They caught you unawares this morning. As smart and strong as you are, you don't have a pair of eyes in the back of your head. You could use someone to watch your back. You said you trust me, let me help you." He hesitated, and I added hurriedly, "I can't sit here not knowing if you're dead or alive. I'm armed. I've proven I can handle myself. Let me come with you, please."

I knew Vrateus would rather keep me in hiding while he did everything on his own. A few days ago, I would have probably preferred to wait it out, too. The mess hall was not my favorite place to visit.

As strong as Vrateus had always been, however, I'd also witnessed his vulnerabilities. In the past couple of days, he had been nearly poisoned to death then almost decapitated by his own crew. He needed me, and I needed to be with him.

I closed the distance between us, circling his waist with my arms.

"What if someone finds me hiding here while you're gone? Can't you see?" I rubbed his nose with mine. "Together we're stronger than apart."

His chest heaved with a long breath.

"Stay close." He tightened his arms around me. "Do not let anyone come between us. And if you have to shoot, aim to kill."

"Don't worry about me." I exhaled in relief, glad he was giving in and we didn't have to part again. "Focus on what you need to do. I'll take care of myself."

He moved his hands over the belts and holsters strapped to my body, inspecting all my weapons.

"Don't let anyone close." He stuffed a spare power cell for my gun into my boot.

"I won't."

"There are benefits to keeping you with me, considering the circumstances." He nodded somberly, as if trying to convince himself. "It's best to stay together."

He shoved aside the shelf unit in front of the gap leading to the library, then turned back to me quickly. His hand on the back of my head, he kissed me, fast and passionate.

"Be safe." He leaned his forehead against mine.

"Good luck," I whispered, smiling as encouragingly as I could manage.

Chapter 23

I'D PROMISED TO WATCH his back.

Now, as we walked down the corridor, I paid close attention to our surroundings. We weren't holding hands, keeping them free for weapons. I held my gun in my right hand and a knife in my left. Vrateus had both of his guns out of their arm holsters and in his hands.

The stench of decomposing bodies hit my nostrils as we approached the doors to my room. The dead aliens that Vrateus and I had killed yesterday lay in the same positions we'd left them. No one had bothered to dispose of them, though some bodies showed clear signs of cannibalism.

Vrateus's jaw muscles clenched as he made his way around the corpses. I followed less than a foot behind him, glancing over my shoulder once again.

As we turned around the bend in the wall, the entrance to the mess hall came into view.

It was much quieter here than I remembered. Some males lay by the wall in the corridor, impossible to tell whether they were alive or dead.

One got up to his feet at the sight of us.

"You again..." he gaped at Vrateus, quickly giving a sign to someone inside the mess hall.

More crew members rose from the floor, joined by a few rushing out to join them. Armed with long, jagged pieces of metal, they menacingly moved our way.

"Keep back, or I'll shoot," Vrateus warned, raising his weapons.

Snarling—their teeth bared, jaws and mandibles snapping—they kept advancing on us.

Vrateus opened fire. I jumped aside, ducking from a piece of metal hurled my way. The sharp edge caught my upper arm. Thankfully, the material of my suit held. The blow hurt but left no cut.

I bit my lip, swallowing the cry of pain, afraid it would divert Vrateus's attention to me. He couldn't afford to be distracted right now.

Two aliens snuck up behind us somehow, rushing us from the back. I aimed and shot quickly, leaving neither of them a chance to throw the long rods they wielded.

"Are you all right?" Vrateus asked over his shoulder, his attention on the entrance to the mess hall.

"I'm fine. Let's go."

Holding both guns up, he moved forward. A few of the males piled by the wall stirred.

"Down," Vrateus ordered, pointing one of his guns in their direction.

Either realizing the threat or out of the habit of obeying his authoritative tone, they froze.

He entered the mess hall. Keeping my gun pointed at those in the corridor, I quickly glanced around him and into the hall.

The room looked like an explosion had taken place. Every piece of furniture had been upturned. Debris, spilled wine, and remnants of food littered the floor, along with puddles of vomit and who knew what else.

The aliens lay and sat everywhere, some still chewing or drinking, others already motionless. A few of the climbing species clung to the walls at various heights.

A huge pile of scrap metal had been erected in the center with a chair placed on the very top of it. Crux reclined in his makeshift throne with the other *errocks* lounging below him. Leaning against the pile, Wyck was chewing on what appeared to be a *vasai* leg. Chained to him, Lesh lay at his feet. All three of his heads were gnawing on a long bone.

Everyone who was still alert snapped to attention as Vrateus entered.

"What a mess you've made, crew." He curled his lip in disapproval. "It's disgusting. You've been without your captain for barely a day and look at this place!"

A few of them shifted uneasily, glancing around the trashed mess hall.

"They have a new captain." Crux rose to his feet.

Due to his massive size, he looked impressive, towering over the room from the height of the metal junk pyramid.

There was no graceful way to climb down it, though. Crux scrambled to the ground, sliding and tripping over his feet. Once on the floor, he stood tall again, his fists on his hips.

"Great to see you here," he smirked. "Now, you'll finally be executed. The female is mine, as she should've been all along."

Other *errocks* moved closer, flanking their leader. The rest of the crew, however, stayed where they were, staring with confusion at the two men who both claimed the title of the captain.

"Relinquish your claim to my position," Vrateus said calmly. "Or deal with the consequences."

"I'm *relinquishing* nothing!" Crux spat on the floor. "Hey boys!" he shouted, "Grab this phoney. As your captain, I give you my permission to do with him as you please." He shifted his weight to another foot. "And bring the girl here. Will you?"

Everyone in the room seemed to freeze for a moment. Back to back with Vrateus, I moved my gun in a slow arch, gauging where the next attack would come from.

One of the *kreers* let go off the wall. With a high-pitched wail, he grabbed a loose cable dangling from the ceiling and swung our way.

I shot. The *kreer* crashed to the floor, blood trickling out of the smoldering wound in his chest.

"You're good?" Vrateus asked me, keeping his gaze on Crux.

"Fine," I bit out, forcing myself to relax my grip on my weapons, since my hands had started to cramp and shake with tension.

He addressed his rival, "You can't just proclaim yourself the captain, Crux."

"Well, *you* did."

"Right. After I'd killed Raex in an honest fight. I didn't *poison* him in secret, like a coward." He swept the room with his gaze, raising his voice to get the attention of anyone who could still focus on what was happening. "You have to earn the title by winning it."

"Do you want to fight me?" Crux folded his arms over his chest.

"Yes."

"Well, you're too late, I'm already the captain."

It surprised me that Crux wouldn't jump at the chance to fight. He seemed to be the one who would welcome any opportunity for aggression. I wondered if he felt intimidated by Vrateus, despite the *errock's* obvious size advantage.

"You're not." Vrateus shook his head. "I'm still here. And I challenge you to fight for the title if you want to keep it." He spread his arms wide, slowly turning around the room. "What say you, the dwellers of the Dark Anomaly? Do you want to watch me fight Crux for the chance to be your leader once again?"

Crux twitched uneasily.

"He'd force you to work again!" he yelled quickly. "He'd lock up the wine and make you fight under his rules. He'd forbid you to eat whatever and whoever you want!"

He said all of that as if those were all bad things. How could forbidding them from eating each other be viewed as a negative?

It boggled my mind.

"I will bring order and discipline back," Vrateus said, loud enough for his voice to carry across the entire room. "With me, you will never have to worry about running out of food or wine. We'll always have lights on and enough oxygen to breathe. If you follow my rules, you will not have to fear for your life or your safety."

Now, *these* promises sounded appealing to me. The males, however, didn't jump at his words. They weren't rallying behind Crux either, which was better than nothing.

"Do you want to see a fight?" Vrateus knew his people better than I did, for they all perked up at that opportunity. Even some of those who had appeared to be corpses piled up by the walls stirred, coming to life. "No rules. The winner becomes the one true captain, with no further challenges from the loser."

This sounded really good if Vrateus won. If he lost, however…I dreaded to think what it would mean for him. For us.

A swell of approving screams and roars rolled from wall to wall. Everyone seemed to be eager to watch a brutal battle with no rules.

I kept my guard up, making sure no one would jump in, in their excitement. Everyone seemed impatient for the fight to start—many might want to join in themselves.

"No weapons." Crux moved into the center of the room, finally accepting the challenge. "I'll rip you to pieces with my bare hands."

I stepped closer to a wall.

"No weapons." Vrateus nodded, backing up to me. Tearing his shirt off over his head, he unbuckled the gun holsters from his thighs and forearms then the dagger's sheath from his chest, tossing them all on the floor at my feet.

With a brief encouraging smile for me, he walked to the center of the room. Broad-shouldered and bronze-skinned, he moved with grace and efficiency.

This was the first time I'd seen Vrateus without his shirt.

The wide strip of white fur peppered with gray and black on his head and nape continued down between his shoulder blades, thinning into a narrow trail along his spine that disappeared into his pants. The fur on his forearms tapered at his elbows, leaving his upper arms and shoulders bare from it.

Three long, rugged scars ran across his left side, parallel to each other. They must have been left by a set of claws some time ago. A crescent of small round scars on his right shoulder could have been from fangs and teeth.

Strangely, seeing the scars on his body gave me some encouragement. They were a reminder that Vrateus was a survivor. He had fought for his life ever since he was a little boy. I had to trust his skills and his abilities.

Still, my heart ached at the sight of him next to the massive form of Crux when they stood facing each other. Whereas Vrateus looked strong and tall, wired with thick ropes of well-defined muscles, Crux was a mountain of hard flesh, capable of crushing a person to death under one of his enormous fists.

"You're dead, *captain*." Crux smirked. "As will be the female when I'm done with her."

"We'll see—"

Crux didn't let him finish, rushing him without waiting for the signal to start.

No rules.

I tightened my grip on the gun, my hands slick with sweat.

Leaping aside, Vrateus narrowly escaped being knocked off his feet by Crux. Leaner than the *errock*, Vrateus was faster on his feet, too. Though Crux still showed some unexpected agility for his size. He landed a blow on Vrateus's shoulder, making him stagger back several paces.

I gasped, my heart speeding up with worry. My attention on the fight, I nearly missed a *kreer* creeping my way along the wall. His hands and feet splayed flat on the surface for a better grip, he snaked one skinny tail my way. A smirk slanted his lipless mouth, drool dripping to the floor from both corners of it.

"Back off." I pointed my gun at him, stepping over the pile of weapons Vrateus had left for me to guard. One of the *kreer's* tails twitched that way, too, and I fired, shooting it off.

He wailed, scurrying away and up the wall. No blood dripped from the stump of his tail, the small wound fully cauterized by the laser blast.

With a loud roar, Crux launched at Vrateus who rolled out of his way at the last second. Following the momentum, Crux slammed into the wall, crashing into the *kreer* who'd tried to attack me.

Enraged by his failure, the *errock* pivoted on his heel, searching for Vrateus with blood-shot eyes.

The night of drinking obviously slowed his movements. I was glad now that Vrateus had been wise enough to get some rest. *His* moves remained quick and efficient.

Lowering himself into a crouch, his tail swaying to aid his balance, Vrateus met Crux's next attack with a well-placed kick to the groin.

No rules. It worked both ways.

Howling in pain, Crux doubled over, both hands pressed between his legs.

Not giving him a chance to recover, Vrateus leaped onto the *errock's* back, hooking his arm around Crux's massive neck.

The *errock* growled. Clawing at Vrateus's arm, he arched his back, attempting to toss him off. Vrateus grabbed his wrist, squeezing his arm harder and crushing the *errock's* windpipe.

Crux's face turned deep burgundy. The veins in his forehead bulged as if ready to burst. His legs shook. With a strangled grunt, he collapsed to his side, crushing Vrateus's leg under his bulk.

A wave of shouts, growls, and roars rolled throughout the room. It was impossible to tell if it was the noise of approval or aggression. Either way, the crowd obviously appreciated the fight, whether or not they cared about its outcome.

Eyes glistening with aggression, a *dimo* moved toward Vrateus and Crux as they wrestled on the floor. He obviously intended to join in the violence.

"Back!" I yelled at him, raising my gun.

He paid me no attention. Cracking his knuckles and licking his lips, he hungrily eyed the fight.

"I said *back*!" I yelled louder. A surge of adrenaline rushed through me with heat and cold.

Getting no reaction from him, I pulled the trigger. The laser blast seared through the plated layer on the *dimo's* shoulder.

Turning his attention to me, his eyes glowing red with rage, the male rushed my way.

"Stay back," I gritted through my teeth, aiming at his face where his plated armour was thinner.

He didn't slow down, and I pulled the trigger again.

The laser blast burned through his eye, incredibly, hardly slowing his advancement on me. I kept pressing on the trigger, holding the gun steady until the ray worked its way through the *dimo's* brain and he crashed to the floor.

"Anyone else?" I pointed my gun at the room, trying hard to stop my hands from shaking. Everything inside me vibrated with tension. No matter how many I'd killed, it didn't seem to get easier.

Thankfully, not that many of those present were paying attention to me, the focus of most was on Crux and Vrateus.

Holding his opponent in the headlock, Vrateus kept squeezing.

The *errock's* eyes finally closed, and he croaked, "Mercy..."

Vrateus released Crux from his grip, freeing his leg then climbing to his feet.

My heart fluttered with relief and gratitude at seeing him standing tall.

Victorious.

He faced his crew.

"I am your one true captain," he said, slowly moving his gaze across the room. "You live under *my* rules, or you don't live at all."

One thing this bunch of criminals and degenerates seemed to understand better than anything was the pure power of dominance.

Vrateus had no weapons on him. They could rush him, crush him, destroy him—had they had the will to act together. Instead, they remained where they were, held in place by the authority in his voice. Submitting to the winner of the fight.

He knew his people well. He had already made them submit once before. And he had just done it again.

"Now, clean up this mess." He tipped his chin at the garbage littering the floor. "And bring me the key to the wine storage, this instant."

Shifting from their position and peeling off the walls, the crew moved to obey their captain's orders.

Grabbing the holsters with his weapons off the floor, I stepped closer.

Vrateus stretched his arm my way.

"Come here. How are you?" He pulled me in for a firm hug.

"Relieved that we're both still alive." I smiled.

Crux groaned on the floor, rolling to his belly.

Vrateus released me from his embrace, watching the *errock* gather his arms and legs under him.

"What are you going to do with him?" I asked, taking a step back, just in case.

"Accept me as your captain," Vrateus demanded from the *errock*. "Or die."

Crux rose to one knee, rubbing his neck.

"You are my captain." He scowled, tossing Vrateus a glare from under his thick brow ridge.

"You can't let him live," I said to Vrateus, quietly.

A few weeks ago, I would not have believed myself capable of this kind of bloodthirsty ruthlessness, but things had changed. The time I'd spent on the Anomaly had changed me, too.

Keeping Crux alive would be like having a knife aimed at Vrateus's throat. Having been publicly humiliated by his defeat, Crux would strike again. I had no doubt about that.

"He asked for mercy, I have to grant it to him," Vrateus objected, adding, "How can I demand from others to respect my laws if I don't follow them myself?"

He then addressed the room again, "Crux will be whipped for usurping my power. A hundred lashes. Tomorrow morning. He is no longer my second in command." He gestured my way, unexpectedly. "Svetlana is."

The combined roar of everyone thundered through the room. The males paused in their tasks for a moment, eyeing me—their jaws dropped, mandibles slackened, mouths hanging open. Astonished, I turned around to face Vrateus.

"The fuck she is!" With a filthy curse, Crux slammed into me from behind. His meaty arm around my chest, he squeezed my neck with his other hand. "You'll do as I say, or I'll snap her neck in half."

"Don't hurt her!" Vrateus raised his hands, pure horror flashing through his eyes.

My arms pressed to my body, my feet lifted off the floor as Crux crushed me with his brute strength. I couldn't even draw a breath, there was no room for my chest to expand.

The sensation of the gun handle in my hand registered with me.

I bent my arm, wedging the barrel between my back and Crux's front. I angled it at his belly, then pressed the trigger.

He howled in pain. His arms flexed, squeezing the last drops of air out of my lungs, then fell off me. The massive *errock* crashed to the floor at my feet, and I leaped away from him in horror.

"Svetlana!" Vrateus caught me in his arms.

"I broke your rules," I rasped, my throat sore and closing in on itself. Wrapped in Vrateus's embrace, I glanced back at the disemboweled Crux, his legs contracting with their last spasms. "I killed the loser of the fight."

"It wasn't your fight." Vrateus kissed my face, stroking my hair.

He was wrong.

Every fight involving him was now mine, too. Anyone who threatened Vrateus was a direct threat to me. I had a feeling this was not our last fight, either. But at least, there were two of us.

From now on, we would fight all our battles together.

And together we were twice as strong.

His arm wrapped tightly around my shoulders, Vrateus addressed his crew again, "Anyone who dares to touch her again will be shot on the spot. Svetlana has my permission to carry weapons." He met my eyes. "Because she is the only one whom I trust. Completely."

Chapter 24

JUSTICE ON THE DARK Anomaly was swift.

Vrateus ordered some whippings as punishment for disobedience. Those were to be carried out the following morning.

Considering the sorry state of the habitable sector, most punishments ended up being an increased amount of labor for everyone.

Vrateus questioned Tunkrox, the wiry alien who'd handed him the canteen with the poisoned wine. The male confessed that he stole some *fuhnid* mushrooms from the gardens while Crux was distracting Malahki.

Together, they then squeezed the juice and mixed it with wine. Apparently, Crux had promised Tunkrox an unlimited supply of berry wine for the job. And judging by the state and appearance of Tunkrox, the *errock* had fulfilled that promise.

The Tunkrox's execution was ordered for the very next day.

"How about the *errocks*?" I asked Vrateus when we finally returned to his room for a few hours of sleep later that night.

"They'll be whipped," he replied, taking off his clothes then removing all his weapons.

"Do you still want to keep them as your personal guard?"

"They have been very effective in that role."

"*Have been*." I made a face. "Until they betrayed you. What if they do it again?"

"The better reason to have them close—easier to keep an eye on them."

"So, you want them to resume their positions?"

"Yes. Wyck will be their lead now. I'll announce it tomorrow." He crawled under the covers of his narrow bed and joined me.

I scooted aside, to give him space, but he drew me closer.

"Are you sure about Wyck?" I thought back to the moment I caught the young *errock's* glare after I had shot Crux. Wyck's bright, yellow eyes were full of undiluted hatred for me. I had no illusions I'd made a mortal enemy of him by killing one of his kind.

The better reason to have him close.

"All right. Wyck it is then." I drew in a deep breath. "Tomorrow will be a long day."

"Try to get some sleep." Vrateus kissed my forehead.

The metal frame of his bed cut into my side, and I made a mental note to have the bed from my room moved into his. It was much wider and would be more comfortable for the two of us.

A lot of things still needed to be done, big and small. I remembered how exhausted Vrateus always seemed to be before. Now, I was there, to share the burden and the responsibility of running the Dark Anomaly with him.

And together, we were stronger.

THE WHIPPINGS ALL TOOK place in the mess hall. Vrateus wanted the entire population present to witness the punishments.

He'd ordered the *errocks* to flog each other. They growled and glared with hatred at those whipping them. That was why Vrateus did it in the first place. By pitting *errocks* against each other, he ensured they wouldn't be as quick to unite against him any time soon.

Maybe, his crew learned their lesson while watching the red welts swell on their comrades' backs after each blow of the whip. Or maybe, they mostly enjoyed another display of violence.

Either way, the punishment had been served.

Afterwards, we all moved to the airlock across from the storage room with the spacesuits. Two of the *errocks* brought Tunkrox out from his holding cell.

"I did it!" he yelled, kicking his long legs out, lashing with his thin tail, and thrashing in the *errocks'* grip. "I drank the wine, ate the mushrooms, and chewed on the flowers... And I'll do it all again!"

"Do you understand why you're being executed?" Vrateus asked at the entrance to the airlock.

I recited the charges, finishing with, "Under the law of the Captain of the Dark Anomaly."

"Captain?" Tunkrox turned to Vrateus with a sly smile. "Fuck you, Captain!" He broke into a series of uncontrollable giggles that turned to loud hiccups after a while. "We don't need a captain here. We need more wine!"

Vrateus gave the signal to proceed, and the *errocks* shoved Tunkrox into the airlock, closing the door behind him. The lanky alien swayed on his feet, glancing over his shoulder once. Then the outer door opened, blowing him out into open space.

I watched the chitin on Tunkrox's body crack and tear as his flesh underneath expanded in the vacuum of space. What was left of him was strewn over the wreckage of the crashed ships. I felt only the slightest tug of sympathy. The predominant feeling was that of relief that with his death there was one less threat to Vrateus and me.

Vrateus's words from long ago rose in my memory, *"Around here, there is no law but mine."*

The Federation had no power on the Dark Anomaly. Intergalactic laws did not exist here. The Federation Forces didn't matter.

Around here, everything was different.

Apparently, I was now different, too.

Chapter 25

I woke up in my old bed that had been moved to Vrateus's room, replacing his narrow metal one. The sound of running water told me he must be in the shower.

It had been a month since Vrateus fought Crux and won. Twenty-five years had passed on Earth. Combined with the time I had spent here before that, it had been nearly half a century since I'd left that world. Every day added another ten months to that time.

Chances were that almost everyone I'd ever known as adults was already dead. That thought didn't feel as crushingly devastating as it had a few weeks ago.

Oddly, knowing that probably no one alive would know about me made me miss life on Earth less. I still dreamed I was running on the grass or swimming in the ocean, now and then. But those were the same dreams I'd had back on the space station during my mission.

I'd said goodbye to Earth long before I crashed on the Dark Anomaly.

By choosing a career in space exploration, I knew I wouldn't be spending much time on the ground for the rest of my life. Just like my parents before me, I had willingly dedicated my life to working off planet, giving up on personal relationships and the potential for a family.

With Vrateus, I had unexpectedly gained some of that back.

He was closer to me than anyone I'd ever had in my life. Our relationship was more intimate—physically and emotionally—than I'd ever had with anyone else.

Stretching under the soft, puffy covers, I rubbed the remnants of sleep out of my eyes.

"There you are." I smiled at Vrateus as he walked out of the bathroom naked, drying himself off with a towel.

I couldn't leave the Dark Anomaly, but I'd gained a different kind of freedom here. I was free to spend the rest of my life with the man I loved. Something my parents never had. Something I'd never thought I could do, either.

"Morning." The fur on his head was still soaking wet, water dripping from the large, soggy curl over his forehead.

"Come here." I sat up, patting the mattress next to me.

When he sat down, I took the towel from his hands, drying his head and shoulders for him. The damp fur stood up in spikes when I finished, and I smoothed it with my hands the best I could.

He smiled at me while I arranged the curly wave over his forehead. The luxurious softness of his fur clashed with the rest of this man who seemed to be made entirely of hard planes and sharp edges.

"Here you go." I fluffed it up a bit, whipping it into its usual shape. "Looks good." I placed a kiss on the corner of his smiling mouth. "Devastatingly handsome. Like always."

"How about this?" He swung his soggy tail into my hands.

"You want me to groom *all* of you?" I tilted my head, raising an eyebrow.

"Could you?" His smile grew teasing. Mischief twinkled in his eyes, brightening their burnt-orange color.

"Well..." I pretended to be annoyed but wrung the water out of his tail with the towel. "If you insist."

He smiled wider. I enjoyed touching him, and I knew he treasured it. Deprived of any physical contact most of his life, he soaked in my attention like a sponge.

From the base of his tail, I moved the towel to his chest, trailing it down his chiseled abs and lower.

The grin slipped from his face as my fingers brushed by his erection. It immediately jumped from half-mast to fully erect.

"Now what?" I glanced up at his face.

He lifted an eyebrow at me, expectantly.

Dropping the towel, I stroked him with my hands. The dark, hard ridges swelled along his shaft, making me tingle with anticipation, for I knew how tantalisingly sweet they rubbed when he was inside me.

"Now, it's my turn to do some *grooming*," he growled, rolling me onto my back. "Only, I'll do it with my mouth."

He dragged his long tongue between my legs, and I rolled my head on the pillow, moaning deep in my throat. Heat flooded me, prickling my skin with pleasure and making my toes curl.

We had things to do this morning. I knew we did. Only I could no longer remember what they were. Nothing seemed to matter.

Even as an inexperienced virgin, Vrateus had been able to make me feel things no one else ever could. Now, after a month of eagerly learning everything about my body, he masterfully played it like a well-tuned instrument.

Easing out his claws, he lightly scraped along the skin of my thighs then up my sides to my breasts. I moaned louder as he found my nipples, squeezing them lightly between his fingers.

He swirled his tongue inside me, and my hips jerked as pleasure rushed through me.

Promptly sliding up my body, he fitted himself between my thighs. I opened my legs wider, lifting my hips to meet him as he fitted himself at my opening then slipped inside.

"It's like coming home, Svetlana..." he murmured in my ear, starting to move. "Every. Single. Time."

I was his home now, and he was mine.

Hugging him closer, I let the pleasure roll through me with his every thrust.

After a few pumps, he flipped me to my stomach. I bent my knees, lifting my hips up for him, and he entered me again, from behind this time.

The ridges along his length tugged and rubbed all the right places inside me. The soft fur of his tail brushed around my thigh. Then the tip slid between my legs, finding my most sensitive spot.

Vrateus growled, gripping a handful of hair on the back of my head. The sting at the roots spread pleasure along my scalp and the rest of my body, making me groan in delight.

He thrust harder. The growls of his pleasure mingled with my loud moans. The intensity was building up as he pumped his hips with increasing speed and ferocity.

"Oh, yes..." I breathed out as the orgasm exploded through every cell of my body.

Throwing his head back, he growled through his clenched teeth as his release rocked us both.

When he collapsed next to me, I held him close. Raking my fingers through his fur, I whispered, "We're going to build a good life here, Vrateus."

At that moment, I truly believed that it was possible. We had found our kind of happiness on the Dark Anomaly. As long as we stayed together, everything was within our reach.

That was how he made me feel—happy, even in the middle of hell.

IN THE AFTERNOON, VRATEUS took me out to the surface of the Dark Anomaly. He needed to check the power supply panels. They converted the Anomaly's lights into energy, which was used to power the life inside it. One of them seemed to be malfunctioning, possibly requiring some repairs.

Dressed in spacesuits, we exited through the airlock, then walked along the surface of the giant disk, just a few feet away from the edge. Vrateus checked the connection of each panel, while I fell behind.

Stopping between two power panels, I took out the two polished metal balls I'd made from some parts collected from my ship.

I made sure that the camera on my helmet was on and that it was connected to the computer on my arm. Lowering myself into a crouch, I set one ball on the surface. With the tool I'd brought with me, I shot the ball to roll toward the center of the Anomaly with a predetermined speed. It bounced and hopped over the uneven surface, rolling to a complete stop about a hundred feet away from me.

The gravity along the circumference of the disk seemed to be the same as it was inside.

I glanced up, toward the bulging center of the Anomaly. Far in the distance, it rose from the disk as a smooth, perfectly rounded dome the size of a mountain, completely black. Not even the vivid dancing lights around us reflected in its hemisphere.

Setting the second ball on the ground, I shot it to follow the exact trajectory of the first one, with a higher velocity. The second ball rolled faster, slamming into the first one and knocking it forward.

Brought back into motion, the first ball rolled toward the center, slowing down again.

When it reached a certain point, however, the speed of the first ball increased again. Speeding up, it rolled faster and faster, until the shiny, silver shape of it blended far in the distance with the bulging mass in the middle.

On the surface of the disk, the Anomaly pulled things to its center. I took a note never to wander past the power panels, lest I be dragged there myself.

I made sure that everything I'd just done had been recorded on the camera on my helmet. I had already inputted the exact mass and dimensions of the two balls. And the computer now calculated the speed and rate of increase in their velocity.

When I got back to the library, I would add all this data to what Vrateus and I had collected so far. I'd also add the new calculations I was planning to do.

I'd left Earth to explore the unknown. Crashing here was a tragedy. But it gave me the opportunity to be closer to the Anomaly than any human had ever been. For as long as I lived, I would study it.

I would never stop exploring.

EPILOGUE

"There is the man I love," Svetlana greeted him as soon as he entered their room.

She looked stunning. The bright, flowery dress she wore made the lights of the Anomaly behind her pale in comparison. She had always been the most beautiful thing to him.

A warm trickle of pleasure rippled down his skin at her words. This was the first time he heard the word "love" from her. Judging by the gaze she gave him—her dark eyelashes fluttering like the wings of a bird he'd only ever seen in videos—she knew what she'd said, and she meant it.

"I love you, too." He gathered her into his arms, burying his face in her hair.

She sank her fingers into the fur on the back of his neck, stroking down his spine. The pleasure of her touch flooded his groin with heat. It happened so much more often than it used to before her.

Nuzzling the side of her neck, he nibbled on her skin.

"What took you so long? It's way past dinnertime," she murmured. "I was starting to worry."

Every now and then, he still forgot about dinner, getting caught in one of the many tasks that needed to be done in order to keep life on the Dark Anomaly going.

"Sorry, I lost track of time. How are the gardens?"

"Good. The flour we made from the *laahon* grain worked out amazingly well."

The only reward for saving Vrateus from the poison that Malahki had asked for was to spend more time with Svetlana. The request puzzled Vrateus, but Malahki had explained he needed someone knowledgeable and trustworthy to help with gardening.

Svetlana had easily agreed to that, eager to learn more about plant life on the Dark Anomaly. Vrateus had spent several days with them until he was completely satisfied he could trust the *damirian* to protect Svetlana. He felt comfortable leaving them alone for a couple of hours a day.

Besides the gardening, Svetlana had also taken over meal preparation on the Anomaly, under the condition that no one except for Vrateus or Malahki would be allowed to enter the kitchen.

Taking these two tasks completely off his shoulders and helping him with many others, she'd considerably lightened his workload. Now, he even had some free time, which he always preferred to spend with her.

"Hungry?" she leaned back, smiling. "I made *pizza* for dinner." Delight sparkled in her dark eyes, bringing out the golden specks of happiness he loved seeing in them.

"*Pizza*?" he asked, confused. He wished to share in her excitement, but the translator failed to deliver a word he'd understand.

Svetlana had been gathering various bark, seeds, and roots from the garden. She then used them as ingredients while cooking different dishes and experimenting with flavors.

"Look!" She proudly gestured at the low table she had set with pretty dishes he had collected from various storage rooms for her.

A bunch of large, bright flowers stood in a jewel-encrusted carafe. Berry wine glistened blood-red in two crystal goblets.

"I have been playing with this recipe for a week now, testing different ingredients from the kitchen and the garden." Svetlana pointed at the flat disk of dough covered with black melted goo that suspiciously reminded him of tar. "It's a bit scary-looking," she admitted, with a slight frown. "But it tastes just like a real *pizza* from back home, I swear."

He must have been staring at the offensive disk a little too long, since she shifted uneasily. "If you don't like it, I have some stew from the kitchen, too.

"No. I'll try it." He drew some air in through his nostrils. "It smells delicious."

After a lifetime of eating some variation of the same dish, trying all her cooking experiments felt exciting. Even if they turned out truly inedible sometimes.

"Let's have some *pizza*." He took her in his arms again. "Just right after I do this."

He lowered his mouth to hers.

A rush of familiar calm and pleasure descended upon him as he kissed her.

Just like coming home.

"HEY, CAPTAIN! THERE'S another crash!" Valmo, one of the few *akuks* on the Dark Anomaly, panted out of breath and choking with excitement. "Nocc and Wyck are fighting over the female. And they're not following the rules!"

Immediately, Vrateus thought of Svetlana being the female in question. Wrath and terror flared in his chest, making his heart leap.

He had left her in the gardens with Malahki just a little while ago. Had something happened he'd not accounted for?

"Where are they?" He dashed out of the storage room, leaving Enkail to service the spacesuits on his own.

"On the very edge of the habitable segment, past the gardens." Valmo was running slightly behind him, struggling to catch up despite the eight pairs of legs on the wiggling bottom half of his yellow-spotted body.

The main corridor seemed endless as Vrateus rushed from one end of it to the other. His heart burned with worry, threatening to burst out of his chest.

"Malahki!" He yelled into the entrance of the gardens as he passed by. The *damirian* was nowhere to be seen, which only intensified his panic.

He rushed further.

Around the last bend in the corridor, he nearly tripped over the cutting tool left on the floor. The outer wall gaped with a freshly cut opening. A couple of his crew members stood by, peeking inside it.

"Svetlana?" he asked, shoving them out of the way.

"She returned to your room a while back," someone said.

"She did?" Vrateus turned to face the speaker, Xoqaek, one of the few *ognats* who had survived the devastating effects of berry wine the day Crux had taken over.

"Malahki said she left," Gahot, a *yourlu*, added, his tentacles splayed on one side of the opening in the wall.

She was safe.

He let the thought trickle through his mind with a calming bliss.

"Malahki? Where is it?"

"Um..." Gahot looked around, confusion spreading on his face. "It was just here..."

Vrateus glanced inside the opening, into the interior of a brightly lit ship he had not seen before.

Only now Valmo's words about the crash had fully registered with him. Then, the understanding for the reason for the fight rushed in.

An unknown human female crouched low by the far wall of the room. Lesh kept hissing, tied to a piece of wreckage nearby. Wyck stood over her, his chest heaving fast and heavy, his gaze unhinged, and his knuckles bloody.

Standing on one knee, Nocc glared at him, blood trickling out of his nose and down his face.

At least two more humans lay on the floor behind them, their heads twisted at unnatural angles. Either they had died during the crash or had been killed shortly after, but they were obviously dead now.

"What is going on here?" Vrateus climbed inside, adjusting the grip on the guns in his hands.

"This does not concern you," Nocc rasped, smearing the blood on his face with the back of his hand. "You already have a female. You can't have them all."

A familiar combination of annoyance and worry rushed over Vrateus.

Another female.

He didn't talk to her. He refused to spare her a glance. A wave of fear and resentment rose in his chest. This female was not just a threat to the barely re-established order, her mere appearance here put the relatively safe existence of Svetlana into danger all over again.

He had managed to force his crew to view Svetlana as their superior. There were no more weekly sessions in the mess hall. With the new arrival, they could easily revert to treating her as an object to relieve their sexual tension—not to mention the disturbance that was already happening.

"So, you have fought, I see." He moved his gaze from Nocc to Wyck. Judging by their positions, Wyck had won the last round. However, if Vrateus didn't stop them now, there could be many more. With the others now coming in, aggression buzzed in the air.

If he let the situation slip out of control now, many more of his crew might end up joining the dead humans on the floor.

"Wyck won?"

Wyck nodded as Nocc leaped to his feet, raising his fists.

"He is not getting her!"

"He *did* best you." Vrateus turned to the two at the entrance. Xo-qaek and Gahot had entered, with many more of his crew climbing in or poking their heads through. "Was it a fair fight?" he asked Xo-qaek and Gahot.

"Um... Sure." They nodded.

"It's not over yet!" Nocc roared.

"*I* say when the fight is over around here!" Vrateus raised his voice and his weapons. "And I'm saying this one is."

"Wyck can't have her," Enkail rumbled. The *dimo* obviously hadn't stayed behind to finish servicing the spacesuits. Vrateus made a note to discipline him later for not doing his work. "If she is the prize, then we all have to get a chance to fight for her, too!"

That was met with a loud rumbling of approval from everyone.

"No one is getting the female!" Vrateus shouted over the noise, lifting his arm to call for silence. "No one!"

Hostile glares of his crew clashed with his as he turned around the room.

"The rules will stay the same," he said firmly. "The female belongs to no one and to all of us."

"What do you mean?" The same question came from many mouths.

"She will be brought to the mess hall, weekly." The solution had worked well enough before. "You'll be getting your entertainment back!"

Svetlana had disliked the sessions in the mess hall. He had reasons to believe the new female might not be fond of them either. However, the priority was to dissipate the aggression crackling in the air.

And hopefully save some lives.

Another wave of rumbles rolled through the room. To his relief, it was thick with approval for his decision.

It occurred to him that the presence of another female on the Dark Anomaly might work to his benefit. Ever since he had discontinued the sessions in the mess hall, he had overheard plenty of comments and caught enough disgruntled glances tossed Svetlana's way. Having another female to resume the sessions would take the attention from Svetlana and ease the tension.

An unpleasant feeling scratched inside him, as if he were tossing the female to the pack of predators. And in a way, that was very much what he was about to do.

For Svetlana's peace and safety.

He would do anything for her.

"I won't be the one touching her, though," he said to his crew.

"Who will?" the crowd perked up, expectant.

Vrateus gave the new leader of the *errocks* an assessing stare. Younger than the rest of his brutal group, Wyck still shared most of the characteristics of his kind. He was just as aggressive, hot-minded, and rebellious as all the *errocks* on the Dark Anomaly. Since the death of Crux, Wyck had also shown signs of hostility toward Svetlana.

How long would a human female last in his care?

He glanced at Lesh. The ill-tempered *mahdi* had been one of several dozen of the animals, chained and caged in the cargo hold of a *yourlu* ship. It had crashed about nine years ago. All the *mahdi* had been killed and eaten within days. Some had been forced to fight each other—bloody, brutal battles instigated for entertainment. Both winners and losers ended up being butchered afterwards.

Only after Vrateus had taken the power had Wyck come to him with Lesh. He told Vrateus that he had saved the animal, hiding it in one of the side tunnels. He had fed it, trained it, kept it alive, and in return, the *mahdi* gave him his undivided loyalty.

Could Wyck's patience and kindness to the animal be translated into better treatment for the female?

There was no way to tell for sure, but Wyck was the best choice Vrateus had. Wyck had the power and the strength to defend someone in his charge. He would also have Vrateus's full support in doing so.

"As the leader of my personal guard, Wyck will have the honor of taking care of the female," he announced, loud and clear, making sure that none of the doubt he felt made it into his voice.

Nocc growled. Spitting on the floor he threw a heated glare at Vrateus, then stormed out, shoving everyone out of his way.

Vrateus added another mental note to his already longer-than-his-tail list: to watch Nocc more closely.

Wyck shuffled from foot to foot, uncertainly. *"Take care of the female"* obviously didn't make much sense to him in terms of specifics.

"Put her in Svetlana's old room. Bring her meals. Make sure no one touches her." Vrateus rubbed his face. No matter what, every new arrival was his responsibility. He was the captain, after all. He needed to make sure, though, that Wyck understood it differently, in this case. "She is fully under your protection. Do you understand? Her life and wellbeing are your responsibility."

Wyck threw a glare toward the female who sat quietly, a calculating expression on her face.

"Captain..." The *errock* shifted closer, turning his back to the rest of the crew and lowering his voice. "I don't want her."

"What?" Vrateus felt his eyebrows shoot up to his fur line. These must be the most shocking words he'd ever heard from a male on the Dark Anomaly. "Why did you just fight for her, then?"

Wyck rubbed the back of his neck, seemingly unsure about his own motives.

"I found Nocc between her legs. She shrieked and fought... He looked like he would kill her."

"So, you stopped him?"

"He was so much bigger than her. It didn't seem fair..." the *errock* mumbled. His voice trailed off, as if Wyck realized he wasn't making much sense, not enough to continue.

The little he'd said, however, only reinforced Vrateus's conviction to keep the new woman in Wyck's care.

"Keep her safe," he ordered. "If you want someone else to bring her to the mess hall instead of you, let me know by tomorrow night. You don't need to touch her yourself, but you do have to keep her well and alive. Understood?"

Wyck made a half-nod, half-shrug in reply. That would have to do.

"What about the second female?" the *errock* asked unexpectedly.

"What second female?" Vrateus replied sharply. Wyck better not be talking about Svetlana again.

"When I got here, there were two females, at first."

"Two?"

Wyck turned around, scratching his bald head in confusion. "Where did she go?"

"Xoqaek and Gahot. Have you seen another female here? Besides this one?"

Both stared at him with their mouths agape.

"Um... No, Captain."

"Just this one here."

Vrateus took a closer look at the bodies on the floor. There were actually four in total. All four appeared to be male. However, since they all wore the same pale-blue bodysuits as their female, it might be difficult to determine their gender right away.

"Could you have mistaken one of *them* for a female?" he asked Wyck. "This one seems to be as slim as she is." He pointed at one body with the toe of his boot. "Or this one. He has a rather soft, feminine face."

"Maybe..." Wyck frowned, uncertainly.

The female chose this moment to finally speak to Vrateus.

"You're the leader here," she stated, her voice shaky but firm enough considering the circumstances.

"Was there another human female on the ship?" Vrateus asked her. "Where did she go?"

She blinked.

"Another? No. Just me. I'm the only one left alive," she said, quickly. "Listen, I'm appealing to you as the leader—"

"No." Vrateus cut her off, shaking his head. "Wyck is in charge of you. Tell him anything you need." He turned on his heel, already assessing the amount of work that had to be done on this ship before he could call it a night. "Wyck, take her out of here, the rest of you..." he faced the males filling in the space. "You all will have to help me remove the equipment tonight."

"Captain!" the female snapped sharply, demanding attention.

"Listen." Wyck spoke to her directly. "What's your name?"

"I'm not talking to *you*," she bit off.

It looked like Wyck had his work cut out for him. This might be the most challenging task Vrateus had ever assigned to the young *er-rock*.

Well, they all had their share of work to do around here.

THE END

POWER

Dark Anomaly, book 2

CHAPTER 1

The impact was enormous. Much harder than I'd expected. The hull of our spaceship groaned and screeched. The walls warped and bulged. The panel closest to Val, one of our pilots, caved in, somehow breaking through the protective energy barrier around her chair. She screamed in pain as the armrest snapped, digging into her side.

Jose, the captain, had lost control during the landing, which turned into a crash. I'd caught the moment it happened. His eyes grew larger as he frantically ran his fingers over the control panel. His skin paled, and perspiration beaded on his forehead. No matter how hard he worked, he couldn't prevent our ship from slamming into the edge of the anomaly harder than even the worst of the landings during our training sessions.

Then, all went still and dark.

A moment later, the auxiliary system kicked in, flicking on the lights.

"Val!" Jose climbed out of his seat and rushed to his second-in-command who doubled over in her seat. "Are you okay?"

"I'm pretty sure I broke my rib," she groaned, pressing her hand to her side. "And I think I'm bleeding."

Like all of us, Val was wearing a pale-blue suit, covered with colorful logos from the collar to the boots. I saw no tearing in the material and no blood. It didn't mean she wasn't bleeding underneath it.

Lee, the scientist on board, clicked his seat belt off and jumped out of his chair. "We need to get her into the medical capsule."

Val groaned softly as Lee led her to the wall with the medical bed concealed inside.

"How is everyone else doing?" Jose rose to his feet, surveying the rest of us—two on-board engineers and me, the movie producer.

Yes, that was what I was—the movie producer. My sole purpose on the team was to record everything that could later be assembled into a movie, a documentary, or a series to air for profit. The footage would also provide visual evidence of whatever we discovered here.

The Earth Space Coalition had stopped exploration of the Anomaly GR-A8502 shortly after the disappearance of the scientist Svetlana Kostyk. She had been part of the team studying the mysterious anomaly from a station that orbited the nearby water world Omphi. She'd gone missing during a solo mission a little over fifty years ago. Her ship had lost all communications with the station, and neither the ship nor Svetlana Kostyk had ever been found.

Passionate about her work and new discoveries, it was believed that Svetlana might have come too close to the Anomaly and had been sucked in along with her ship.

Instead of shedding some light on the mysterious Anomaly, Svetlana had only added more mystery to this celestial body. Her disappearance sparked a number of speculations on what might be inside of it.

Five years ago, it had been proven that a solid core lay at the center of the unpredictable force field, renewing keen interest in exploring it further. The mission was deemed too risky by the Earth governments who refused to finance it. Luckily, several private corporations had stepped in, outfitting our expedition.

"Nadia? Are you okay?" Jose glanced my way, not leaving Val's side.

I climbed out of my chair, unsteadily. "I'm fine, I think—"

A screeching noise cut me off, then a fountain of sparks shot from the wall. Another malfunction? Were we not done crashing yet?

Both engineers rushed to the wall but were forced to keep their distance as the spray of sparks fanned in a wide circle. The melting paneling material dripped to the floor.

"Get in the suits, everyone!" Jose ordered. "We have a hull breach."

Lee quickly turned Val toward the hatch where our suits were kept. I ran after them.

With a slamming sound, an uneven oval cut-out of the wall fell in, followed by a smoky cloud with a chemical smell.

"What the—" I heard the confused voice of one of the engineers who was fully enveloped into the smoke. His voice was cut off by a wet crunching sound that I couldn't place at first.

A tall, dark figure emerged from the dissipating smoke that rolled off his shoulders like a cloak.

Then the motionless body of the engineer came into view. He lay on the floor, his neck twisted at an unnatural angle. My stomach roiled when it dawned on me what that wet-snappy sound had been. The monster that had just barged onto our ship had snapped my teammate's neck.

I stepped back, frozen in shock and horror. I'd never witnessed a murder before. Heck, I'd never seen any crime being committed right in front of me. Crime, in general, had been all but eliminated on all the main planets of the Federation, including Earth.

I kept staring at the motionless body on the floor, unable to move a muscle. The man who'd been a living, breathing, thinking individual just moments ago, was nothing but a corpse with its neck snapped.

Jose recovered first.

"We are a peaceful delegation!" He faced the newcomer—the *errock*, I recognized his species.

His yellow eyes narrowed as he gave each of us an assessing glare.

At least a few inches taller than the biggest man of my crew, the *errock* seemed twice as broad. His reddish skin darkened to gray on the hard ridges running along his arms and bald head. Wearing black pants, dark boots, and a wide utility belt, the male was topless.

Errocks were a civilized nation. Yet this individual's behavior was that of a feral, murderous animal.

The second engineer suddenly leaped on the newcomer's back with a laser knife clutched in his hand.

With a grunt, the *errock* grabbed the engineer's head and yanked it, twisting it with his hands. The human's neck snapped with the same wet cracking noise I'd heard earlier. I swayed on my feet, ready to barf.

"Oh, my God..." Val whimpered. She staggered backwards to the wall while pressing an arm to her side. Her face as white as the wall behind her, she slid to the floor.

"Run!" Jose shoved me aside, grabbing a long, heavy tool from the shelf in the suit storage.

Run! But where?

According to the glowing sign over the airlock by the control panel, outer space lay behind it. I had no time to get into my spacesuit. We were trapped on the ship, with the huge, murderous *errock* blocking the only exit he'd created. Where did he come from? Why was he killing everyone unprovoked?

I had no idea, but it was clear he wasn't going to stop. A murderous glimmer in his eyes, lips curved in a menacing smile, he faced Jose.

I anxiously darted my gaze along the walls and the ceiling around me, searching for an escape route, a place to hide, anything. Running to our sleeping cabin would only make it easier for the *errock* to corner me there.

My body shook. Everything inside me vibrated with horror and the need to escape.

The escape capsule!

Tripping over my feet, I dashed for the round door next to the suit storage.

From the corner of my eye, I caught the sight of Jose being hurled against the wall by the monstrous *errock*. Our captain's head dangled awkwardly, only attached to his body with muscles and skin.

Lee ran for the opening the *errock* had cut out, probably hoping to escape that way.

Val was lying on the floor next to the round table in our common area in the middle of the ship.

"Val!" I yelled. "Here!"

Curled into a ball, she didn't move. Was she dead, too? The monster must've gotten her already.

"Lee!" I screamed, stabbing my fingers into the control panel next to the entrance of the escape capsule. The door slid open, and I climbed in.

I poked my head out, searching for Lee. The *errock* held him over his head. He slammed our scientist over his knee, snapping the man's spine in half.

My head spun, terror lodging tight in my throat. I hit the panel on the other side of the door, locking myself inside.

The capsule was designed to take us off the Anomaly upon completion of our mission if the ship failed.

My entire team had been annihilated in seconds. Screw the mission, the documentary I was supposed to make, and the astronomical reward I'd been promised.

With trembling fingers, I strapped myself into one of the six seats inside the capsule and initiated the take-off sequence on the on-board computer.

I was the last survivor of our ill-fated expedition, and I was getting out of here.

A red warning flashed on the control panel in front of me.

"Not enough power to complete the take-off sequence."

What exactly did it mean? I feverishly searched my brain for any mention of this message during my year-long training for this mission.

The capsule was much smaller than the spaceship. Its engines, however, were many times more powerful than the ship's. The sole purpose of this thing was to take us off the Anomaly. Why wouldn't it do just that?

Had something been damaged during our crash landing? I punched more buttons on the control panel, trying to troubleshoot the problem.

The dreadfully familiar sound scraped against the capsule door from the outside.

The *errock*!

He had murdered my crew and was now cutting through the door of the capsule to get to me, too.

Again and again, I re-started the launch sequence, getting the same message.

"Not enough power."

The shower of hot sparks blew into the capsule. The *errock* was cutting through the door, and I was trapped here, like a mouse in a jar, with nowhere left to run.

Panic shot through me.

"How much power do you need? To lift off a capsule the size of a bus?" I yelled at the control panel. Shaking with anger and fear, I punched it with my fists.

I heard a loud thud behind me. The fine hairs on the back of my neck stood up as I sensed *his* presence inside the capsule. His heavy breathing reached my ear.

I didn't want to turn around and face him. Everything inside me urged me to curl into a ball and make myself invisible. Only, there was no place to hide in the capsule.

I'd been cornered.

"Where do you think you're going?" the *errock* growled, mockingly.

Hearing him speak somehow made him even more monstrous. He obviously was a self-aware, intelligent being, not an enraged animal. Yet, he had killed my entire team in cold blood.

His words spurred me into action. I scrambled to the wall, avoiding his hands as he reached for me, then scurried for the opening he'd just made.

If I made it past him, I could get off the ship the way he had come. Fingers crossed, there were no more creatures like him out there.

Tripping over my hands and feet in panic, I climbed out of the opening and back into the spaceship.

"Not so fast." The *errock's* heavy hand swiped me off my feet.

I fell face down. Then the enormous weight of the *errock* crashed on top of me.

Nearly crushed under him, I could barely breathe. Clawing at the floor tiles with my fingers, I attempted to crawl from under him, but that was like trying to shift a tank off me.

"I'll fuck you fast before anyone gets here," he growled in my ear, yanking at my suit. "But I *will* fuck you, even if it's the last thing I do."

He hooked his fingers into the neckline of my suit from behind, and tugged it down, almost choking me. The material held, frustrating him. Painfully grabbing on to my shoulder and hip, he flipped me over.

I came face to face with my attacker. The look in his yellow eyes terrified me even more than his actions. There was no thought in them, no emotion other than the unhinged, feral lust.

Pinning my hips under his pelvis, he straddled me.

The moment his chest lifted off mine, I greedily sucked some air into my oxygen starved lungs.

"Female," he smirked, pawing at my breasts through the suit. Leaning closer, he sniffed my neck. "Smell good, too. Good enough to eat." He dragged his tongue down my throat.

"No. Please..." I whimpered, already knowing that my pleas would make no difference to him. He acted as if he didn't even hear them, sniffing down my body.

Hooking his arms under my knees, he yanked them open and dropped his head between my thighs.

Around my core, I felt the heat of his mouth through the suit. Then a sharp pain blinded me as he bit down.

Anger cut through the terror from the pain. I thrashed in his arms, slamming my fists at his bald head. The three hard ridges running along his skull hurt my hands, but I didn't care. I didn't care about anything other than getting as far away from this monster as possible.

"Yeah, fight me." Satisfaction was thick in his growl as he effortlessly caught my both hands in one of his and fisted his other hand in my hair.

Tears sprang to my eyes at the pain on my scalp as he yanked.

"You didn't wait for me, Nocc," a new deep voice suddenly sounded from above us. "It's against the rules to board a new ship on your own."

Through the blurry film of tears, I saw another *errock* standing by. His arms folded across his chest, he seemed unaffected by the horrors that one of his species had inflicted on my spaceship and my person.

Did he come to join my attacker?

The thought made me wish I'd been killed along with Lee, Val, and the rest of my crew.

"Fuck off, Wyck," the one called Nocc gritted through his teeth. His hand in my hair, he yanked my head back, grinding his crotch against me.

I screamed again at the sudden pain in my neck. It felt like it would snap any minute. Maybe he would kill me sooner than later?

Wyck, the second *errock*, grabbed Nocc around his throat and shoved him off me. I was able to draw a full breath once again.

"What the fuck!" Nocc leaped to his feet with a speed shocking for his size.

Wyck shifted from foot to foot, as if confused by his own action. "You're killing her," he muttered.

"Not yet. First, I'm going to fuck her!" Nocc bellowed, lunging for me again. "You can stay and watch, but don't you dare get in my way."

I rolled on the floor, scrambling away from him. Nocc tripped over my foot with a long, filthy curse.

Wyck quickly stepped over my legs, placing himself between Nocc and me.

"Kill those who are aggressive," he said. "Let the captain deal with the rest. Those are the rules for each new ship's arrival."

"Since when do you care about *his* rules?"

AVAILABLE NOW

More by Marina Simcoe

PARANORMAL ROMANCE

Madame Tan's Freakshow
Call of Water
Madness of The Moon

Demons, Complete Series
Demon Mine
The Forgotten
Grand Master
The Last Unforgiven - Cursed
The Last Unforgiven - Freed

Stand Alone Novels Set in Demons World
The Real Thing
To Love A Monster

Midnight Coven Author Group
Wicked Warlock (Cursed Coven)

SCIENCE-FICTION ROMANCE

Dark Anomaly Trilogy
Gravity
Power
Explosion

My Holiday Tails
Married to Krampus
My Tiny Giant

Standalone Novels
Experiment
Enduring (Valos Of Sonhadra)

About the Author

MARINA SIMCOE LIKES to write love stories with characters, who may or may not be entirely human, because she firmly believes that our contemporary world could always use a little bit of the extraordinary.

She has lots of fun exploring how her out-of-this-world characters with their own beliefs, values, and aspirations fit into our everyday life.

She lives in Canada with her very own captain, their three little offsprings, and a cat, who is definitely out of this world.

For updates on her books please visit Marina Simcoe Author page on Facebook or www.marinasimcoe.com.

Please Stay in Touch

Newsletter signup: http://eepurl.com/c__RGn
Facebook Readers' Group
Marina's Reading Cave
www.instagram.com/marinasimcoeauthor
www.marinasimcoe.com
www.facebook.com/MarinaSimcoeAuthor/
www.amazon.com/author/marinasimcoe
www.bookbub.com/profile/marina-simcoe
www.goodreads.com/MarinaSimcoe